DARK DAYS
AT SADDLE CREEK

OTHER BOOKS BY SHELLEY PETERSON

Dancer
Abby Malone
Stagestruck
Sundancer
Mystery at Saddle Creek
Christmas at Saddle Creek

Jockey Girl

DARK DAYS AT SADDLE CREEK

Shelley Peterson

Originally published by Cormorant Books, Inc., Toronto, 2012

Cover image: istock.com/debibishop
Printer: Webcom

Library and Archives Canada Cataloguing in Publication

Peterson, Shelley, 1952-, author
Dark days at Saddle Creek / Shelley Peterson.

(Saddle Creek series)
Previously published: 2012.
Issued in print and electronic formats.
ISBN 978-1-4597-3954-3 (softcover).--ISBN 978-1-4597-3955-0 (PDF).--
ISBN 978-1-4597-3956-7 (EPUB)

I. Title. II. Series: Peterson, Shelley, 1952- . Saddle Creek series.

PS8581.E8417D37 2017 jC813'.54 C2017-903970-9
C2017-903971-7

1 2 3 4 5 21 20 19 18 17

Conseil des Arts du Canada
Canada Council for the Arts
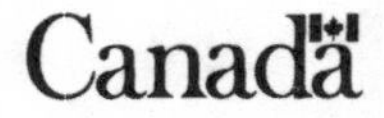

We acknowledge the support of the **Canada Council for the Arts**, which last year invested $153 million to bring the arts to Canadians throughout the country, and the **Ontario Arts Council** for our publishing program. We also acknowledge the financial support of the **Government of Ontario**, through the **Ontario Book Publishing Tax Credit** and the **Ontario Media Development Corporation**, and the Government of Canada.

Nous remercions le **Conseil des arts du Canada** de son soutien. L'an dernier, le Conseil a investi 153 millions de dollars pour mettre de l'art dans la vie des Canadiennes et des Canadiens de tout le pays.

Printed and bound in Canada.

VISIT US AT

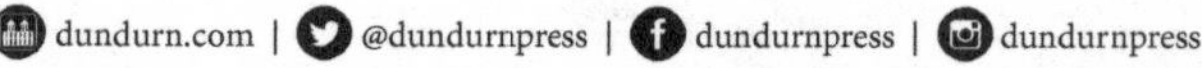
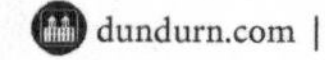

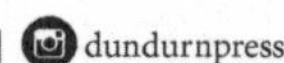

Dundurn
3 Church Street, Suite 500
Toronto, Ontario, Canada
M5E 1M2

To my remarkable family:
Together,
We celebrate the great gift of life,
Discovering joy and beauty in every precious day,
While accepting the inevitability of death.
In memory of Clarence Peterson who inspired the character of Pete Pierson, and whose life galvanizes us still.

Two Wolves

One evening an old Cherokee told his grandson about a battle that goes on inside people. He said, "My son, the battle is between two 'wolves' inside us all.

"One is Evil. It is anger, envy, jealousy, sorrow, regret, greed, arrogance, self-pity, guilt, resentment, inferiority, lies, false pride, superiority, and ego.

"The other is Good. It is joy, peace, love, hope, serenity, humility, kindness, benevolence, empathy, generosity, truth, compassion, and faith."

The grandson thought about it for a minute, and then asked his grandfather, "Which wolf wins?"

The old Cherokee simply replied, "The one you feed."

If you stand high on the cliffs behind Saddle Creek Farm, the shape of the river below forms the outline of a saddle. The water twists and winds its way through the rocky, dramatic landscape of the Niagara Escarpment in Caledon, connecting all who cross its well-worn path.

Wild animals — deer, raccoons, squirrels, porcupines, coyotes, and foxes — come to drink. Hawks and owls compete for field mice, and songbirds trill in the treetops. Beavers dam off sections to build their homes, and fish are plentiful in the cold, deep pools.

If you were to paddle a canoe down the creek from The Grange to King Road, you'd pass Owens Enterprises, Merry Fields, the Malones, Hogscroft, Bradley Stables, and, of course, Saddle Creek Farm. It is a tightly knit community — a place where people care deeply for one another, and for the land around them. It is also a community that is passionate about its horses.

And what horses! Those in the area are famed for their talent and strength: the legendary Dancer, Sundancer, and Moonlight Sonata. All were foaled within walking distance of Saddle Creek, and all have carried themselves and their riders to victory — both in the ring and beyond. Some wonder what secret the area holds, to bring forth such amazing creatures. Some say it's in the water.

1 DARKENING SKIES

There was a time when all the people and all the animals understood each other and spoke the same language.

— Elder Betsy Anderson, Tadoule Lake Dene

Alberta Simms studied the black clouds gathering overhead and hoped the rain would stay inside of them for just another few minutes. All day long the sky had swirled with indecision, but now it darkened with the inevitability of a massive downpour.

Easy does it, boy.

There it was again. The voice. Her heart quickened. She examined the crowd at the horse show, her eyes darting from one person to the next, alert to every facial movement and gesture. Nothing. Was she imagining things?

Twice now, she'd thought she'd heard a mental transmission, but both times she hadn't been able to locate the origin of the voice. It was unique, somehow. Was it a human, and not an animal, that she'd heard? She set her jaw. Forget it, she told herself. If it's real, it'll come again.

Alberta, or Bird as she was known, heard a distant rumble of thunder. She wondered if her sister's class would have to be cancelled. Now her fingers were crossed.

Determined to remain undistracted by the weather or the voice, Bird leaned on the white rail fence and refocused her attention on the action in the show ring. Her younger sister, Julia, was doing a great job of steering her chestnut pony around the course of jumps. Theirs was the fastest time so far, and all the rails were still up. Julia had talked of nothing but showing since her first-place finish at the Palston Classic in June. Now it was August, and they were back for the Summer Summit.

It was the last class of the day, and Julia was the last rider. The skies blackened dramatically as the pair made the final turn into a line of jumps. Small raindrops were beginning to fall.

Earlier that day, Bird and her formidable horse, Sundancer, had won their class, setting high expectations for the other riders from Saddle Creek Farm. Bird replayed the moment in her mind with considerable pleasure. It had been close to a perfect ride. Sunny was responsive and brave, and Bird was on her game. Horse and rider were totally synchronized — listening and moving and thinking as one.

After that, though, the entire day had felt odd — ominous, even, with the weight of humidity and the threat of rain hovering. Red-haired Kimberly and her mare, Moonlight Sonata, had gone off course and were whistled out. Liz and Pastor had crashed through a jump. But perhaps the barn's luck was about to change. If Julia and Sabrina kept this up, there'd be two first-place ribbons for Saddle Creek Farm.

Sabrina, Julia's pretty Welsh pony, was certainly intent on winning. Her tiny pointed ears strained forward and her mouth was tense with effort as she cantered over the blue and white oxer and took three quick strides to the red and green vertical. One stride, then over the yellow boards with her knees tucked up neatly under her chin. They landed safely and raced through the finish gate.

Julia's face broke into a huge grin.

Bird slapped her sister's calf when she trotted out of the ring. "Good job, Julia!" She gave Sabrina a pat on the neck. *Good job, Sabrina! Did you have a little trouble on the far corner?*

A huge flower popped up!

Bird smiled. A woman had opened her yellow umbrella just as Sabrina and Julia were cantering past. It might have seemed like a surprisingly big flower to the pony.

You did well to stay focused, Sabrina.

Think I'd spoil my ride because of a stupid flower?

Bird laughed out loud. Other horses would have spooked.

Julia slid off Sabrina and removed her helmet. "I wish Mom had stayed to watch that."

Bird hugged her little sister. "She'll wish she did when we tell her." Eva had been around earlier in the day, but something had "come up" and she'd left before Julia's class. Bird snorted. Probably a manicure or a shoe sale. Maybe lunch with a gossipy friend.

Big drops of rain landed on their heads. Julia looked up at the sky. "It's really starting now."

And start it did. Thunder rolled and the clouds let loose their burden. All around, people hurried for cover. Umbrellas opened and horses were dragged into trailers. People crowded under trees, dashed for their vehicles, and ducked under overhangs. Within seconds, Bird and Julia were soaked to the skin.

"Let it rain!" yelled Julia as they ran for the trailer with the pony. "I had the best time of my life out there!"

"I think you won first," called Bird, running beside her.

You think? *We won for sure!* corrected Sabrina.

Bird dropped the rear ramp of the horse trailer, and Sabrina trotted right up beside the other horses. The sisters jumped in, and together they stood dripping as the rain pounded on the aluminum roof.

"Holy," said Julia. "I'm glad this waited till we finished."

Bird nodded. "Yeah. Your ride would've been called off with this thunder."

The rain was coming down so hard that a curtain of water streamed down the trailer door opening, inches from the girls. Julia put out her hand and squealed as water sprayed everywhere.

"Bring it on," laughed Bird. "We couldn't get wetter if we tried!"

That's just stupid, commented Sundancer. The big chestnut gelding stood on the other side of Sabrina. *I was perfectly dry until now.*

Suck it up, Sunny, answered Bird. *A little water never hurt anybody.*

Tell that to a cat!

Sundancer always took an animal's point of view, Bird observed. *Where is everybody?*

Moonie and Pastor are here in the trailer. Duh.

I can see that, smartass. I meant Aunt Hannah, Liz, and Kimberly.

They're in the truck.

Bird spoke aloud to Julia. "Let's go for it. When I count to three, get out. We'll close up the trailer, run to the truck, and beat the rush out of here."

"And go home? Before the ribbons?"

Bird saw the disappointment on her sister's face. "Okay, maybe we can wait here a little longer. Aunt Hannah knows where we are." Their aunt owned and operated Saddle Creek Farm, and was also their coach.

Julia looked much happier. "Holy. It's really pouring."

Bird squinted and peered through the sheet of water falling off the trailer roof. All around them, vans were pulling out. The show was over, and except for the eight riders who'd placed in the last class, no one had any reason to stay. Bird looked over to the entrance: a long line of trucks, trailers, and cars was waiting to leave the grounds.

The rain began to abate as quickly as it had started. Within minutes it had completely stopped, and the sky began to clear.

"Bird? Julia?" Hannah's worried face peeked around the corner of the trailer. "You look drowned!"

"I think I won, Aunt Hannah!" crowed Julia.

"Good girl. I'll run down to the office and find out what's going on," said Hannah. "You girls change into your spare clothes before you start shivering, and don't forget to rub Sabrina down."

"I've got to tell Liz and Kimberly first!" Julia leapt off the trailer like a flying squirrel and dashed to the truck.

Bird slipped the saddle and bridle off Sabrina and carried them to the tack room at the front of the trailer. She placed the pony's saddle on the rack and hung up the bridle, wet girth, and saddle pad. From the trunk she got out her old green sweatsuit, and, after peeling off her wet riding clothes, she stepped into the soft flannel and pulled her rubber boots over dry socks. Much better, Bird thought. She grabbed a big towel to dry off Sabrina and stepped out of the tack room.

Julia appeared just as Bird was leaving. "I forgot to pack dry clothes," she said through chattering teeth.

"Here's a wool cooler." Bird rubbed Julia's head with the towel and grabbed a soft horse blanket. She threw it over her sister's shoulders before splashing through deep puddles to the back of the trailer.

Before she could get to work on Sabrina, Bird's attention was drawn down the hill to a galloping horse. A teenaged girl with a lead shank and halter was chasing a handsome bay horse with mud-splattered legs. He must have broken free, Bird guessed. The girl's face was red with exertion and contorted with frustration. Bird recognized her at once. It was Wanda, a groom for the professional trainer Dexter Pill.

Bird put her hands on her hips. What was Wanda thinking, she wondered. Horses never come to people who chase them, especially when those people are yelling. It's too scary for them.

Just as she was deciding how best to help, Bird was startled by a clear mental message.

Easy. Settle down, boy.

That voice again! Where had it come from? It had an authority and a clarity that made her certain it had been transmitted by a person, not an animal. Bird was puzzled. She'd never heard a person do that before.

The horse's eyes and nostrils widened. He stopped, surprised. She watched as a man appeared from the trailers. He casually stepped up to the horse and reached out his hand. The horse relaxed at his touch.

Although Wanda was still visibly upset, the crisis was over. She nodded her thanks to the man, slipped the halter over the runaway horse's head, and led him back in the direction from which they'd come.

Bird looked at the man closely as he walked away. He intrigued her. He was slightly built and moved with a quiet athleticism. He wore jeans, white sneakers, and a green T-shirt. His unruly hair was jet black, and his skin was weathered. Who was he?

Bird had considered it a possibility that other people might communicate telepathically with animals, but actually witnessing this was a first.

Wait! she messaged. *I want to meet you!*

Bird threw the towel over Sabrina's wet back and raced down the hill, tracking the man's steps. She ran around the stall tents and remaining trailers looking for him, but he was gone. There was absolutely no sign that he'd ever been there at all. Bird wondered if he was in one of the trucks or trailers that were moving out of the parking lot. If so, it was too late.

When Hannah returned from the show office, she found her nieces with Kimberly and Liz, busily hanging wet clothes and saddle pads out to dry on the Saddle Creek trailer. The truck doors were open, draped with drying objects, and the mounting block, flatbed, and even the hood of the truck were in use. There was no surface uncovered.

"Girls?" Hannah's brow wrinkled. "What are you doing? No, I see *what* you're doing. *Why* are you doing it?"

"To dry things," answered Julia.

"The sun's out," added Kimberly.

"Wet things get m-mouldy," Liz said helpfully.

Hannah wasn't fooled. "I wasn't going to leave before Julia got her ribbon. *If* that's what you're thinking."

The girls broke out laughing.

"Thanks, Aunt Hannah," grinned Julia. "I'll put everything back in the trailer."

"Leave it out until we go. Wet things get mouldy." Hannah chortled.

"What did they say at the office, Aunt Hannah?" asked Bird.

"The jump-off is cancelled, so winners will be ranked by time and rail faults. They'll announce when they're ready."

"Do riders have to be mounted?" Julia asked. She glanced down at her strange ensemble of borrowed apparel. Her dripping breeches, shirt, and jacket hung on the truck door.

"No, lucky for you. Most of the horses have already left. The show was over anyway, except for the last class ribbon presentation."

"Whew."

Just then, the announcer called for attention over the intercom system. "The judges are ready to pin the last class. Those concerned should come to ring four. Now."

Hannah clapped her hands. "Let's go find out how you did, Julia."

"I can't wait!" Julia jumped up and down.

Kimberly grabbed the younger girl and spun her around. "I knew I was out of the ribbons as soon as I went off course. Maybe that was better — no suspense now about getting placed."

"And I landed right in the m-middle of the oxer!" exclaimed Liz. "P-Pastor was so upset, p-poor guy."

The Saddle Creek contingent hurried down the hill to the office together. It was a small room, and already crowded. Bird recognized a good portion of the crowd. The same people returned to horse shows time and again, especially if they were winning.

A tall woman in her mid-sixties stood behind the desk with a sheaf of papers, a pair of half-glasses perched on her nose. This was the judge, Bird surmised.

"Hello, people, and well-ridden!" The judge's tone was gracious and warm, and her eyes sparkled. "I have the honour of presenting your ribbons." She smiled at each person individually.

Bird smiled back. This woman really enjoyed her job.

"I don't normally judge the jumper classes — hunters are my specialty — so it was a lot of fun for me today. I hope to judge again next weekend, so do come out and compete for the silver trophy."

There was a lot of nodding and smiling and nudging of elbows.

"Every one of you did a wonderful job. I wish each of you could get first place. You kids all worked hard, and each one of you deserves praise. But I won't keep you in suspense any longer. I'll award your ribbons from first to last for a change. Now, for the presentation!"

"About time!" grumbled Julia under her breath.

"Hush!" Hannah looked at her sternly.

"The first place winner is ... number three-nine-seven. Julia Simms and Sabrina!"

"Oh my gosh!" Julia's face beamed with pleasure as she rushed up and grabbed her ribbon. "Thanks *so*, *so*, *so*, *so* much!"

"You're most welcome," said the judge warmly. "You rode fast enough to beat the rain!"

Hannah and the girls hugged Julia briefly, then listened politely while all the others got their rosettes. Once the ceremony was over, Liz and Julia jumped up and down together.

"I can't believe I won first!" Julia whispered.

"So f-fabulous!" enthused Liz.

Bird noticed the dark looks her sister was getting from the other contestants. She poked Julia in the ribs and spoke quietly. "Don't rub it in."

Julia's face dropped. "I didn't mean to."

"Take it outside."

Liz took Julia's hand, and they raced off together giggling.

Kimberly sighed. "They're so-o-o eleven."

"Yeah," said Hannah dryly. "You fourteen-year-olds are over the hill. Let's go."

Kimberly obeyed Hannah's orders, but just as Bird was about to follow, a remark from within the crowd caught her attention.

"My horse is crazy. Totally."

Bird strained her ears.

"Dex says nobody can train him. He bucks. My father is going to have him put down."

Bird studied the person who was speaking. She was a short, blond teenager with braces on her teeth. Bird had seen her competing many times on her black and white pony, and she remembered that her name was Sally. She rarely made it to the ribbons, but always gave her best effort.

Bird wondered if she should interfere. Sundancer had been considered crazy, and was about to be euthanized when Bird got him. She had spent a lot of time and used a lot of patience — along with her special skills — to help him settle down. Now he was a champion.

Hannah was waiting at the door. Bird couldn't help but listen.

"No sense getting hurt." The woman was talking now, and she spoke with authority. "If that's what your father thinks, you're doing the right thing. Some horses are just bad."

Bird cringed at the woman's words. Horses, and people, for that matter, were often deemed to be "just bad." But just like bad people, bad horses sometimes had a reason to be bad. Maybe the handling was rough, or something hurt, or they just didn't feel appreciated or understood. Rarely were they "just bad."

Hannah stared at Bird pointedly. "Well? Are you coming?"

"One minute."

"What's up?"

"If I tell you, you'll say no." Before Hannah could open her mouth to respond, Bird walked over to the blond girl and the woman.

"I couldn't help but overhear," said Bird. She tried to appear friendly and helpful, instead of nosy and interfering. "Are you having a problem with your horse?" Now Bird recognized the woman. She was Kelsey Woodall. Bird recalled that she'd wanted to lease Moonlight Sonata for her daughter Candace until she fell off.

"I might be able to help," continued Bird. "I've had experience with troubled horses."

The woman's brow furrowed. "For someone so young, you have a very high opinion of your horsemanship. Who do you think you are?

"My name is Alberta Simms, Mrs. Woodall."

The woman studied Bird's face. Recognition dawned, and she blushed slightly. "I don't wish to continue this conversation." Kelsey Woodall turned and walked away.

Bird could understand her embarrassment. Earlier that summer, they'd had an unfortunate interaction. Candace had broken her ankle falling off Moonlight Sonata. Their trainer, Dexter Pill, had flown into a rage, and Kelsey Woodall had been rude and high-handed to Aunt Hannah. But Bird couldn't give up. This horse's life might be worth saving.

"I'm sorry to be a pest," said Bird.

"I've heard of you. They call you Bird."

Bird nodded. "And you're Sally."

"Yes, I'm Sally Johns. I can't believe you remembered my name! I mean, everybody knows you, but I'm not … you know … famous."

It was Bird's turn to blush. "I'm not famous," she mumbled, then changed the subject. "I saw you ride your paint, Peasblossom. He's cute. You did great today."

"Thanks! Eighth is still in the ribbons!" Sally's smile faded. "My father bought me a new horse because I'm outgrowing Peasblossom, but it's not working out so well."

Hannah had pushed through the flow of departing adults and kids. When she finally reached Bird and Sally, she wasn't pleased. "The horses are standing on the trailer and the girls are waiting."

"Aunt Hannah, this is Sally Johns. I heard her say that her horse is going to be put down."

"My dear Bird." Hannah let out an exasperated sigh. "You cannot save every horse on the planet. This is her business, not yours."

"It might be very simple, though! An aching muscle or rough teeth."

"I'm sure they've had the vet out. Come now, Bird." Hannah smiled at Sally. "Sorry to pull her away, but you know how it is."

Sally nodded. "I know. But Bird? The horse's name is Tall Sox. He's stabled with Dexter Pill at Moreland Farm on the Fifth Sideroad."

Hannah reacted to that information. She began pulling Bird outside by the arm.

"Do you live close by?" called Bird over her shoulder.

"I'm with my mom right now. She's on Kennedy Road in Cheltenham."

"Okay. I'll be at Saddle Creek all weekend."

"I know where it is. It's not far from my mom's place, and Moreland Farm, too."

"Come over tomorrow!" Bird spoke loudly enough to be heard across the room. Sally nodded enthusiastically as Hannah slammed the door behind them.

As soon as they were outside, Hannah muttered under her breath, "Dexter Pill!" Her voice got louder and louder as they neared the trailer. "Bird, you know how I feel about him. Dexter Pill! You're to have nothing to do with this, do you hear me?"

"This is about the horse, not the trainer."

"The horse is stabled with the trainer, Bird! You cannot deal with the horse *without* dealing with the trainer. You know that."

"Please don't be mad."

"Don't you remember how he treated Moonlight Sonata at the show just a couple of months ago?"

Bird certainly did remember. It had been ugly. "All the more reason to help Sally's horse. Just think what Tall Sox must be going through!"

"Dexter won't even allow you on the property! He hates us for rescuing Moonie and then winning firsts with her. It makes him look bad."

"But this isn't about him!"

"You're not listening, Bird! Dexter will not *let* you help!"

"And *you're* not listening, either! I don't care about Dexter. I don't need him!"

"You need him to allow you in his barn!"

Bird and Hannah stood face to face, yelling at each other. Bird looked around and realized they were causing a bit of a scene — people were starting to stare. She didn't care. This was important.

Hannah's shoulders slumped and her expression softened. "I'm sorry, Bird," she said quietly. "I didn't mean to lose my temper. I'm upset at the thought of Dexter Pill, not at you. No matter how charming people think he is, that man makes my blood boil."

Bird was still angry. "I know, but you don't understand. I'm not like other people. I can help this horse no matter what you or Kelsey Woodall or Dexter Pill say."

"I hear you. Nothing I say is going to change your mind."

"Finally." Bird exhaled noisily.

"Did you say Kelsey Woodall?"

"Yes. She was the woman talking to Sally when I went over."

"About putting the horse down?"

"Yes."

Hannah looked thoughtful. "Interesting."

"What are you thinking?"

"I'm not sure, but I have a funny feeling. I know she's been looking for a new horse for Candace. Are they trying to sell Sally the previous one?"

Bird looked at her aunt. The Woodalls stabled horses and trained with Dexter Pill. Maybe there was more to this than Bird had first thought. "One thing I know about funny feelings," she said, "is that we should pay attention to them."

Hannah smiled. She put out her right hand for Bird to shake.

"Friends again?"

Bird accepted her handshake. "Friends again."

"Then let's get back to Saddle Creek Farm and look after these horses." Hannah took Bird's arm, and together they joined the others at the rig.

2 TALL SOX

In any great undertaking, it is not enough for a man to depend simply on himself.

— Lone Man, Teton Sioux

The horses were all outside in the cool evening air, bathed and fed, grazing in their fields. The heavy rain had greened up the grass, and the leaves sparkled with drops of rain. It had been a very successful day. After cleaning the tack and bringing the laundry inside to wash, everybody was ready for dinner and bed.

Once Bird had helped with the dishes, she went upstairs to shower and change into her pyjamas. She looked around her old room with pleasure — the open window facing Sunny's field, her cozy bed, the scratched dresser and cracked mirror — she was so happy to be back at Saddle Creek Farm! She and Julia had made a deal with their mother, Eva: they would stay over with Aunt Hannah whenever there were shows. This arrangement worked well for everybody. It gave Eva a chance to be alone with her new husband, Stuart, and it allowed Bird and Julia to concentrate on the horses and the shows.

For Bird, the chance to stay with her aunt was welcome for an entirely different reason. Ever since her mother had returned from her honeymoon a few months earlier, things had been strained. Lately, they argued about every little thing. Bird sighed. She felt much more relaxed here.

As she dried her hair with a blue towel, she observed herself in the mirror. Her hair was growing in very nicely. It had been singed in a barn fire in June, and she'd had it all cut off and styled quite short. She liked it much better now that it was a little longer. It felt more like it belonged to her.

Her body was starting to change, Bird noticed, but not enough to be embarrassing, like her mother, whose large breasts made every outfit look too tight. At fourteen, Bird still had a girlish look. She hoped she'd always stay that way. She didn't feel ready to be a grown-up.

She noted the darkness of her skin and eyes. She liked her colouring, especially in the spring, when other girls looked strangely transparent until the sun gave them substance. Eva was blond with blue eyes, as was Julia. Bird had always known she had a different father than her sister; she'd just never met him. She tried not to dwell on it, but now, drying her dark hair in the mirror, questions resurfaced. Did she get her dark eyes and hair from him? She'd always thought so, but the truth was, she had no idea. All she knew was that her father had met her mother at the Calgary Stampede, where he was a broncobuster, and that he'd disappeared shortly thereafter. She desperately wanted to know more. He was her father, after all! But Eva constantly rebuffed her questions. It was always "someday" or "not now" or "later." Mostly, Eva just lost her temper.

There were a few other things on Bird's mind as she dried her hair in the mirror.

Firstly, Alec. Bird smiled. Her reflection smiled back, happy and content. Alec was away at Camp Kowabi for the summer as a counsellor-in-training, but he was her boyfriend again. Pamela was out of the picture. For good, Bird hoped. She wasn't going to worry about it. When Alec had gone back to camp last time, he'd left her with his favourite sweater — to keep her warm in his arms, he'd said. Bird shivered with joy and her reflected grin grew even wider.

Secondly, and amazingly, the strange man who'd spoken telepathically at the show. She felt shivers up her arms. Would he be at the show on Friday? Was there really someone who could speak to animals in the same way she could? And, most urgently, there was Tall Sox. Bird didn't care how angry Hannah might be, she would try to get to the bottom of the problem with Sally's horse. She vowed to do that the very next day, which was Sunday. Bird needed to visit this horse before he could be euthanized. Put to sleep. Killed. Vets usually didn't work on weekends except for emergencies, so tomorrow would be her best chance.

Bird girl. Bird's thoughts were interrupted.

Cody? Is that you?

It is.

Is there a problem? Cody was a small coyote. He always knew what was going on, and he was usually the first to alert her when there was trouble. They'd had many adventures together. How he always knew when she was there was a mystery to Bird.

No problem. I am glad you are back.

Bird released her breath.

I'm glad to be back, Cody. And I'm glad you came to say hello.

Bird looked out her window, but the coyote was nowhere to be seen.

She gazed into the growing dusk and searched the field across from the farmhouse with her eyes. She could just make out two shadows. Sundancer and Charlie were at the fenceline at the far end, heads down, feasting on the refreshed August grass.

Happily, Bird slid between the covers and rested her head on the pillow. She was proud of the way she and Sunny had ridden at the show. Tomorrow she would find Tall Sox. Next week, if he was at the show, and she was lucky, she would speak to the mysterious man. Soon she would kiss Alec. Within minutes, Bird had fallen into a contented sleep.

Bird? Are you awake?

Bird rolled over to get more comfortable.

Bird? Wake up!

Bird sat up. She waited. Was she dreaming, or had Sundancer just called from …

Bird!

Sunny? What is it? She was fully awake now.

You have human company. Look out your window.

Bird jumped out of bed and stepped over to the window. On the ground below, somebody was looking around furtively. A young girl. Bird watched as she fidgeted and fussed. She seemed very uncertain of what she should do.

Bird removed the screen and leaned outside. "Hello?" she said quietly. "Who's there?"

The girl let out a weak scream and clutched her chest with her hands.

From the kitchen below, Hannah's dog, Lucky, started to bark.

Lucky! Quiet! It's all right!

The barking stopped. *If you say so. If you say so.*

Good dog, Lucky. Good dog!

Bird spoke to the girl. "Don't be afraid. I'm up here. In the window."

The girl looked up, and the moonlight revealed her face. Sally Johns.

"Sally! Stay there. I'm coming down."

"Bird! I'm so glad —"

"Shh! Don't wake everybody up."

Sally nodded and slapped her hand over her mouth.

Bird quickly pulled some clothes over her pyjamas and slipped on her runners. She crept downstairs and out the kitchen door with Lucky at her side. The brown dog raced over to Sally, who was standing under the big maple tree at the fence. He sniffed her, then took off to follow his nose.

Sally looked like she might cry. "Bird, I'm not so sure I should've come. I'm scared! And I don't have a driver's licence!" She glanced to the end of the driveway, where a car was parked on the road. "That's my mother's. She doesn't know I took it."

Bird guessed that Sally wouldn't have come over in the middle of the night without a good reason. "Something new with Tall Sox?"

Sally nodded wildly. "They're taking him away first thing in the morning. Wanda — she's a groom at Moreland's — told me. I don't know where he's going, but they're going to kill him, I just know it. I've been dying to talk to you since I heard! Can you come with me now?"

"Do you have your beginner's?"

Sally's head bobbed assertively. "I know how to drive."

"And you have a plan once we get there?"

"Of course I do!"

"Then what are we waiting for?"

Sally's face relaxed. The two girls headed for the road. They ran on the grass to avoid making any noise on the gravel. As quietly as possible they got into Sally's mother's car and pulled shut the doors.

Lucky's furry head appeared at Bird's window. *Can I come? Can I come?*

No. Good dog. Guard the house while I'm gone.

The dog's tail began to wag. *Yes, Bird! Yes, Bird!* He disappeared from sight.

Sally started the engine. The car jerked into gear and sped into the road. She jammed on the brakes, causing the car to skid in a wide arc and throwing gravel in all directions.

"I thought you said you could drive!" cried Bird. She willed her heart to stop pounding.

"I can! I've driven the lawn mower since I was ten!"

"How old are you?"

"Fifteen."

"You said you had your beginner's."

"No, I didn't. I said I could drive. Another chance? Please? I can do better."

It was one thing to help Sally save a horse. It was another to risk her life. "No offence, but I'm going to ride my bike." Bird got out of the car.

"Really, I can drive! I'll show you!" Again the car lurched forward as Sally put her foot to the gas pedal.

"I've got bikes," said Bird. "You shouldn't be driving. You're terrible."

"What'll I do with Mom's car?"

"Just leave it. We'll worry about it later."

Sally frowned, but she followed Bird back to the house. Bird's bike was leaning against the bricks, and Hannah's stood next to it. Bird wasn't too sure about

Sally's bike riding skills, either, but there was really no other way. She gave her own bike to Sally and rode Hannah's.

The girls pedalled fast, and soon they neared Moreland Farm. Sally stopped, out of breath.

"What?" asked Bird. She braked her bike as well.

"Now that we're here, I don't know what to do."

"You said you had a plan!"

"I did. My plan was to figure it out when we got here."

Bird decided not to scream at her. "You stole your mom's car, got me out of bed, and you don't have a plan?"

Sally's mouth tightened. She looked hurt.

"Don't worry." Bird got back on the bike and pedalled slowly so that Sally could catch up. "Let's leave the bikes at the gate and walk in."

"No!" Sally whispered urgently. "There are security lights and cameras at all the gates."

"That's a good thing to know," said Bird sarcastically. They'd been within a few feet of discovery. If they'd triggered the lights, their adventure would've been over before it had begun.

"There's a trail over there that leads to the stable." Sally pointed to the right, and Bird peered into the darkness. She could vaguely see a path through the tall grass.

"Okay. That's where we'll go."

They trespassed over the adjacent neighbour's field and left their bikes in the bushes. Bird looked around. The night was still, and eerily quiet. Nothing moved — not even the blades of long grass in the meadow. Through the dimness, she took a good look at the barn. It was a huge old clay brick building with a separate arena off to the side. The Dutch doors were open at the top, letting in the night air, but the place looked dark and forbidding.

Silently, two large German Shepherds came racing around a corner. Their noiseless arrival put Bird on edge. She knew that a dog intent on catching something didn't bark. A bark is a warning. No bark means business.

"The guard dogs!" gasped Sally. "I forgot!"

"What else did you forget?" Bird groaned. She was beginning to feel like a fool. She held out both hands and messaged the dogs. *Stop. We are not here to harm you or the horses or the property.*

The dogs halted their approach. One dog began to whine. The dog that wasn't whining demanded, *State your intentions.*

Bird identified him as the alpha. She answered with respect. *We are here to help the horse named Tall Sox. Some humans believe him to be a bad horse. They will remove him and destroy him.*

Tall Sox. Now the whining dog spoke. *We call him Sox.*

The lead dog slowly wagged his tail. *He's a good horse. Come with us. We know the way.*

Bird followed them.

"How did you do that?" Sally stood still. She looked bewildered and afraid.

"Are you coming or not?"

"Aren't they vicious?"

"No. They're good guard dogs."

Sally was still unsure. She tentatively stuck her foot onto the Moreland property. When the dogs ignored her she quickly caught up to Bird. "I don't know what you did or how you did it. Everybody knows these dogs are killers!"

Bird was too busy to respond. *Are people here?*

They sleep.

Are there cameras to watch our actions?

The leader answered, *Up in that corner.*

Bird looked. A camera was mounted in the corner of the doorframe, but it looked dusty and disused. There was no light to indicate it was working. It was too late anyway. If it was working, it already had their faces on tape.

Bird and Sally followed the dogs along the hall and around a corner until they stopped at a stall door and sat. Bird looked inside. *Tall Sox?*

A dark horse with a wide white stripe down his nose turned and gave her a looking-over. In the dim light he appeared to be in good shape. As well as the white blaze, he had tall white markings on all four legs. Tall Sox. Apt name, thought Bird. She guessed that he was a thoroughbred, built for speed and agility, and was probably close to ten or eleven years old.

Now the horse answered, *Tall Sox is what humans call me. Animals call me Sox. When I raced against all the others, my name was Silk Stockings. That was a long time ago.*

So she was right — he was a thoroughbred racehorse. And friendly. He didn't seem to have a bad attitude. Why would a horse like this become a problem?

Do you have soreness or pain anywhere?

Once I bowed a tendon. That's when I stopped racing. It hurt.

But now?

I feel good all over, except for a sore spot on my back.

Bird noted that he had an exceptionally handsome face, and clear, intelligent eyes. She asked another question. *This girl beside me. Do you like her?*

She is not a good rider, but she is kind. I will look after her if I'm allowed.

And the man we call Dexter Pill? Do you like him?

Tall Sox backed into the far corner of his stall and began to shake.

Bird reassured him. *He's not here.*

I do not like him. He puts something sharp on my back where he sits. It hurts when I move. It doesn't hurt now, but it aches.

Can I look? I want to help.

Yes.

Bird opened the stall door and entered. She gently worked her fingers along his back in the saddle area. Tall Sox flinched. *There! That's where it hurts!*

There was a raw spot in his coat. It was warm to the touch, and swollen. Bird felt the sticky residue of blood. With this sore, right where the saddle would sit, any horse would react to the pain. She gasped. Had Dexter Pill purposely made this horse misbehave?

Sox, messaged Bird. *Dexter is going to take you away tomorrow. Do you want to go with him?*

No. I don't trust him.

Then can you come home with me now?

Where do you live?

Bird knew that the unknown was sometimes worse than the known to a horse, however bad the known might be. *Not far. I live with Sundancer and Moonlight Sonata.*

I know them. And now I know you. You go by the name of Bird.

Yes.

I will come with you.

Let's go now, before anybody wakes up.

Bird opened the stall door wide and together they walked out.

"What are you doing?" asked Sally, aghast. "You can't just kidnap him!"

Bird looked at the girl, surprised. "Then what do you want to do? Why are we here? Tell me."

"I don't know," Sally whined. She seemed confused and fidgety. "Can't you just tell me what's wrong with him? You said you could help!"

Bird felt the girl's uncertainty, and took her time to explain the obvious. "You told me they're taking him away first thing in the morning. If he's here in the morning, that's what'll happen."

Sally nodded jerkily and began to speak quickly. "Okay. You're right. I know! I'll clean out his stall and fix it up so the grooms will think it was meant to be like this. Then they won't call for help right away. I mean, if it looks messy and everything, it'll look like he was kidnapped. Like he was."

Bird said, "Great idea. I'll start walking with Tall Sox, and you catch up when you can."

"You'd leave me alone in the dark?"

"We don't have a lot of time, Sally."

She nodded. "Okay, I'll be quick. But go slow!"

"Okay." Bird walked down the hall with the gelding following. Horses nickered softly from their stalls as he said goodbye to his barn-mates. Once outside, the guard dogs escorted them to the path.

Thanks, Bird messaged. *Watch out for the girl, and make sure she gets back here safely. And try not to make her nervous.*

They wagged their tails. *Yes, of course.* Then they were gone, silently, into the barn.

Bird picked up Hannah's bike, and she and Tall Sox began to walk along the road. He kept close to her, and together they enjoyed the silence of the night until they heard the sound of bicycle tires on gravel behind them.

"I made it look perfect!" exclaimed Sally. She jumped off Bird's bike and walked along with them. "They won't notice anything unusual until Dexter comes to get him."

"Good work," said Bird. "That gives us a little time to figure things out."

"What things?" asked Sally.

Bird stared at her. Sally seemed to be completely unable to think ahead. "Things like, what to do with your horse," she replied, trying not to get irritated. "How we get Hannah to agree to keep him at Saddle Creek. How we convince your father that Tall Sox is not a crazy, untrainable horse that needs to be euthanized. How we get your mother's car home. Things like that."

"Oh my gosh. You're right." Sally began to fret. "Oh my gosh. What'll we do?"

"Can you drive your mother's car home? I mean, without killing yourself?"

"Of course I can! I drove it here in the first place."

"This might be a bad idea," Bird said, "but why don't you leave Tall Sox with me and drive your mom's car home. Slowly. And I mean slowly, Sally."

"I'm insulted you think I'm such a bad driver."

"That's not important," said Bird. "What is important is to think out a good plan for Tall Sox."

"Oh, yeah, I agree." Sally sounded confused. "Which is ...?"

By now they were nearing Sally's mother's car, parked at a very odd angle on the road.

"Which is this," Bird stated firmly. "You go home. Slowly, remember? I'll put Tall Sox in the barn for the night. You and your mother come here tomorrow morning. By then I'll have talked things over with Hannah, and we go from there. How's that sound?"

Sally looked relieved. "It sounds great! What time should I come?

"Early. As early as you can."

"I know, but when?"

"Seven-thirty? Eight o'clock?"

"Too early. My mother likes to sleep in on Sundays. How about eleven?"

"This is a *big deal*, Sally. We've just kidnapped your horse! We have to figure this out before Dexter finds him missing. Wake your mother up. The last thing Aunt Hannah needs is to be charged with horse theft!"

Sally's eyes rounded. She nodded. "Right. See you tomorrow morning. Early." With that, she dropped Bird's bike on the side of the road and got in the car. She started it up and jerked forward. Bird and Tall Sox jumped out of the way.

"Slowly, Sally!" pleaded Bird.

Sally tried again. She began the arduous task of turning the car around. She backed up and halted, backed up and halted, moving her wheels inch by inch.

Bird left her to it. She rescued her bike and walked up the Saddle Creek lane with two bicycles and a horse. On the bright side, Bird thought, Sally hadn't run over her.

Tall Sox settled in calmly and seemed to enjoy the roomy stall with fresh hay and water. *This is a nice place*, he messaged. *Can I stay here?*

I think so, answered Bird. *At least for now.*

I'm glad to be here. I feel safe.

Bird was reminded how sensitive horses were. There was not much they couldn't figure out from people's demeanour and moods. They just took it in, like drinking water. *I'm glad you're here, too. Tomorrow you'll meet*

Hannah. She owns the barn, and it's important to make a good first impression.

I always do. Tall Sox put his head back down and munched more hay.

3 A NEW BOARDER

Humankind has not woven the web of life. We are but one thread within it. Whatever we do to the web, we do to ourselves.

— Chief Seattle, Suquamish, 1854

Bird was up very early, and was already in the kitchen when Hannah came down at six to make coffee. Bird immediately offered her a steaming cup with milk and a bit of sugar, just the way she liked it.

"Toast?" asked Bird. "Bacon and eggs? Sunday brunch?"

"What are you up to?" Hannah rubbed her eyes and yawned.

"I'm just trying to be nice."

"Sorry, Bird. I shouldn't be suspicious! How awful of me." She sat down at the table and took a sip of coffee. "Delicious. Thanks, sweetheart."

Bird sat with her. "Actually, you should be suspicious. I have an ulterior motive."

Hannah's sleepy eyes cleared. "Speak to me."

"Remember yesterday? The conversation I had with Sally Johns?"

"The blond girl with braces?"

"Yes."

"The girl with the horse at Dexter's?"

"Yes."

"The horse that I forbade you to rescue?"

This was not going to be easy. Bird took a deep breath and decided to go for it. "Well, he's here."

"Who's here? Where?"

"The horse, Tall Sox. He's in the barn."

Bird waited for Hannah's reaction.

Hannah scratched her head. She took a sip of her coffee. Finally she said, "I can't say I'm surprised. I don't want to know how he got here. It might incriminate me." She gave Bird a sideways look. "What's he like?"

Bird exhaled. "He's really nice looking, Aunt Hannah. And sensible. He has a small, deep gouge on his back where the saddle sits. I think Dexter did it, and that's why everyone thinks he's untrainable."

Hannah tapped her finger on the coffee cup. "Let's not jump to conclusions. We're in a lot of trouble. I'm assuming you had Sally's permission to move the horse" — Bird nodded as Hannah continued — "but you didn't have her parents'. There are laws about things like that. I'm going to get dressed. I'll think this over. When Paul wakes up I'll ask his opinion." She rose from the chair and left the room, then called back, "And Bird? Paul needs to see this gouge."

"Right. I'll wait here." Bird leaned back in her chair, relieved. She couldn't have asked for a better reaction. Paul was a veterinarian. He would fix up Tall Sox's back.

Minutes later, Hannah and Paul came downstairs, and after Paul sleepily grabbed a coffee, they went out to the barn.

"Who's this new gelding?" asked Cliff, the farm manager, as he met them at the door. "Why didn't I know about him?"

Bird explained. "His name is Tall Sox. He belongs to Sally Johns. She asked me to bring him here last night because Dexter was going to euthanize him today."

Cliff's eyes widened. "Why? He looks healthy and sound to me. And he's making friends with everybody, so it's not that he's a nutcase."

The four of them walked to Tall Sox's stall and looked over the half-door.

Hi, Sox. Did you sleep well? messaged Bird.

Very well. I like it here. He stuck his nose over the stall door and sniffed Bird. She patted his head.

"He's handsome," said Hannah. "I'll give him that."

"Let me see this sore on his back," said Paul. He'd brought his vet bag from his truck, and now he donned latex gloves. "Put him on cross ties for me, will you, Bird?"

She did as he asked, and watched as he methodically examined the animal's back.

"There's a pus pocket under the surface. Sitting where it is, it doesn't drain well." Paul cleaned the wound thoroughly and disinfected the area. "I don't know why it hasn't been looked after."

"Especially with the money they charge over there," added Hannah.

Paul stripped off his gloves. "When we get permission from his owners, put him on sulphur, Cliff, will you?"

Cliff nodded. "Ten days?"

"Yep. That should clear it up." Paul shook his head. "I don't know how this particular injury would occur," he said, "unless he was poked hard with a sharp object, and the wound was kept open and allowed to fester."

Their conversation was interrupted by the sound of tires crunching across gravel. A car stopped at the door of the barn. Bird watched as Sally and a short blond woman got out. The woman did not look happy, but Bird steeled herself. She walked over to them with a welcoming smile on her face.

"Hi, Sally! And hello, Mrs. Johns. I'm Bird."

The woman smiled feebly. "I'm Sally's mother, but my name is Cindy Farr. Can anybody tell me what's going on? It's early, and Sally makes no sense at all."

Hannah ushered them over to Tall Sox's stall. She introduced herself and Paul, then said, "Your daughter asked for help with her horse. How much do you know about the situation?"

"Only what Sally told me on the drive over — which wasn't much. Harold looks after the horse part of Sally's life. She insisted I come, but I stay out of all this craziness. It's easier that way."

Hannah and Paul looked at each other. Cindy was not going to be much help. Paul spoke next. "We need to speak to someone who can authorize stabling and treatment for this horse."

"That would be Sally's father. I'll call Harold." Cindy Farr took a cellphone out of her small shoulder-strap purse. She pressed a number on speed dial, and handed it to her daughter.

Sally stared blankly at the phone. "What do I say?" she asked her mother. "That I stole my own horse?"

"Not my problem," Cindy answered.

Bird could hear a man's voice on the other end of the line. "Hello? Hello?"

Sally regained her composure. "Daddy? Sorry to call so early. I'm at Saddle Creek Farm with Tall Sox. I brought him here. They want to talk to you to get permission or something."

"About what? You say you're at Saddle Creek?"

"Yes." Sally's voice faltered. "I don't want Tall Sox to go … anywhere. I love him."

There was a pause, then Bird heard Sally's father sigh loudly. "I'll call Dexter," he said curtly. "I know where Saddle Creek Farm is."

Sally hung up without another word, but her face told Bird everything she needed to know. This girl was worried about being in trouble. Bird knew just how she felt.

Tall Sox's head appeared over the stall door, and Sally stepped over to stroke his nose. "You're a good boy, aren't you? They're wrong about you, I just know it."

I'm glad you all believe in me, the horse messaged.

We won't give up, replied Bird.

Cindy fidgeted with her car keys. She was ready to

leave. “I don’t want to be here when he arrives. Can Sally stay here?”

Hannah nodded. “No problem.”

Cindy kissed Sally lightly on the head as she prepared to go. “Call if you need a ride,” she said. “Good luck with your father.”

When Cindy was out of earshot, Sally whispered to Bird, “They just got a divorce.”

Cindy stepped into her car and turned it around. Bird gasped when she saw a fresh, long, deep scratch along the entire right side of the car.

“Did your mom see that?” whispered Bird.

“Thank gawd, no. I hope she doesn’t look until she gets groceries. That way she’ll think somebody did it in the parking lot.”

“You’re lucky it’s the passenger side.”

“Yeah,” Sally sniffed. “Not my fault Mom’s garage is so narrow.”

“Right,” whispered Bird. “Couldn’t possibly be your bad driving.”

“Okay, folks,” said Hannah, using her take-charge voice. “Since you’re here for the day, Sally, we’ll put you to work.”

“Can I get a banana or a muffin or something first? I didn’t have breakfast.”

“Sure. Bird, get Sally something to eat, and wake up Julia. I want the three of you out here pronto. We have a lot to do today.”

Kimberly and Liz arrived shortly after, and everyone pitched in to get things done quickly — they cleaned tack, washed out the truck and trailer, and organized boots, blankets, saddle pads, and bandages. After that, they went for a quiet hack on the horses that had been at the show the day before, to calm their heads and work out any stiffness. Sally rode Charlie, and became friendly with Julia, Liz, and Kimberly.

Sally's father didn't arrive until noon. The girls had just returned from riding. Bird was in the tack room putting out food for the barn cats when Harold Johns strode up the aisle. "Hello?" he called out. "Hello?"

"Daddy!" cried Sally, running into his arms. "I'm having so … much … fun!"

Bird decided to stay where she was.

"I'm glad you are, Peaches!"

"The kids here are *so* nice, and we actually went for a ride outside! On the trails! It was so-o fun!"

"That's wonderful."

"What took you so long? I called hours ago."

"Dexter said Tall Sox was still there, so I went golfing."

"Golfing?" Sally pouted. "You thought I made it up?"

"I thought you were pulling a joke on me, like last time." He sounded kind, but serious.

Sally dropped her voice. "It wasn't like last time at all! Bird and I brought him here in the middle of the night because Wanda told me that Dexter was sending him away today. It was real this time."

"I know that now, Peaches." Harold spoke to his daughter gently. "Dexter left a dozen messages while I was golfing. A guy came to transport Tall Sox and he wasn't there. Nobody noticed him missing until then."

"That's because I fixed up the stall to look like it was supposed to be empty. It worked!" She sounded happier now. "Wait till I tell Bird!"

In the tack room, Bird smiled. She'd congratulate Sally later, but now she wanted to listen undetected. Often you learned more that way. Like that Sally played jokes on people. Bird was glad she hadn't known last night — she wouldn't have gone to Moreland's with her.

Hannah approached them from the arena, where she'd been sweeping the kick boards. "Mr. Johns? I'm Hannah Bradley, the owner of Saddle Creek Farm. I'm glad you're here."

"Sally, can you keep yourself busy for a few minutes?"

"Sure!" Off she ran to the wash stall, where Charlie stood waiting for his shower to be continued.

Harold Johns watched her go. "I haven't seen her so happy for a long time." Bird heard the scrape of a barn stool as he sat down, and another scrape when Hannah sat down on the other.

"She's a lovely girl," said Hannah warmly. "She's helpful, and fits in well with the others."

"Really?" Harold sounded surprised. "She's had a hard time since Cindy and I split up. Maybe she's finally finding her feet."

Hannah got down to business. “We need to talk about your horse, Mr. Johns.”

“Go ahead. And please call me Harold.” He sat still and listened.

“I’ve put my reputation at risk here, and I need to know what you want done. We don’t have a lot of time. As soon as Dexter figures out where Tall Sox is, he’ll come right over.”

“Dexter already knows he’s here. I told him when I called him back. But, please tell me, how have you put your reputation at risk?”

“By having Tall Sox in my barn without your instruction. And being party, albeit after the fact, to a horse being removed from Moreland Farm without permission. Dexter is within his rights to be very angry, as are you.”

“I see.”

“So,” continued Hannah, “before the proverbial manure hits the fan, I need to know what you wish to do.”

“What are my choices?”

“Keep Tall Sox here or send him back.”

“I’ve already decided not to keep him at all,” answered Harold. “I authorized Dexter to get rid of him, and that’s what I intend to do.”

Hannah softly replied, “That, of course, is your choice to make.”

Harold sniffed. “I made a mistake buying him. I liked him a lot, and thought he looked great, but what do I know? I should’ve let Dexter choose the right horse for Sally in the first place.”

"Why do you say that?"

"Well, as soon as Tall Sox got to Moreland Farm he started to buck! Dex said he must've been drugged when I bought him. He told me it happens all the time. That's why people should trust the pros to buy for them. They don't get fooled."

Hannah didn't say anything.

Bird pictured the wound on Sox's back and almost interrupted, but she clamped her mouth shut and listened. She waited for Harold to continue.

"He wasn't cheap, either, but it seemed like a fair price. At least I thought so at the time. Dex doesn't think he's worth a nickel." Harold snickered at himself. "They say a fool's born every minute."

"So, does Dexter have another horse in mind for Sally?"

"Yes," Harold answered, sounding surprised that Hannah would guess. "A lovely gelding. And very well trained. Now *this* one is expensive!" Harold's laugh was forced.

There was a pause. Bird strained to hear.

Hannah's next question was cautious. "When Dexter told you that Tall Sox had no value, did you decide to put him down rather than sell him?"

"No! Why do you ask?"

Hannah paused again.

"Did Sally say that?" asked Harold.

"Yes."

"I'm afraid my daughter has a vivid imagination. I hadn't even considered putting him down."

Hannah spoke thoughtfully. "I see."

"Dexter did say that it would be best to cut my losses and move on," said Harold. "That seems sensible to me. He'll send Tall Sox to a sale barn for as little cost to me as possible, and then we'll try out the more suitable horse."

The oldest trick in the book, thought Bird. Horse dealers will often try to convince a buyer that they are the only ones to trust — especially when the buyer doesn't know anything about horses. This way Dexter would get commissions selling and buying — selling Sox and buying a new horse for Sally — and perhaps inflate the commission to boot. But first he had to convince them that Sox wasn't good enough.

"Let me show you something." Hannah rose from the stool, and Harold did the same.

Bird heard their footsteps echo on the concrete hall floor. She peeked around the tack room door as Hannah led Harold to Tall Sox's stall.

"See for yourself." Hannah put a halter on the horse's head, walked him out, and clipped on the cross ties in the aisle. Sox was gentle and responsive.

Bird thought it was time to become part of the action, and joined them. "Mr. Johns? I'm Bird. I went with Sally last night to get Tall Sox."

"It's very nice to meet you, Bird," said Harold heartily. "I've seen you ride Sundancer. He's quite the horse! I'd love to find one of those for Sally."

Bird bit her tongue. Sally could no more handle a horse like Sunny than drive her mother's car.

Hannah directed Harold's attention back to Tall Sox. "Look at this. What do you think?"

Harold took a look at the oozing sore on the gelding's back. "I've never seen this before!" he exclaimed.

"Dexter should have treated it," Hannah said sadly. "And Tall Sox should not have been subjected to the pressure of a saddle on his back until it was healed."

"The question is how he got it in the first place," said Bird. "It sure would've made him buck."

Harold stood still. "I hear you. Let's just say that it's opened up some questions."

As Harold had predicted, Dexter Pill arrived in his truck and tagalong horse trailer. He came to a halt at the barn door and got out. He was tanned and fit, with a shock of short blond hair. His eyes were blue, and he was always showing his perfect teeth in a perpetual smile.

Another man sat in the passenger side of the truck. It was Ed Cage, one of Dexter's grooms. Bird had seen him around the shows. He was as dark as Dexter was fair, and just as good-looking. All the girls were in love with him. Bird recalled that he was married, but that didn't prevent him from being a flirt.

Hannah put her hand on Bird's shoulder. "Be careful what you say. Just listen."

Bird nodded. "You forget. I'm the master of silence."

Hannah smiled, and they held eye contact for a second. Bird was indeed the master of silence. It wasn't long ago that she hadn't spoken at all. She had a condition called selective mutism, which caused her to lapse into periods where she couldn't utter a word aloud. She was never sure when these periods would occur, or why. Bird made a silent wish that she would never suffer another bout.

Dexter worked hard to control his feelings as he entered the barn, but Bird felt his irritation hit her like a wave.

"Harold! Good that you're here!" Dexter grinned boyishly and stuffed his hands in his pockets. Bird understood how people considered him charming. With his easy laugh and his rancher's down-to-earth manner, he quickly gained people's trust. He had a reputation of getting ribbons for riders, too, which was good for business. "So," he chuckled, "Sally's being dramatic again. No worries! Let's get Tall Sox back to Moreland's and call it a day." He indicated the waiting horse trailer.

"Dexter," said Harold. "Come over and take a look at this." He showed Dexter the sore. "We were just talking about how it could've happened."

Dexter clacked his tongue as he examined it. He opened his eyes wide. "What have you done to this horse, Hannah?"

Hannah stared at Dexter in shock. "What are you suggesting?"

"Hannah didn't do it!" Bird shouted. "It was like that last night in your barn, before he ever got here. I saw it!"

Dexter's face brightened. "You admit you were there?" He smiled broadly. "You admit to trespassing and horse theft?" He laughed and pointed his finger at Bird. "Gotcha! Just kidding!"

Hannah shot her niece a knowing glance and Bird cringed. *That's* why Hannah had wanted her just to listen.

Harold Johns spoke. "Let's slow this all down. I need to have a talk with Sally and find out what she wants to do with the horse. I bought him for her, after all. He's Sally's horse."

Bird sensed that Harold's emotions were stronger than he was showing.

"Let's be serious, here. She's a kid, Harold," said Dexter. He stepped closer to Harold and spoke confidentially. "I know better than she does about what she needs in a horse. And we had a plan, which I was putting into action. With your approval, I might add."

"I understand, and I'm sorry, but things have changed."

Dexter frowned. "You leave me in a bad situation."

"I'll be fair to you financially." Harold stood firm. "I always honour my debts."

"Okay. I get that you want to give Tall Sox another chance. Let's get him home and talk this over." Dexter began to unclip the horse.

Harold stopped him. "I want to keep Tall Sox here. At least for now."

"Here?" Dexter threw out his arms and looked around. "Moreland's is a far superior facility, and you're paid up for the month. With me as Sally's coach, not Hannah." He shot her a disparaging look.

"It's my decision to make, and I've made it. Tall Sox stays at Saddle Creek. If I change my mind, Dexter, I'll certainly be in touch."

"And what about that other gelding? The owner's turned down several offers!"

"She can take any offer she wants, and she knows it." Harold continued to speak calmly, but his tone was increasingly firm. "I never promised to buy that gelding."

"You've made the wrong decision for Sally. You'll see." Without another word, Dexter stalked out of the barn. Ed Cage stood beside the truck. As soon as his boss appeared, they both got in, shut the doors at the same instant, and drove away.

Bird felt the atmosphere clear with their departure, but she doubted it was the last of them.

Hannah and Harold let out their breath at the same time.

Harold spoke first. "I'm sorry you had to hear all that. And I'm sorry to have put you in this position. Thank you for stepping up."

"I had nothing to do with it. It was Bird and Sally who brought him here."

"But you didn't send him back."

Hannah considered this. "I might have, if not for the sore on his back. It made me wonder."

"That's what made my mind up — when Dexter tried to put the blame on you. Even a novice like me can see that the sore didn't happen last night."

Hannah nodded. "May we treat it? Paul, Dr. Daniels, has already looked at it, and he tells me the horse needs antibiotics and regular cleansing."

"Absolutely. You have a new boarder. If you'll take us."

Hannah smiled. "Of course."

"I'll start paying board today. Lessons, too. Sally likes it here."

"I really, really do!" Sally had finished bathing Charlie and came running to join them. "I'm so happy!"

"We really like Sally," enthused Bird. "And Tall Sox, too."

"I'm glad, Bird." Harold Johns smiled at her as the three of them walked out of the barn.

"See you tomorrow?" called Sally.

"See you tomorrow," answered Bird. "Oh, Sally? Can I show you where to put your tack?"

"Sure!"

Bird showed Sally into the tack room and closed the door behind them.

"I actually wanted to ask you something in private," she said.

Sally looked wary. "What?"

"Why did you tell me that your father was going to put Tall Sox to sleep?"

"He was!"

"The truth?"

Sally looked at the floor and mumbled, "Okay, I didn't know exactly. But I knew he was going somewhere. I don't trust Dexter, and nobody was telling me anything."

Bird decided to accept that. "Fair enough. But from now on be honest with me, okay?"

Sally smiled sheepishly, and nodded agreement. The girls walked out to join the adults.

Sally waved goodbye as she and her father drove away. Bird watched from the barn door and waved back, hoping that Sally could keep her promise.

Can I stay here? asked Tall Sox. *Did I make a good first impression?*

Looks like it, answered Bird. *But I have to keep your sore cleaned out. You're not going to like it, and it has to be done.*

If you're gentle.

And you have to eat all your food, even with the medicine stirred in.

I will.

Good. When it heals enough, I'll get on you and find out how much you've been taught.

I can run fast, and I know how to jump, but I'm not ready to go into competition.

Would you like to?

Yes!

And will you be nice to Sally?

Yes, if I can stay here.

Deal.

Bird laughed in surprise as Sox leapt joyfully in his stall, playfully shook his ears, and bumped Bird gently with his soft nose. Whatever happened next, Bird knew she'd made this horse very happy.

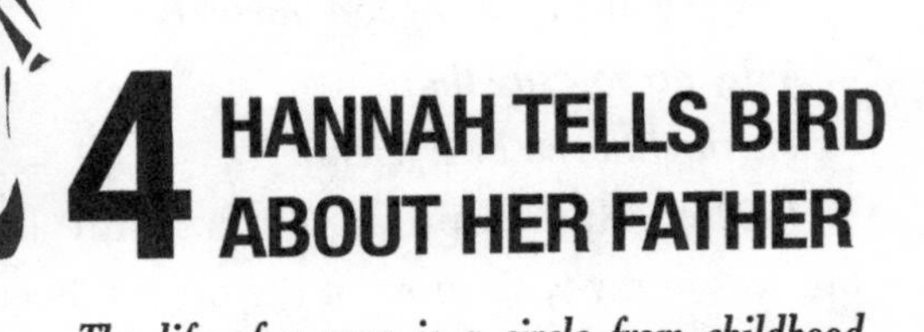

4 HANNAH TELLS BIRD ABOUT HER FATHER

The life of a man is a circle from childhood to childhood, and so it is in everything where power moves.

— Black Elk, Oglala Sioux holy man

Bird put Tall Sox outside with a barrel of fresh water and headed to the farmhouse for a late lunch. The others were already eating sandwiches outside under the big maple. On the way down the lane, she walked past Sundancer's field.

Sunny threw his head up. *You're paying a little too much attention to the new guy.*

Jealous, Sunny? Don't be! You're my best friend.

All the horses want you to ride them.

Bird climbed the fence and sat on the top rail. Sunny came over to get his ears scratched.

It was fun at the show yesterday, wasn't it? Bird messaged.

Yes. That jump in the first corner was tricky.

The vertical? Yeah. We might've come in too fast.

No, we didn't. It wasn't measured out right.

In a class like that, the distances would be accurate.

It wasn't right.

You know these things, Sunny. Bird grinned at her stubborn horse.

Sox is going to be a good horse, Bird.

Why do you say that?

He might even be a friend.

Really? This surprised Bird. Sunny liked Charlie, but was bossy with most of the others. Even Moonlight Sonata, whom he liked, was in danger of the occasional shot from his rear hoof.

Yes, really. He's smart.

High praise from Sundancer. *We'll see.*

Bird jumped down from the fence and continued to the house. Hannah was on the phone when she came through the kitchen door. As Bird made a peanut butter sandwich, she couldn't help but overhear.

"I hope he feels better soon, Laura. Do you need me to drive him? … How about groceries?" Hannah wore a slight frown on her face. "What do you think it is? … Hmm … Well, let me know what I can do … Okay, keep in touch … Bye."

"What's wrong with Mr. Pierson?" asked Bird, as Hannah replaced the phone on the wall.

"Oh, he'll likely be fine. He woke up feeling nauseous. It's probably the flu, but Mrs. Pierson worries about his heart, now that he's getting older."

"*Getting* older? He's close to ninety!"

"Bird! You'll be that age one day, if you're lucky, and sooner than you think."

"I'm just saying that Mr. Pierson *is* old, not *getting* old. I love Mr. and Mrs. Pierson!"

Hannah nodded. "I hear you. But understand that to say a person is old is to say they're getting close to death. It's a hard concept to accept."

"I never thought about it like that."

"That's because you're still young. Anyway, I'm sure Mr. Pierson will be fine. He's quite healthy."

Bird bit into a crunchy apple. She liked apples with her peanut butter sandwiches. "Can I stay here tonight? Or do I have to go, you know, back home." She tried to sound casual.

Hannah raised an eyebrow. "This sounds like a loaded question."

"No! Well, not really. I'd like to stay here, of course — I always do. And with Tall Sox here, and the show next Friday, I could be useful for the week." She took another bite and avoided Hannah's questioning gaze.

"Sit down, Bird. Do we need to talk?"

"Why? It's a simple question!"

Hannah put her elbows on the table and looked at Bird thoughtfully. "Just sit down for a minute, will you?"

Bird sat, her back rigid.

"Are you having trouble with your mother again?"

"Wow. You don't waste time."

"Are you?"

"Why do you ask?"

"I'm getting a sense of it, that's all. From you and Eva both."

"Okay. You're right." Bird decided not to pretend otherwise. She slumped. "I don't know why. We can't agree on anything, even to agree to disagree."

"Anything specific?"

"Everything specific! She hates my haircut, hates my clothes, can't imagine why I prefer my friends to the kids of her friends, and walks around the house modelling her new clothes and asking for compliments! She buys me skanky outfits and wants to teach me how to get a boy! She points out makeup tips and wants me to practise walking in heels! I'll probably smack her!"

Hannah listened carefully. "Is that all?"

Bird was offended. "Isn't that enough?'

"Plenty. But I hear more real pain in your voice than those trivial things merit."

Bird decided not to react to the "trivial" comment. She sat silently. After a moment, she spoke in a low voice. "It's happening all over again. She makes me feel ... inadequate."

"How so? You're talented, smart, accomplished in many ways, as well as being attractive. How can you possibly feel inadequate?"

"I don't know, I just do! After Mom met Stuart, we got along so well. I thought things had magically become perfect. I should've known better. I guess I just wanted it to be true."

"I know what you mean," agreed Hannah. "What does Eva complain about most?"

Bird gave Hannah's question some serious thought. "That I'm a freak, an alien. She doesn't use those words, but she definitely thinks I'm odd. She wants me to be just like her. She doesn't understand how I think, or why I do the things I do. I feel like I'm in the wrong family."

"And what bothers you most about her?"

"That she wishes I looked like Julia." The words popped out of Bird's mouth before she'd even thought them through. Still, Bird knew it was true.

Hannah tilted her head. "You mean like Eva?"

Bird nodded, her eyes filling with tears. "Like them both."

"You're a beautiful girl, Bird. You must know that!"

"I wish my mother thought so."

"I'm sure she does." Hannah sighed. "Eva can be insensitive. She's always been that way. She most likely has no idea what you're feeling. You need to talk to her, Bird. She won't figure this out on her own."

"I've tried, Aunt Hannah. Many times. But I went too far, and it only made things worse."

"How do you mean?"

Bird slumped further onto the table. "I need to know, and she never tells me, and I know she wants to forget, but last week I asked her again about my father."

"Oh."

"I only asked her if I looked like him, and she went crazy! She screamed at me and I ran out the door. Is that such a bad question?"

Hannah shook her head. "Not at all. It's an excellent question, and you do look quite a lot like him. But Eva doesn't want to discuss that chapter of her life. It's her story to tell."

"It's her story, but it's my life!"

"I'm sure she'll tell you when she's ready."

"She'll never be ready! I keep asking her! All I know is that he rode in the rodeo." Bird reached across the table and grabbed her aunt's arm. "You can tell me, can't you?"

"I only know what I heard from Eva."

"Please?"

"Bird, you're putting me in a corner."

"Was he so horrible? Was my father a murderer? A rapist?"

"No! Nothing of the sort!"

"Then why can't you tell me about him?" Bird was in tears. She let them fall down her face.

Hannah reached across the table and wiped them away with her hand.

Bird said quietly, "Please, Aunt Hannah? Tell me about my father?"

Hannah studied her. She nodded slowly. "Okay. Eva may never speak to me again, but I'll tell you everything I know." Hannah took a deep breath and released it slowly. Bird waited while she found the right words.

"I'll have to tell Eva I told you, Bird, and I don't look forward to it, but I'll start at the beginning as I understand it." She paused, and began. "My sister, your mother, was a gorgeous, headstrong young woman. She loved having fun. Still does, but she makes better choices now."

Hannah smiled and briefly shook her head. Bird knew the two sisters had had a troubled relationship over the years, but since Eva's visit the previous summer, things had been much better.

"Eva met Fred Sweetree at the Stampede in Calgary, Alberta. That's why she named you Alberta, but you knew that."

"Sweetree," Bird repeated. "Fred Sweetree. Wow. I never even knew his name until now."

Hannah stretched her back and got comfortable. "Fred was a broncobuster of enormous fame. He won more rodeos that year than anyone ever has, before or since. People said the horses bucked better for him, and less viciously, than for anybody else."

Hannah looked at her niece and smiled fondly. "Your father was a star. No — a legend. And above all the women flirting with him, he noticed Eva. They happened to be in the same bar one night, and he bought her a drink. Then another. Eva fell head over heels. It didn't hurt that all the other women were jealous. They left the bar together, and spent the Stampede week as a couple."

Bird could imagine the whole scene — Eva would have loved every minute of being with the toast of the town. The charismatic cowboy and the glamorous party girl.

Hannah continued, but her voice was more guarded now. "The last day of the Stampede, things went terribly wrong. Rumours circulated that Fred drugged horses. Some of the cowboys, not all, believed what they heard because of the change that came over the horses when Fred was around." She paused. "They were plain jealous. They couldn't figure out how else he was so successful."

Bird could guess the rest, but she let her aunt finish the story.

"The big awards dinner was that night, but Fred knew what people were saying about him and left town before the big trophy and the shiny new belt buckle could be presented." She paused, and her voice dropped.

"He also left your mother. Eva was heartbroken. She really loved Fred, Bird." Hannah moved chairs to sit beside Bird, and put her arm around the girl's shoulder. "When he left town, he took your mother's heart with him. But Bird," Hannah said gently, "he left her with a rare and beautiful gift. He left her with you."

Bird imagined her mother, young and irresponsible, but in love and crushed. Alone and pregnant.

"By the time she found out she was going to have a baby, Fred Sweetree was far away. She tried to contact him through the Stampede and various cowboy associations. After a while she accepted that she was going to have to raise you on her own. She tried her best to forget her dashing cowboy."

Bird remembered something she'd once overheard. "Mom once said that when my father saw her for the first time, he came up to her and asked, 'Do you want to play Cowboys and Indians?'" Bird looked intently at her aunt. "Does my father belong to a First Nation?"

"Yes, Bird. And very handsome. His rodeo name was 'Indian Fred.'"

Bird let this sink in. She was aboriginal. She sat up straight. How astonishing! Why did she not know this until now — this very important fact about who she was? There were so many questions that she needed answered. Which First Nation did she belong to? Did she have aunts and uncles and grandparents? Even brothers and sisters? She resolved to find him and ask.

"Thanks so much for telling me," said Bird. "Where is Fred Sweetree now? How can I find him?"

"Oh, Bird. I thought you knew."

"Knew what?"

Hannah drew in her breath. "Eva's quite convinced he's dead."

Bird felt like she'd been punched in the stomach. "Dead?"

Hannah nodded.

"How?"

"He was in a bush plane accident. There were no survivors."

"Oh, no!" Bird's stomach flipped. "That's horrible! When did it happen?"

"Years ago. I'm so sorry. I thought you knew."

"How could I know? Nobody tells me anything!" Bird's pain turned to anger as she tried to digest all of this new information.

"Don't shoot the messenger," warned Hannah.

Bird relaxed. "I'm sorry. It's not your fault. My mother should've told me a long time ago."

"I hope I did the right thing, telling Eva's story."

"You did, Aunt Hannah. It means so much to me to finally hear the truth." Bird turned to hug her aunt. "I can always count on you."

Bird simply couldn't understand why her mother had never wanted to tell her about Fred Sweetree. Maybe Hannah was right, her heart was still broken, but Eva was nothing if not resilient. She'd gotten married to someone else before Bird was even born, and she'd had Julia a few years later. And now she was madly in love with her new husband, Stuart Gilmour.

Bird snorted at the thought. The solid, predictable public school principal was the polar opposite of the dashing, carefree rodeo star.

Just then, Eva flew through the screen door, letting it slam behind her and startling both of them. Aunt and niece were still sitting side by side at the kitchen table. "Speak of the devil," whispered Bird.

Eva was out of breath. "Hannah, I have a big, *big*, favour to ask."

"Sure. What is it?"

"Can Bird stay over for a few days? Stuart and I have been invited to visit some old friends at their cottage in Muskoka. They have a daughter Julia's age. Bird would have nothing to do, and I'm sure she'd much rather stay here!"

Bird frowned. "Hello? I'm here? Can I make my own decisions?"

Eva waved a freshly manicured hand in Bird's direction. "You'd only cause trouble, and you know it."

Bird jumped up from her chair. Her heart was pounding. She wanted nothing more than to break something over Eva's smug, over-painted head. Instead, she looked at Hannah and said, "Can I move back in with you? Not just for a few days but forever?"

"Bird!" said Eva sharply. "What a hurtful thing to say!"

"Hurtful?" Bird stopped trying to control herself. "You ignore me, exclude me, say I'll cause trouble, and you call *me* hurtful?"

"It was better when you couldn't talk!"

Hannah tried to intervene. "Enough! Look, folks. If I could make a suggestion —"

"Hannah, my daughter and I will work things out our own way. Can she stay here or do I have to find a sitter or leave her alone at home?" Eva looked pointedly at her wristwatch.

"Of course she can stay." Hannah's face was flushed. "I love having her here. You don't have to ask. It's not a favour."

Bird was ready to explode. "I was unacceptable when I couldn't talk, remember? That's why you sent me here last summer. You wouldn't even admit to being my mother! And now you have the absolute nerve to say that it was better then? Well, now I can talk! And I'll say whatever

I want to say! I hate you! I wish you weren't my mother! And you can just … go! … just go! … to Muskoka or wherever you want. Because … I … don't … care!"

Bird ran outside, letting the screen door slam. She clambered over the rail fence and raced across Sunny's field, only stopping when she'd climbed the fence on the other side. She flopped down in the soft grass and closed her eyes. Hot teardrops warmed her face. She hadn't felt this miserable in a very long time.

Her mother was utterly foreign to her, that much she knew. Lucky for her that she had Aunt Hannah. Otherwise, who knew where she might end up? Maybe on the streets. Or foraging in the woods like her Uncle Tanbark, Hannah's half-brother, before he'd gotten help earlier in the summer.

And then there was her father. She'd just found out two rather large pieces of information. One, he was aboriginal, and two, he was dead. She would never be able to meet him. She would never be able to ask him about her family. Never be able to ask him why he'd left her before she was born. And why he had never even tried to meet her before he died. Not once. She really wished Alec were here to talk to. He always understood.

Bird girl.

Bird opened her eyes. *Cody!*

The small coyote stood close by, his head tilted. *You're making water from your eyes. Are you in distress?*

Yes, but not in danger.

I will help you.

Thanks, Cody, but there's nothing you can do.

Call on me. Cody disappeared from view.

I have my animals, thought Bird. What do I need Eva for, anyway? She doesn't understand anything about me. A revelation hit Bird — she really didn't understand anything about her mother, either. Eva was a complete mystery.

Bird sat up and looked across the field at the Saddle Creek farmhouse. She watched as Eva rushed Julia from the house. Eva was full of energy, and even from across the field Bird could see that she was happy, now that she'd gotten her way. She ushered the limp, resistant Julia into the car, closed the door with a flourish, and spun girlishly to wave goodbye. Hannah stood at the kitchen door. She waved absently as the car drove down the driveway to the road.

Once the car was gone, Bird stood and brushed the grass off her jeans. Her anger had dissipated, but she still felt the sting of her mother's rejection.

While Bird had been watching the house, Sunny had strolled over. Now he stood at the fence looking at her. *Hey, Bird.*

Hey, Sunny.

Don't be sad.

Bird patted his soft nose. *I'll be fine. Really.*

People confuse me. You were happy before you went in your house, and sad when you came out. Is something bad in there?

No, Sunny. My mother made me sad. I'll get over it.

Good.

Sunny bent his neck and resumed grazing. Bird rubbed his neck and breathed deeply. She was starting to feel better already.

For dinner, Hannah made her special dessert, rhubarb and cream cheese pie. It was Paul's favourite, and he had two pieces.

"I love your cooking, Hannah," he sighed as he leaned back in his chair.

"I love cooking for you," replied Hannah. "You're so appreciative!"

"I'm appreciative, too," said Bird. "I just don't gush as much."

Hannah chuckled. "You don't need to. I saw how you ate every bite and asked for more."

I like Hannah's cooking, too. Lucky thumped his tail under the table.

You like anybody's cooking.

I do. I do.

"You made an extra pie," noticed Bird. "Is that for tomorrow?"

"No, that's for the Piersons." Hannah filled Paul in on her conversation with Laura. "Pete is under the weather, and he really likes this kind of pie."

Paul rubbed his belly. "Can you blame him? It's amazing."

"Do you have time to run it over to them, Paul?" Hannah asked with a smile as they cleared the table. "Do you mind?"

"Anything for you," he answered, and kissed her on the cheek.

"Why don't I go instead?" Bird asked. "I haven't seen them for a while. I could ride Sunny, and leave you two alone to get mushy with each other."

"One day you'll understand." Hannah grinned as she began wrapping the pie.

"I understand already. I'm the three in the 'two's company and three's a crowd' rule."

"Never!" exclaimed Hannah.

"I want to ride over and see the Piersons anyway, if it's okay with you."

Paul looked at Hannah, who nodded. "Great," she said. "Just be home before dark, okay?"

"Okay."

Can I come? Can I come?

"Can I take Lucky with me?"

"Sure." Hannah added. "Be careful on the road."

"Okay." *You can come.*

Hooray! Hooray!

Bird helped Hannah put the wrapped pie in a cloth bag with handles so she could safely carry it on horseback. She left the house with the brown dog happily following her.

5 MERRY FIELDS

Honour all with whom we share the Earth; four-leggeds, two-leggeds, winged ones, swimmers, crawlers, plant and rock people.

— anonymous Native American Elder

Sunny and Bird took their time getting to the Piersons' farm. Leisurely, they hacked down the gravel road, followed by Lucky, who sniffed every bush happily. Bird smiled with pleasure. There was nothing she liked better than to ride her horse bareback in the cool, fresh evening air.

Hannah's pie smelled delicious. Bird was sure that Laura and Pete would be delighted. The Piersons had always been good to her. She counted them among the people she could rely on in times of need. They'd helped her when her grandfather had tried to sell Sundancer, and counselled her wisely whenever she needed to get on the right track. They cheered her up, too, Bird thought. They had a wonderful, sunshiny, practical outlook on life. Merry Fields was the perfect name for their farm.

Bird could just picture them now, sitting by the fire in their roomy kitchen, chatting about the day's events as Laura stitched a ripped pocket or mended a worn sock. The house would smell of fresh flowers and home cooking, and the kettle would be on, ready to offer a friend or neighbour a cup of tea. It was always like that.

Merry Fields was not far from Saddle Creek, and soon Bird and Sunny were strolling up the driveway. Lucky was busy somewhere, but Bird wasn't worried. Cody was likely around, and he'd keep an eye on the pup.

Interesting, Bird thought. There were no lights on in the kitchen, and the truck wasn't parked in its usual spot beside the house. Maybe the Piersons had gone out somewhere. But where would they go if Pete was not feeling well?

Bird slid off Sunny and removed his bridle so he could graze. *Don't go far, Sunny. I don't know how long I'll be.*

Right you are. I won't move. This grass is delicious.

Bird took the pie and walked up to the kitchen door. She peered through the glass. There was no cheerful fire burning in the hearth, no fresh flowers, and no home cooking. The house seemed empty and forlorn.

She knocked on the door. Nobody came.

She glanced at Hannah's pie. Leaving it outside wasn't an option. The ants, raccoons, and squirrels would get at it within minutes.

She tried the door. To her surprise, it opened. Bird called out, "Hello? Mrs. Pierson? Mr. Pierson? Is anybody home?"

There was no answer, so Bird put the pie in the refrigerator and found some paper and a pencil to write a note. They'd find the pie when they returned.

A wheezy, whining noise coming from the hall stopped her in her tracks. She put down the pencil and strained to listen. The noise came again. It was faint, but something or someone was definitely in the hall.

Bird gathered her courage and crept to the hall door. She put her ear to the space between the door and the frame. She heard it again, this time more clearly. It was a rasping sound, like tortured breathing. Fear gripped her. Should she run? No. She had to know what was going on.

Hands shaking, Bird opened the door a crack to take a look, having no idea what she might see.

Pete! Bird gasped involuntarily. Lying on the floor! He was hunched over in an awkward position with his head jammed against the wall.

Bird rushed to him. "Mr. Pierson! Are you all right?"

Pete opened an eye, and then closed it.

Bird pulled his legs with all her strength to straighten his body, and carefully moved his head to relieve the stress on his neck.

"What happened?" Bird whispered. Pete didn't react. "Where's Mrs. Pierson?" His skin was yellowish grey and his mouth hung open. Bird felt panic rise in her chest. This was all wrong.

Suddenly, Pete's breath rushed noisily from his open mouth. Bird jerked back in fright. He coughed hoarsely.

He opened one eye again, then shut it, as he had done before. There was no sign that he had seen her at all.

Bird shot to her feet. Mr. Pierson needed help. She'd call 911, then Hannah. She ran to the kitchen and picked up the phone. There was no dial tone. She replaced the receiver and wondered what to do.

Lucky began to bark wildly. Bird looked outside as the Piersons' truck stopped with a screech of the brakes beside the house. Bird ran outside.

"Mrs. Pierson! Mr. Pierson needs a doctor!"

Laura got out of the passenger side, and Dr. Collins stepped quickly down from the behind the wheel. He grabbed his bag and ran past Bird into the house.

"Bird, dear!" said Laura. "Pete had a spell. The storm knocked out the phone and I had to drive over to get the doctor. I hope you didn't worry."

Not worry? Bird's eyes grew round. She'd just seen a very old man gasping for air on the ground! "I brought over a pie from Aunt Hannah," was all she could think to say. "I put it in the fridge."

"Thank you, dear. How very thoughtful." Her eyes glanced to the house and back to Bird. "Can you visit another day? I must join the doctor now, and help Pete."

"Yes! Of course!" Bird backed away from the house. "Call if there's anything that we can do." Then she remembered. "Is somebody coming to fix your phone?"

"They're on their way. Don't you worry."

"Aunt Hannah and Paul will help. Just call. Me, too!"

"I will, dear, I will. Thank your aunt for the pie." With that, Laura rushed into the house and closed the door.

Bird stood on the walk and gathered her thoughts. She hated to leave Pete in the condition he was in. And to leave Laura to handle it alone. But Dr. Collins was there, Bird reasoned, and he would call an ambulance on his cell if needed. There was nothing she could do. It was so upsetting!

Sunny, come. We have to go.

So soon?

Yes. Bird took the bridle from the branch where she'd hung it and slipped it over the horse's nose. *Mr. Pierson is sick. Really sick. We have to go home.*

I like him, Sunny messaged. *He's a good man.*

That's what Cody calls him. The Good Man.

Bird silently rode Sunny home. Lucky followed along, but it was a very different ride from the one to the Piersons' farm. All the joy had left Bird's heart. For the second time in one day, she felt that the wind had been knocked out of her.

When they got back to Saddle Creek, Bird let Sunny out in his field, and she and Lucky entered the kitchen. No one was there.

"Hi, Bird," called Hannah, from the next room. "Did they like the pie?"

"Mrs. Pierson said thank you," answered Bird hollowly.

Hannah's head appeared in the doorway. "What's wrong? How's Pete?"

"Oh, Aunt Hannah," said Bird. The words came pouring out. "He's awful! Nobody was there so I put the pie in the fridge. Mr. Pierson was on the floor and he could hardly breathe and it was horrible. Mrs. Pierson came with the doctor and then we left." Bird flopped into a chair with glazed eyes.

"I'm sorry you had to see that," said Hannah as she brushed the hair from her niece's face. "It must have been upsetting."

"Yes, but more upsetting for Mr. Pierson! He was all scrunched up and he couldn't see or hear me."

Hannah looked at the phone. "I wonder if I should give them a call. See if there's anything we can do."

"Their phone is out. It'll be fixed soon. I told Mrs. Pierson to call us if she wants us."

Hannah pursed her lips. "I hope she will."

Paul joined them, and Hannah filled him in. Paul shook his head. "He's a wonderful man. I hope they can fix him up as good as new."

Bird hoped so, too, but the memory of his unhealthy colour and unresponsive behaviour gave her doubt.

It took Bird a long time to get to sleep that night. She couldn't get comfortable. She tossed and turned and flipped and flopped, unable to get the sight of Pete out of her mind. When she wasn't worrying about him, she was thinking about her father — what Hannah had told her, and how he'd died before they could meet. Finally though, when she slept, she slept deeply.

When the morning sun came through her window, Bird sat up in bed and stretched. It was Monday. She would help Cliff with the chores, and maybe Sally would come over to see Tall Sox. There was another show on Friday, and again on Saturday. Maybe they could bring Sox over to see what a horse show looked like. It would get him used to the activity and confusion of the show grounds without the stress of competing in the ring. She'd talk to Hannah about that.

Bird made a wish for Pete, and then jumped out of bed.

When she entered the kitchen, Hannah and Paul were sitting together having coffee.

"Good morning, folks," Bird said as she got a cereal bowl from the cupboard. "Another day in paradise."

"Morning, Bird," said Paul. "Mrs. Pierson called."

Bird spun to face them. "And?"

"Mr. Pierson was taken to Headwaters Hospital last night. He's feeling better, but not great. He doesn't want to be there, that's for sure."

"I don't blame him," said Bird with feeling. "I hate hospitals."

Hannah spoke up. "Apparently, they got the dosage wrong on his new medication, and he had a nasty reaction."

"Not good," said Bird. "Are we going to visit him?"

"Soon," answered Hannah. "He's not ready for visitors yet. Mrs. Pierson said she'd let us know."

Bird got the milk from the fridge and cereal from the shelf. "I'm glad he's at the hospital, even though he hates it." She sliced bananas on top and sat down with a spoon. "He sure looked bad yesterday. In fact, I thought he was going to die right there on the floor." She shuddered at the thought.

Paul looked thoughtful for a moment. "Death is normal, Bird. All living things must die. It's the way it is."

"Death is the price we pay for living," Hannah added. "We make that deal the minute we're born."

"Yeah," said Bird. "I know, but I can't *really* believe it. I mean really believe it."

Paul chuckled softly. "Like everybody else in the world. It's different when it's somebody we love or yourself that's dying."

"We don't need to worry about Pete dying just yet. More coffee, Paul?" offered Hannah.

"Just half, thanks." Paul was not ready to drop the subject. "I deal with life and death daily, Bird. Being a vet puts you in touch with it in a very tangible way. Helping my clients through is a big part of my job."

"That can't be the nicest part," said Bird.

"No, but it's a reality. If I didn't accept it, I couldn't do my job." Paul sipped his coffee.

"Sorry, folks, but I've got to get out to the barn," interrupted Hannah. "Lessons await."

Paul glanced at the kitchen clock. "I've got to get going, too."

"Is Sally coming today?" Bird asked Hannah.

"I think so. And her father wants us to take on Peasblossom. That'll be a problem for Dexter."

"I don't care," Bird sputtered through a mouthful of granola. "That's his problem. Nobody would leave him if he treated his horses better!"

"And was more fair to his clients." Hannah gave Bird a napkin to wipe the milk from her chin as she hurried out the door to begin her day.

"That's part of life, too," Paul told Bird. He rose and pushed back his chair. "Helping people out when things go wrong. And trying to fix things when we can, like helping Sally." He rubbed the top of her head with affection.

Bird was pleased with his approval. She knew Paul was right. And there were always so many things that seemed to be going wrong.

"Oh, Bird?" Paul turned to her as he opened the kitchen door. "Go easy on your aunt. Her father is going in front of a judge today."

Great. On top of everything else — Mr. Pierson's health, Eva's strangeness, sorting out Sox and Dexter — there was the ongoing saga of Kenneth Bradley, her grandfather. Another thing that needed fixing. He'd been arrested and charged with a number of things, including insurance fraud, obstruction of justice, and a pile of others that Bird didn't want to think about. She zipped up her chaps and squared her shoulders. No sense dwelling on it. There were horses to ride and chores to do.

On her way up to the barn, she climbed Sunny's fence and gave him a carrot.

Are we riding today? he asked.

Only if you want to. You deserve a day off to relax.

I'll take it.

Bird rubbed his forehead and kissed his nose. *You're awesome.*

You're not so bad yourself.

Is it okay if Tall Sox lives with you and Charlie?

Yup.

As Bird walked through the field, she gave Charlie a carrot, too. *Thank you, Bird!* He munched it happily and continued to graze. When she got to the other side, she climbed into the small paddock with Tall Sox.

Hi there, Sox! she messaged.

Bird! He trotted up and took the carrot she had in her open hand.

Have you decided who you want to go outside with?

Charlie and Sunny have a very big field with lots of grass.

You know that Sunny sometimes kicks.

He told me. I'll be careful.

Okay, then.

While they were discussing the field arrangements, Bird took a good look at the gelding's back. It was healing. Already the inflammation was reduced, and he didn't wince when Bird pushed on it.

What if I pop on your back without a saddle, Sox? The sore was located behind where she would sit bareback.

It's worth a try, so long as it doesn't hurt.

If it hurts, I'll get off.

Bird ran up to the barn and returned with a bridle. After making a few adjustments for size, she slipped the snaffle bit into his mouth and the headpiece over his ears. She used the fence as a mounting block and got on.

Okay so far? she asked.

Okay.

Tall Sox and Bird walked around the paddock, then picked up a trot. Bird was pleasantly surprised. The horse had very smooth and powerful action. After a few laps, Bird asked for a canter. Tall Sox easily moved into an athletic lope, covering ground without effort.

Very nice, Sox!

Thanks, Bird.

Sally Johns and her father, Harold, drove up the lane and stopped at the paddock. Sally jumped out and ran to the fence.

"Hi, Bird! He looks so, *so* good!"

Harold joined her. "Wonder of wonders. He's not bucking."

Bird slowed Tall Sox and met them at the gate. "That was all about the sore on his back. He's a really good horse. You did great buying him. He'll have a spectacular jump — he uses his body well."

Harold smiled broadly. "So he's not useless after all?"

"Not at all." Bird slid to the ground. "Sally, do you want to get up? You won't irritate his sore. It's further back."

Sally looked at her father, who nodded approval, then ran to the car to get her helmet.

"Turns out that Tall Sox was going to a man in Montreal."

"Really? What did Dexter tell you?"

Harold laughed. "Not a thing. We heard through the groom network at Moreland's."

"But you didn't know about it?" asked Bird.

"Not a thing. I thought he was going to a sales barn. I was to pay board and training fees until he was sold."

"Did the man come to ride him?" Bird asked.

"Apparently."

Holy, Bird thought. Dexter was pulling a real fast one. "So let me get this straight. Dexter was going to bill you to transport and stable Tall Sox at a fictional barn until he was 'sold,' which might have taken many months, and all along he already had him sold for real?"

"I don't know." Harold shrugged. "Maybe he was planning on telling me."

Sally had returned wearing her helmet and chaps. "Dexter wants us to buy the other gelding he has for sale, but I love Tall Sox now!"

Bird was curious. "Who owns the other horse?"

"Kelsey Woodall," answered Sally. "She bought him from Dexter for Candace."

"He's too much horse for Candace," stated Harold proudly. "Dexter thinks he'll be just the right amount of challenge for Sally."

Bird listened with skepticism. If Candace Woodall was having trouble with the horse, Sally would too. But what did Dexter care? He would still get a commission for selling them a new horse.

Sally puffed with pride. "Even Wanda says so. And Ed Cage, too. I think she's got a thing for him." Sally giggled.

Bird rolled her eyes. Ed was totally a flirt. She gave Sally a leg up. "Grab his mane."

Harold watched his daughter and her horse. "Sally and Tall Sox look good together. He's a good-looking animal," he said.

Sally sat up proudly. They began to walk in a large circle around the paddock. "He feels so-o comfortable!" she called. "Dex never let me ride him, not even once!"

"Have fun, sweetheart! Gotta run." Harold left for work, promising to pick Sally up later that afternoon.

When Hannah saw Sally riding Tall Sox, she came down from the barn. "Let's get your lessons started!" she said. Soon, Sally and her horse were having fun trotting through poles.

Bird watched Hannah teach Sally in the paddock, feeling quite happy about how horse and rider were getting along. Sally giggled and shrieked as she slipped and slid without a saddle, but Tall Sox kept shifting his weight to help her stay on. It was a very good match, Bird thought with satisfaction. This was one time that getting involved had worked out well.

When the lesson was over, Hannah joined Bird and leaned against the fence. Bird told Hannah what Harold had said about Dexter's plan, as Sally stretched her aching legs and cooled out her horse by leading him around.

"You're kidding!" exclaimed Hannah. "That must be why Kelsey urged Sally to put Tall Sox down! She wants the Johnses to buy her horse."

Bird wasn't so sure. "It was Sally who talked about Sox being put down. Kelsey just went along with it."

"Well, it sure got you on board."

"True. But Kelsey probably only believed what Dexter told her — you know, that Sox bucked and was mean and everything. Would she have known about the deal to sell him?"

"Maybe not. But she'd be happy to unload a problem horse that she bought for a lot of money." Hannah shook her head. "Shoot me if I ever get like that!"

"You mean a horse trader like Dexter Pill? Fat chance!"

They were interrupted by a horse van turning in the driveway.

"Must be Peasblossom," said Hannah. She walked through the gate and waved to the van driver. "Come on up!" she called.

The driver saw her and continued to the barn. Bird watched the brown, black, and white paint pony unload. He sniffed the air with his perky nose.

"Peasblossom!" yelled Sally. "I'm so glad he's here!"

Bird took Sox's reins so Sally could run up to the barn to join her pony. Bird led him out of the small paddock and opened the gate to Sunny and Charlie's big front field.

Thanks for your good work, Bird messaged as she took off the bridle.

Thanks for helping.

Bird looked over at Sunny and Charlie as they grazed across the field. *Don't crowd them, okay, Sox? Remember, this is their field. Be humble at first. A guest. Just until they get used to you, and then they'll forget you were ever the new guy.*

Good advice. They're going to be my best friends!

The other horses looked up as Sox walked into the field. Together they trotted toward him with flattened ears and threatening postures.

Bird knew it was a game of "who's the boss," and horses are big and strong and can really hurt each other. They'd been beside each other overnight, and had gotten used to each other over the fence. Now they needed to accept the new fact of shared grazing territory.

Sox stopped and put his head down. He avoided direct eye contact and let the others approach. Sunny sniffed him and pushed him hard with his nose. Sox didn't rise to the challenge.

Charlie dropped to his knees and began to roll, indicating that Sox was no threat. Sunny turned his backside to the newcomer and kicked up in the air. Sox refused to take offence, but stood his ground.

Bird relaxed a little. This should work out fine. She checked her watch. They'd been together for five minutes. She'd stay here for fifteen more. Twenty minutes was the magic number. That was when horses had either accepted each other or decided on war.

While Bird waited at the fence, Kimberly and her mother drove up the lane. Lavinia drove too fast, as always, and didn't see Bird waving. Bird laughed at the look on Kimberly's face as they sped by. Kimby was constantly telling her mother to slow down, and Lavinia was constantly ignoring her.

Bird thought about her own mother. Eva and Lavinia should have been great friends, since they were so much alike. Both were self-centred, vain, and impatient. But they couldn't stand to be in the same room.

Kimberly came running down to the fence and joined Bird. "Mom's here to pay Hannah next month's board and the show bills. What are you up to?"

"Just waiting to be sure the horses are happy together."

"Oh. Moonie likes where she is, with Sabrina. I think Peasblossom should go out with them, too."

Bird thought he'd probably rather go out with Timmy, who was a gelding and a pony too.

Kimberly yawned and stretched. "He's a cute pony."

"Yeah, I think so, too."

"Hey, Bird, can I tell you a secret?"

"Sure. What?"

"It's about Sally. I heard it from Danielle. You know, at Dexter's barn?"

Bird had seen Danielle ride at the shows. "What?"

"Everybody's glad Sally's gone. Nobody liked her."

"Why?"

"She lies. She makes things up. Once her father called the police because she told him somebody stole Tall Sox."

So *that's* what Harold had meant when he referred to the "last time," thought Bird. "And he wasn't stolen?"

"No! Sally hid him in the neighbour's shed!"

"Why would she do something like that?"

Kimberly shook her head. "Dunno. It's crazy."

"Or a call for attention." Bird paused, remembering how it felt when nobody seemed to care about her. "Her parents just got divorced. And I'll guess she wasn't in the cool group at the barn."

"Well, lying about her horse didn't make it any better," said Kimberly with a toss of her head. "It made her look like an idiot."

"Maybe so." Bird considered. "But she got her father's attention, didn't she?"

Liz and her mother, Patty, were the next to arrive. Liz waved out her window. "Hi, g-guys! Is Julia h-here?"

Liz's question reminded Bird of how Eva had ditched her. "No. She's with our mother at a friend's cottage."

Liz scrunched up her face. "Too b-bad."

Patty stopped to let her daughter out of the car, and waved to Bird and Kimberly. "Good morning, girls! Beautiful day, isn't it?"

"Sure is, Mrs. Brown," called Bird.

"B-bye, Mom." Liz joined Kimberly and Bird at the fence. She watched with them as the horses got used to each other. "They look p-pretty together," she said.

"A b-bay, a b-black, and a chestnut, and all g-good-looking."

"What do you think of Sally?" Kimberly asked Liz, changing the subject.

Bird shot her a warning glance.

"Sh-she's nice," answered the younger girl. "Wh-why?"

Bird jumped in. "Nothing. She's new, that's all. She's moved her horse and pony here, so it'd be great if we all got along."

Kimberly got the message, but couldn't help herself. "She lies, just so you know."

"That's not fair!" Bird turned on her friend, outraged. "That's gossip! Just remember how gossip hurt us last June, when everybody thought we were in the middle of all the bad stuff that was happening when Sandra Hall died."

Liz stepped back. "B-Bird, don't be m-mad!"

"It's not the same at all!" Kimberly stated, defending herself. "We were innocent!"

"How do you know Sally isn't?" Bird couldn't contain her feelings. She continued. "Tanbark was innocent, too, and everybody thought he was guilty!"

"Calm down, Bird!" Kimberly yelled.

"Calm down yourself! All my life, people have gossiped about me — about not talking, about being a problem, about causing trouble. It's not a nice feeling. I don't care what anybody says, Sally is going to feel welcome here!"

Without looking back, Bird turned and strode toward the farmhouse, leaving Liz and Kimberly speechless.

6 MISSING PIECES

Abuse no one and no thing, for abuse turns the wise ones to fools and robs the spirit of vision.
— Chief Tecumseh, Shawnee Nation, 1768–1813

Bird didn't care what Liz and Kimberly were saying about her. She didn't care that she'd spoken to them the way she had. It bothered her that people liked to gossip and pick on others, mostly because she'd been a victim of it so often.

Bird conceded that Sally might have had a problem with the truth. But that was in the past. She'd moved barns now, and she deserved a clean slate, didn't she?

Whenever she needed to figure things out, there was one person who helped the most. That person was Alec. But he was away at camp and would be there until September. Bird sniffed back a self-pitying tear. He couldn't use his cellphone or even text. She'd write him a letter later, but that wasn't nearly good enough. She needed to talk to someone now.

She knew exactly who. She needed to talk to Pete Pierson. He always understood so perfectly how she felt! But he was sick and in the hospital. She remembered his yellow colour and lifeless mouth with a shudder. Paul had said he was feeling better. Good enough.

Bird walked straight to the far side of the house and grabbed the handlebars of her bike. Up she got and off she rode. Headwaters Hospital was a fair distance by bicycle, but Bird didn't mind. It would feel good to push her legs to the limit.

It did feel good. Bird sailed along the highway as fast as she could. Trucks and cars and trailers and motorcycles sped past, throwing exhaust fumes and dust in her face, but Bird ignored it all. She was on a mission, and nothing could stop her. Somehow, just doing something — anything — made her feel more in control of her life.

An hour later, Bird rolled into the big paved parking lot. It was noon on a hot day, and she was sweaty and red in the face. She coasted to a shady spot under some trees, hopped down, and propped her bike against a trunk. Bird put her hands on her knees and caught her breath, then sat down on the grass to regain her composure before going in.

Bird studied the hospital. It was big and square. She knew the layout well; in June, she'd sneaked into her Uncle Tanbark's room and stopped a man from injuring him. Maybe killing him. She'd managed to sneak out again without getting caught, even though the security people were all over the place. Bird shook her head. Had she really done that? Hannah had been so mad!

Bird sighed as she realized that Hannah would be mad at her again. Very mad. She hadn't told anybody where she was going. Why did she always get herself in trouble?

She lay back in the grass and looked up the thick tree trunk through the leafy canopy. The sky was baby blue, and feathery clouds drifted along on a lazy breeze. A few pleasant minutes passed, and Bird sat up refreshed. The sweat in her hair was almost dry and her face had cooled. Hopefully, she was presentable enough to enter the building without looking like she should go straight to Emergency.

Bird walked up to the woman sitting in the information booth. She was engrossed in a paperback book, with her head down.

"Excuse me, please?" Bird said politely.

The woman looked up. It was the same woman who'd called security when she'd come to help Tanbark!

"May I help you?" the woman asked.

Bird tried to act normal. "I'm here to visit a patient."

The woman studied her face closely. "You look very familiar. Have you been here before?"

Bird smiled in what she hoped was an offhand manner. "Not lately."

"What's your name?"

"Bird."

"Bird? That rings a bell. Bird — like a winged creature?"

Bird nodded. She had to change the subject before the woman remembered. "I'd like to visit Mr. Pete Pierson, thank you. Which room is he in?"

The woman ran her finger down a list in the ledger on her desk. "It says here, 'No Visitors.' Sorry."

Bird tried to read the room number upside down, but the woman's hand was covering it.

"This is really bothering me!" the woman said, jutting out her jaw and squinting her eyes. "How do I know you?"

Bird shrugged her shoulders. "Were we on the same lacrosse team?"

"Bird!"

Bird spun around to see Laura Pierson hurrying over. "Dear, dear, girl! How nice of you to come!" She hugged Bird and kissed her on the cheek.

"I guess I can't visit," Bird said.

"Why not? You came all this way, it'd be a shame. Did Hannah drive you?"

"No, I rode my bike."

"All the way here? My dear child, that's dangerous, with all those trucks. I know Pete would love to see you." Laura took Bird by the arm and headed for the elevator.

"Sorry!" The woman at the booth stopped them. "It says no visitors. I can't let her go up."

"She's family!" exclaimed Laura with authority. "Of course she can go up!"

The woman's eyes narrowed. She looked at Bird and asked, "Why didn't you say so?"

Bird smiled weakly. "You didn't ask."

Pete was asleep when they got to his room. A machine was attached to his arm with long, transparent tubes. His colour had improved, thought Bird, but he still looked ghastly. Unreal. Almost like he was made of plastic.

"Pete?" whispered Laura. "Pete?" She put her hand on Bird's arm and motioned to the armchair beside the bed. "You sit there and wait for him to wake up. I'll fill his water pitcher." Laura picked up the plastic jug and was gone.

Bird sat down, prepared to watch the old man sleep. He opened one eye and saw her.

"Bird. Hello."

"Hi. Are you feeling okay?"

"No. I feel dreadful." He smiled at her weakly, but warmly. "Worse than dreadful."

"At least you're alive. Last night I thought you were going to die."

Pete sighed, and coughed feebly. "That wouldn't have been the worst thing."

"What are you talking about? What's wrong?"

"Nothing but old age. Everything hurts. I can't do anything. I feel as useless as a tit on a bull."

Bird chuckled. "That's pretty useless."

"But it's true. I'm good for nothing anymore."

"You're wrong!" Now Bird was alarmed. She'd had no idea that Mr. Pierson was feeling this way. "Mrs. Pierson needs you."

"I need her, but she doesn't need me. She does everything for me these days. I tell you, I'm worse than useless."

"Well, *I* need you! That's why I rode my bike here."

He turned his head on his pillow. A little more light gleamed in his eye. "Something wrong?"

"Where do I start?" Bird paused. "My mother and I are at each other's throats; my grandfather is in court today; I overreacted to something a friend said; I'm at Hannah's because my mother doesn't want me to come on a trip; I just found out about my father, but he's dead, and I'll never meet him. But the worst thing of all is that you're so sick."

Pete studied the ceiling. "That's a lot on your plate."

"I know, and you're the only one I can talk to."

Pete moistened his cracked lips with his tongue, still staring at the ceiling. "Do you know how stupid I am?"

Bird was startled. "Stupid? You're the smartest man I know."

"Stupid. I liked the new pills so much I took more than I was supposed to. I haven't told anybody else, and I won't, either. They think it was a mistake." He turned his head to look at Bird. "What do you think of me now?"

"You must have had a reason."

"I did. The pills worked wonderfully well. All my pain was gone, or at least I didn't feel it anymore."

"You thought that if you took more pills, they'd make you feel even better?"

"Yup. And they *did* make me feel even better. That's when I blacked out and fell on the floor. I don't remember anything. I gather Laura ran off to get the doctor and you showed up, pie in hand"

"And thought you were going to die."

"I was in a drug-induced coma. And it wasn't half bad."

"You're not thinking of doing it again." Bird was worried. "Are you?"

"No, but I'm in such a *lot* of pain, *all* the time — my arthritis, my shoulder, my back, my legs — I can't get relief from it."

Laura showed up at the door with fresh water. "Oh good! You're awake. Isn't it nice that Bird came to visit?"

"Sure is. Can you go ask the nurse to come?"

"Just press that button right beside you."

"No. Go get the nurse. Please."

Laura looked puzzled, but she disappeared again to do what Pete had asked.

"Don't tell Laura what I told you. About me taking too many pills."

"I won't. I wouldn't have anyway."

"Thank you."

Laura returned with a tall, angular nurse.

"Time for your meds," she said. "Open wide." The nurse gave Pete a small paper cup with pills in it, and a drink of water. "Did you need something?"

"I forgot," answered Pete. "I'll call if I do.

The nurse hurried away.

Laura crossed her arms. "If you want to speak to Bird privately, just tell me. Don't send me running all over God's green earth."

Pete grinned sheepishly. "Sorry, Laura. Bird came to ask me some advice. I don't know why she'd think I could help."

"Don't say things like that, Mr. Pierson! You're the only person who *can* help."

"You're right, dear Bird." Laura's eyes filled with tears. "My darling Pete is going through a rough patch." She smoothed his cheek. "Now, I've got a book to read. I'll do that in the lounge at the end of the corridor."

Once she was gone, Pete said, "I shouldn't even try to fool that one."

Bird laughed. "No kidding."

"So, now that you know you're talking to a stupid man, what do you need my help with?"

"Maybe I should begin with my father. Did you ever meet him?"

Pete wiggled a little under the covers, trying to get comfortable. "I did. He was known as Indian Fred. They called him Indie, and he was billed as the Indian Cowboy. He was a wonder with horses. I watched him take the nastiest, meanest bronc and turn him into butter … bu … tter … bu …"

He was asleep. Bird sat for a minute in case he woke up, but he soon began to snore evenly, and she wondered if the pill the nurse had given him was a sedative.

Bird tiptoed out, feeling better despite all the new questions racing through her head. She didn't know how or why, but Pete knew her father! And even though it wouldn't be today, Pete would be able to tell her things.

She found Laura lying on the couch in the lounge. A book lay on her chest and she, too, was taking a nap. Bird left a note on the book and made her way down to the lobby.

As she was leaving, she walked over to the woman at the information booth. "I just remembered where we met," Bird said innocently.

"You do?" The woman looked pleased.

"Yes. I was the girl who saved Tanbark Wedger's life the night he was attacked in his hospital room."

The woman slapped her hand over her mouth.

"And you tried to keep me from going upstairs, remember? As it turned out, it was a very good thing I did."

Bird walked away as quickly as she could without appearing to hurry. As soon as she was outside, she burst out laughing. The look on that woman's face had been worth the ride to Orangeville.

She hopped back on her bike and pedalled home to Saddle Creek, smiling all the way.

Hannah was definitely not pleased. She stood outside the house with her hands on her hips as Bird rolled up the driveway.

"You can't do that, Bird! You can't just disappear like that! Do you think nobody worries about you? Do you think you can do anything you want any time at all?"

"I visited Mr. Pierson in the hospital." Bird stopped

and dismounted. She stood awkwardly on the gravel in front of her seething aunt.

"I know that!" she snapped. "I called everywhere. I thought something might have happened, so I called the hospital. The nurse at the station in Pete's hall told me you were there and the time you left. Otherwise, my next call would have been to the police."

Bird knew full well she was in the wrong. "I'm very sorry. I won't do that again."

Hannah's voice softened just a bit. "Why did you run off like that?"

"I wasn't thinking straight. I've been worried about Mr. Pierson since last night, and I had an argument with Kimberly. I just needed to go."

Hannah didn't reply right away. "Kimberly told me. She said you were angry, and you accused her of gossiping. She's sorry you're upset." Hannah reached out her hand and pushed the sweaty hair off Bird's forehead. She smiled gently. "All teenagers gossip, Bird. Don't be too hard on her."

"I know," said Bird. "I just got mad."

"But you won't run off again without telling me, right?"

Bird shook her head. "No."

"All right, then. How's Pete?"

"He's okay, I guess. He didn't stay awake long. But he looks way better than yesterday."

"Very good."

"He started to tell me about my father."

Hannah looked at Bird. "Really?"

"Yeah. But he fell asleep. I really want to know more."

"I wish I could help, Bird."

"I'll ask him when he gets better."

Hannah indicated that Bird should put her bike away, and walked with her to the side of the house. "I heard about my father's case while you were gone."

Now Bird felt doubly bad. She'd heaped one worry for her Aunt Hannah onto another. And Paul had even asked her to go easy on Hannah. "What happened today?"

"His lawyer tried to get the case remanded — delayed — and to pay bail to keep Dad out of jail. Like he's done before. But because last year's insurance fraud case is still pending, the new charges of mischief and conspiracy to mislead justice made the judge think Dad's a flight risk."

Bird propped her bike against the wall. She tried to understand. "The old insurance fraud case … plus the new charges … made the judge not trust him? Meaning Grandfather doesn't get bail? Meaning he stays in jail?"

Hannah nodded. "Correct. No matter how his lawyers argue, the judge thinks my father will run from the law. Your grandfather will have to stay in jail until his trial." Her eyes looked hollow. "The date hasn't been set."

"I'm sorry. He deserves it, though." Bird looked directly into her aunt's eyes. "A person who leaves someone to die on the road and then frames his mentally ill son for it doesn't deserve to be free."

Hannah couldn't disagree. "I hear you, Bird." She brushed her hair from her eyes. "Oh, Eva called. They'll pick you up tomorrow evening on their way home from Muskoka."

Bird felt her chest tighten. "Can't I stay here? If I promise not to do anything else wrong? Would you be okay with that?"

Hannah inhaled. "Fine with me. *If* you don't pull any more stunts. Just be prepared to explain to your mother."

"Easy," said Bird. "I'll tell her the truth. She doesn't like me and I don't like her. Why put ourselves through the agony of living together?"

"Hold on, there, Bird. Aren't you being a little harsh?"

"No. It's the truth. No sense denying it."

"Keep an open mind. Things aren't always as black and white as they look."

"They are to me."

Hannah smiled affectionately. "I'd love to have you stay, Bird. But what about Julia?"

"Mom loves her. She'll be okay."

As it turned out, Bird got her wish and was able to stay with her Aunt Hannah. Bird wondered if Eva was relieved to be rid of her. The thought didn't exactly make her happy, but it did confirm Bird's opinion that she and her mother would never get along. No big news.

The week passed with the daily routines of the farm — animal care, lessons, and upkeep — and Friday came quickly. The morning of the show dawned bright and hot. Bird sprang out of bed thinking it was later than it was.

She ran downstairs and surprised Hannah in the kitchen. "Whoa there!" Hannah said. "You almost made me spill my coffee!"

"Are we late?" asked Bird. "We're still going, aren't we?"

"No, we're not late, and yes, we're still going." Hannah smiled broadly at her niece. "I was just about to wake you. Patty dropped off Kimberly and Liz at the barn. Everything is under control."

"Is Julia coming? And Sally?"

Hannah frowned. "Eva hasn't decided yet about Julia, and Sally wants to take Tall Sox, if we have room, to look around the show grounds."

"So, we take Sox if we have room, and Mom hasn't decided yet?"

Hannah looked at the clock. "I told her that the decision would be made for her if she doesn't call by seven o'clock."

"It's five after seven now."

"There you go. Tall Sox is coming." Hannah punched in the numbers to contact Harold Johns. "Hi, it's Hannah … Yes, Tall Sox has a spot in the trailer … Can you meet us at the show? We'll be there a little after eight-thirty … Great. See you later." She turned to Bird. "I woke him up, but he did ask me to call."

Bird ate a big bowl of granola with bananas and berries and vanilla yogurt, got dressed, and rushed out to the barn. Cliff had already packed the trailer with the necessary equipment, and extra bales of hay were piled in the back of the truck. The horses that were going to the show were groomed and ready to load. All except Sox.

"Cliff," Bird called out, "Sox is coming with us. I'll get him!" She rushed back down to his field, but couldn't see any sign of the bay gelding with the tall white socks.

"Bird!" called Cliff. Bird turned. Cliff stood at the barn door, waving. "I brought him in earlier, just in case!"

Bird ran back up. "I should have known."

A car came zooming up the driveway — Eva with Julia. Trouble, Bird thought.

Cliff watched beside her.

"Aunt Hannah already told Harold that Sox can come, and there's no room for little Sabrina on the trailer," said Bird. "Can you be the one to tell Eva? She hates me."

"No way!" Cliff said, screwing up his face. "She scares me!"

"A tough guy like you?" Bird challenged with a smile.

"Yeah, okay." Cliff nodded unhappily. "I'll do it. But she still scares me."

"I'll protect you if she attacks."

"Sure."

"Thanks! I'll groom Sox." Bird raced off before Cliff changed his mind.

She put Sox in the cross ties, scraped the dirt out of his hooves with the hoof pick, and combed his mane. His coat was thick with dust, so she made the decision to bathe him. He might as well look like a show horse.

She and Sox were in the wash stall when Julia appeared, all dressed in her show clothes. "Hi, Bird."

Bird looked around. "Are you okay? I mean, without me at home?"

"Mom is *way* nicer when you're not there to argue with her. No offence."

Bird laughed out loud. "So I shouldn't feel guilty?"

"Well, I miss you!" Julia exclaimed. "You should feel guilty about that!"

"Okay, I do. I'm just glad she's being nice to you, that's all."

"She is. In fact, I think she's trying to spoil me to feel better about you and her." Julia stepped back from the spray of water. "Anyway, I'm really excited. This'll be a really fun day."

Bird thought she was being sarcastic. "Look, sorry about that. Mom was supposed to call Aunt Hannah by seven and she didn't."

"What are you talking about?" Julia looked puzzled.

"That Sabrina isn't coming. We don't have room."

"Cliff told Mom we're coming! I heard it myself."

Bird felt a fork of anger. This was not fair to Sally and Harold Johns. Eva had a knack for always getting her way. She finished washing Sox and scraped off the water. She put him back in cross ties to dry and stomped off to confront Eva.

Cliff stopped her in time. "I thought of a way for them all to go," he whispered. "I'll drive my truck and borrow Lisa and Joe's tagalong trailer." Lisa and Joe had boarded at Saddle Creek Farm for many years, and left their trailer at the barn.

"Did you ask them?"

"I just called. Lisa said yes. Thanks be to the heavens above."

"Cliff, you have no backbone."

"I know that," Cliff laughed. "Hey, I saw how fast you chickened out and left her with me."

They loaded the horses and left for the show. Hannah drove the big rig with Bird and the four horses — Sundancer, Pastor, Moonlight Sonata, and Tall Sox. Eva drove Julia, Kimberly, and Liz, while Cliff trailered the pony, Sabrina, in the borrowed van.

They arrived at the grounds right on time. Sally Johns was waiting in the car with her father at the gate. "Hello-o-o!" she waved excitedly and ran over to the Saddle Creek truck. "I'm here!"

Hannah smiled at the girl and leaned out the window. "Is your dad staying?"

"No, he's got to get to work."

"Jump in. We'll go find a place to park."

Sally waved goodbye to her father and climbed in the back seat behind Bird.

They weren't lucky enough to find a spot overlooking the grounds, but settled on one under a big shady tree. Cliff parked his truck beside it. "We'll have a little ways to go for water," said Hannah.

"We can handle it." Bird jumped down from the truck and opened all the window flaps in the trailer. The horses stuck out their heads and looked around at the activity. Horses, ponies, kids, adults, grooms, riders, vans, trucks, golf carts, motorbikes, bicycles, tents, flags, paddocks, jumps — it looked like a big jumble of colour and movement until you figured out what everything meant, where things belonged, and what people were doing.

So this is what it's like! Tall Sox's nose quivered as he took in all the new smells. *So much is happening!*

You'll get used to it, Sunny answered. *After a while, you learn to ignore what you don't need to notice.*

Bird thought the horse said it well.

Sally came over. "What do we do now?" she asked.

"We'll leave Sox on the trailer until he gets familiar with the smells. In a while, we'll lead him around, just to let him see everything."

Sally nodded happily. "I'm so glad he could come! I've never trained a horse before!"

Bird was surprised that Sally saw herself as a trainer. But really, she thought, it made sense. The most important part of training is reducing fear, which allows a horse to accept what people want to do with him.

"You'll be really good at it," said Bird. "And it'll be fun."

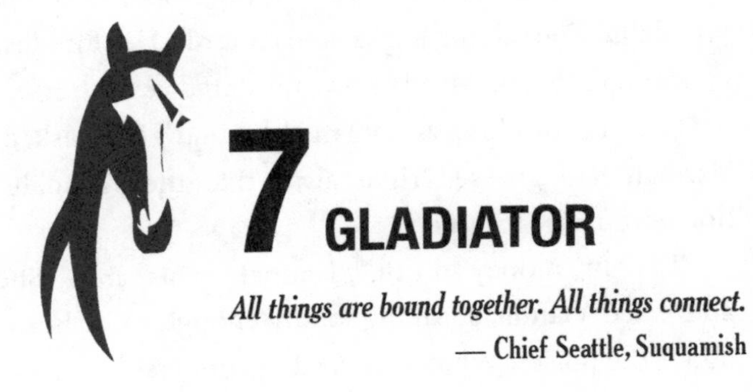

7 GLADIATOR

All things are bound together. All things connect.
— Chief Seattle, Suquamish

Bird walked down to the registration office with Hannah to sign everybody up. The office still had the passports for their horses — they were kept in a box for the season's shows — but Hannah had to write a cheque for the classes and get the girls' entry numbers.

As they made their way down the dirt lane toward the office, Bird noticed a very handsome bay gelding. He was skittery, and spooked at a passing golf cart. Watching him jump clear across the lane, Bird realized it was the same horse that had run away the weekend before — the same horse that had been stopped by the mysterious man!

Bird looked up at the rider. It was Wanda, one of Dexter's grooms.

"Hey, Wanda!" Bird called to the red-haired girl as the horse continued to sidestep and prance.

"Bird! How's it going?"

"Good! What's your horse's name?"

"Gladiator. He's not mine — he belongs to the Woodalls." The gelding jiggled and danced. "He's for sale."

Hannah touched Bird's arm and stared at the horse.

"Are you thinking what I'm thinking?" Bird asked. Hannah had guessed right away that the Woodalls' horse would be for sale.

"I'd put money on it." Hannah whispered. She addressed Wanda, speaking loudly enough to be heard above the noise. "What does he do? Jumpers?"

Wanda rolled her eyes. "He refuses jumps half the time, and is afraid of water, but don't say I said so. They're looking for a lot of money."

"How much?" asked Bird, knowing Hannah would be too polite to ask.

"Fifty thousand."

"Holy!" Bird hadn't expected that. Fifty thousand wasn't out of line for a horse that was consistently in the ribbons, but not for one that stopped at jumps. "He's handsome enough, but fifty?"

Wanda shrugged. "Not my business."

Before Bird could reply, Gladiator decided that the people had chatted long enough. He leapt in the air with a mighty twist. Wanda wasn't ready, and off she tumbled. Gladiator raced away with his stirrups flapping against his sides.

"Stupid horse!" she yelled. "I'll never catch him," she grumbled as she brushed herself off. "And now I'll never get Dexter's clients ready for their classes in time!"

Bird watched as the horse sped away. “Aunt Hannah, do I have time to catch Gladiator for Wanda?”

Hannah nodded. “Lots of time. That’s nice of you. I’ll do the paperwork. See you back at the trailer.” She smiled at Bird and walked on to the office.

“You’d do that for me?” Wanda’s voice was filled with gratitude. “I really, really, really appreciate it!”

“No worries,” Bird said. “Where’s he stabled?”

“At the far end of the third row, closest to the warm-up ring.

“Thanks so much! You’re a lifesaver!” She took off running to do her job.

Gladiator had raced off in the direction exactly opposite from where he was stabled — an indication, Bird thought, that he didn’t want to be there.

She caught sight of him between two trailers, and she began to run. He ducked behind a row of stall-tents and disappeared from her sight.

Gladiator? Are you all right? she messaged.

Who are you?

My name is Bird. Can I come get you?

And give me back to those people?

Is there a reason not to?

The horse didn’t answer.

Gladiator?

Silence. He wouldn’t willingly come to her — not yet, at least. She didn’t blame him, but she didn’t want to give up either. She continued to follow him, and when she got to where she’d last seen him, she turned the corner.

There he stood, with sides heaving. Right beside him stood the man she'd heard at the last show — the man who could communicate like she did. Gladiator had run to him!

After taking a few seconds to think, Bird walked up. "Hello," she said aloud.

The man looked at her out of deep brown eyes with wrinkles all around them. His face was weathered by the sun. His faded jeans had a brown leather belt and a big western buckle, and his messy black hair showed under a faded blue baseball cap. He wasn't tall. He might be as old as Hannah, Bird thought.

While she was examining him, Bird knew he was studying her, too. "Hello," she repeated. "My name is Bird."

"Is this your horse?" he asked.

"No. But I know where he belongs."

"Belongs, you say? He doesn't belong there, or he wouldn't be here."

Bird smiled at him, trying to look friendly and casual. "I feel the same way. But I told them I'd bring him back."

The man took his time answering. He removed his cap to scratch his head, black hair shining almost blue in the sunshine. Bird was wondering if she should say something — the silence was getting awkward — when he said, "Then do what you must do."

He gave Bird the reins and turned away.

"Hold on!" Bird waited for him to turn back. He didn't. "I think I saw you last week." *I heard you speak.*

The man stopped walking. He stood still with his back to her.

I speak the same way, Bird transmitted.

Nothing.

I want to talk to you.

Still nothing. The man didn't turn to her, but he didn't walk away either.

Maybe I have the wrong person. Sorry.

Now the man walked away. He didn't look back.

"Thanks for catching Gladiator!" Bird called to him through a thickening throat. All of a sudden she felt a wave of loneliness. Her eyes burned with tears. *Had* she gotten the wrong person? Had she *imagined* that he spoke telepathically?

The horse gently touched her arm with his nose.

Bird patted him gratefully. *May I ride you back?* she asked.

I don't know. The gelding became nervous again, and shuffled his feet. *I don't want to go back.*

It won't be for long. I'll try to help you.

Okay. You can ride me. I don't like it there, but I will not misbehave.

Fair enough. Bird adjusted the saddle and got up. She tried to put aside her disappointment about the man as she steered Gladiator through the people and horses and fuss. They slowly made their way to Dexter Pill's stall tents.

You're a nice horse. Tell me how I can help you, Bird said.

Can you buy me? I would be happy with you. You understand me.

True. But they're asking a big price for you, which I can't afford.

Soon it will be lower. I do nothing well. I hate my life.

Bird patted his shoulder. *I'm sure you do many things well.*

No, I don't. I used to be a good jumper, and now everything scares me.

Does Dexter hurt you?

Yes. When I don't jump he hits me. Now I never jump and he hits me all the time.

You'll get your confidence back. You're a wonderful animal.

Thank you, Bird. You make me feel good.

I'll watch out for you, Gladiator.

Please don't call me that. I like the name Glad.

Okay, Glad.

It's good luck to find a person who talks like you do.

Thanks. It comes in handy.

But it's great luck to find two.

Bird was confused. *Two?*

Yes, two.

Did he mean the man? Perhaps she hadn't imagined it! *That man? Does he speak like I do?*

Ask him again when he's ready to tell you.

Bird smiled broadly. She would do just that.

When they arrived at Dexter's stabling, Wanda came running. "Thanks so much, Bird! You totally deserve a medal! I owe you one!

"My pleasure," said Bird as she dismounted. "This is a very nice horse."

Wanda rolled her eyes. "Right. Tell that to my bruises."

"No, really," Bird was serious. "If you want to pay me back for helping, be really good to him. And call him Glad."

"Whatever," joked Wanda. Then she looked at Bird. "You're serious."

"I'm serious. Call me if you need help with him. You know where we're parked?"

Wanda nodded. "Yes, and I will."

Bird stroked Glad's neck. *Be a good boy, Glad. I'll check back later.*

I hope so.

Bird gave his chin a rub and headed back to the Saddle Creek trailer.

Sabrina was being shined up for her class, and Julia was nervous. The Champion Pony Jumper was the first class of the day.

"It's too crazy, this course!" Julia wailed. "We start through the gate in the middle, then go right to the fenceline and take the jump with the purple windmill thingies. Then the green hedge, and then the horrible red silo thing. But then what?" She hopped on one foot. "I'll never remember! Never!"

Cliff laughed. "Is this what I miss when you guys go off to shows? Major meltdowns?"

"You try it!" whined Julia. "It's crazy out there!"

Bird took her sister by the shoulders. "Deep breath. You know the course. Get to the first jump and the rest will follow." Bird felt Julia's tension lessen. "Now take another deep breath. And another."

Julia smiled. "Thanks, Bird. I'm ready."

Bird gave her a leg up onto Sabrina and helped them warm up. When the pony and girl were ready, she walked them to the in-gate. They got there just as the announcer called out Julia's number.

"Good timing!" Bird gave her the thumbs up. "Have fun out there."

"I will." Julia looked pale but steady.

Sabrina glanced at Bird. *Ribbon time.*

Bird laughed, and patted the pony's rump as they trotted into the ring.

Cliff stood with Bird. "Where's Eva?" he asked.

Bird shook her head. "Who knows?"

"Does she know Julia's up?"

"How should I know?"

"Should we find her and tell her?"

"You can if you want, Cliff. I'm not doing it." Her mother would watch if she wanted to.

Cliff paused. "I guess you're not getting along too well these days."

Bird turned to him. "It's simple. My mother doesn't care about me and I don't care about her."

A petulant voice from behind startled them both. "How can you say that, Bird?"

It was Eva. Bird sighed and turned to face her mother. "Can we watch Julia now?"

"I can't believe you said that!"

Bird turned back to the ring.

"Don't you turn away from me!" Eva stomped her foot. "If you have something to say about me, you can say it to my face!"

Julia picked up her canter and away they went through the timer. This was not the right time for a big discussion, Bird thought.

"Are you not speaking again?" demanded Eva.

"Can we talk about this after Julia's class? I want to see her ride."

"You've upset me so much, it makes no difference to me if Julia's riding or not." Eva turned with a dramatic flourish and stiffly stalked off.

Bird exhaled. "I really wish she hadn't heard me say that," she said quietly to Cliff.

"Maybe it's better. It's out in the open now, and maybe you two can sort it out. Get it over with."

"Wishful thinking. It never ends with Eva."

Bird and Cliff watched Sabrina fly over the jumps. Up her knees came, and out her neck stretched. Over they went, time after time, like a little well-oiled sewing machine. Sabrina made the jumps look small. Julia's face was earnest and set with determination. Her body moved in harmony with the chestnut pony with flaxen mane and tail. Heels down, eyes up, looking for the next turn, Julia rode with confidence. Bird and Cliff found themselves smiling, in spite of the scene with Eva.

"Wow!" exclaimed Cliff. "She barely landed before she turned and leaped! This is great! I'm glad I came."

Sabrina trotted out proudly, and because she was so pleased, she bucked triumphantly at the exit. Bird wasn't able to grab Julia in time, and off she tumbled.

Julia landed on her feet, laughing. "Sabrina always brings me down to earth!" she crowed.

Bird nodded. "Can't get a big head with this pony!"

Sabrina! You'd be disqualified if Julia came off in the ring! she messaged the mischievous pony.

That's why I did it out here. We won!

There are forty more ponies to go.

Take it from me.

Bird guessed Sabrina was right. It would be difficult in the extreme for anyone to beat her time. She patted her neck and chuckled. Some things never change, and Sabrina was one of them. Eva, too. So why did she enjoy Sabrina's idiosyncrasies but not her mother's? A puzzle for another day.

Julia babbled happily about her ride — the problems and solutions — as they walked back to the trailer together. The show had started well.

Hannah was already back at the trailer. "Great ride, Julia!" she called. "I saw it all!"

"Even my unintentional dismount?" Julia smiled broadly. "Where's Mom?" she asked Bird. "Did she see us go?"

Cliff and Bird glanced at each other.

"That's why she came today," answered Bird evasively.

"Nice ride, Julia," said Cliff quickly. "I didn't know you and Sabrina were so red hot!"

While the other kids in the pony class competed, Julia untacked Sabrina and led her around to cool her out. Bird hoped her sister wouldn't notice that Eva's car was gone.

Kimberly's class was up next, and Bird went over to help her get Moonlight Sonata ready.

"Friends?" asked Kimberly, as Bird brushed out the mare's tail.

For a moment, Bird couldn't figure out what Kimberly meant. She'd forgotten all about their disagreement. "Oh, that! Don't worry about it. I totally overreacted. I was in a funk."

"But you were right about gossip and how bad it is." Kimberly hugged her. "I feel so much better when we're friends!"

Sally came up. "Can you walk Tall Sox around for a while now?" she asked Bird.

"I thought you were his trainer, not me."

"I've never led him before."

"Really? Then it's a good day to start." Bird pointed to a field close by. "Lead him over to the grass and let him graze for a while, okay? He'll feel safe if he can watch from a distance. Then after half an hour or so, walk him around on the paths. Don't go near the stable areas yet. Too busy."

Sally looked uncertain. "You really think I can do this?"

"Of course you can!" Bird said.

Sally straightened with determination as Bird unloaded Tall Sox from the trailer. *Stay cool, Sox.*

I'm a little excited.

Of course. It's an exciting place. Just try to be calm, especially for Sally. She's new at this.

Bird handed Sally the lead shank. "All yours. You'll be just fine."

The horse and girl walked together toward the field Bird had indicated. Bird was satisfied that Sally could handle him — Sox was a very decent animal. She turned back to Moonlight Sonata and put the finishing touches on her grooming, smoothing pine tar on her hooves to make them shiny.

You look the part, Moonie.

I feel the part.

Bird smiled. This mare was special. Talent, quickness, brains, good training, and a big heart. She had it all, and Kimberly knew it and loved her.

"Okay, Kimby," said Bird. "Give it your best shot."

"I will," answered her friend as she mounted. "But I'm a little nervous. Gladiator's the big competition. At least that's what Dexter Pill's saying. He's seriously talking him up."

"Really?" Bird was interested.

"He's a good-looking horse, and Dexter's riding him himself. He's a pro!"

"Don't worry. Just ride Moonie the way you always do. Have faith in her."

Kimberly set her jaw. "I do! She's the best! Aren't you, girl?"

I'm way more solid than Glad, poor guy, messaged Moonie.

You know and I know, and Glad knows. Poor guy is right. Bird patted Moonie's flank as she and Kimberly trotted off. She thought about what a difference it makes for a horse to have the right training and the right rider. Glad had no confidence, and it was all because of Dexter's training methods. Dexter pushed a horse along too quickly, in Bird's estimation. Like raising the jumps higher and higher without letting the horse get comfortable with each height. Then the horse lost heart and wouldn't be able to jump at all. Some horses succeeded with this method, but others became ruined, like Glad. Bird liked to take a lot more time and make each horse feel like a superstar, getting them to believe that there was no jump too tall or wide. Pete always told Bird that patience was the biggest virtue of all when you're dealing with horses.

Bird followed Moonie and Kimberly to the practice ring. They looked calm and ready for a good ride. While Hannah schooled them over some jumps, Bird checked the order of riders, posted with the course.

There were thirty entries. Kimberly was up fifth, and Dexter was riding two horses in this class. One was number twenty; Gladiator was posted sixth.

Suddenly, cries of "Loose horse!" could be heard across the showground. Bird looked around.

Help! Help!

Slow down, messaged Bird to the panicking animal. *Slow down. Don't hurt yourself.*

Bird? It's me, Sox.

Sox? Go to the trailer. It's safe there. I'll meet you.

Bird ran as fast as she could. The Saddle Creek trailer was right in front of her, but there was no Tall Sox to be seen. She got to the rig and bent over, trying to catch her breath. Stupid! She should never have let Sally take Sox alone.

Bird! I'm here!

Bird looked up to see Sox racing toward her. The lead rope dragged on the ground, and Sally stumbled along far behind.

Whoa. Good boy.

Something hit me in the back!

What? asked Bird. *A bug?*

No! Something hard!

Are you hurt?

No. But it stung me and scared me!

Bird could see no blood. She worked her fingers all over his back. *Where does it hurt?*

Right there! The horse flinched as Bird found the spot — a tender bump on his rear.

Bird had no idea what had happened. *You're safe now, Sox. Don't worry.*

Can we go home? Now? I don't like it here!

Not yet. We'll go home soon. Bird felt responsible and wanted this to end on a good note.

Sally arrived, all out of breath. "Bird! I'm sorry! I can't do this! I'm a horrible trainer!"

"Don't worry, Sally. Just tell me what happened."

"I don't know! He just …" Sally huffed and puffed. "He just jumped up and ran away!"

"It's not your fault." Bird put her hand on the girl's shoulder. "Stuff happens."

"I don't want this horse! I want Peasblossom!"

"Give Sox another chance. He spooked at something. All horses do that sometimes. Even Peasblossom spooks."

Over at ring three, Bird saw Moonie and Kimberly waiting at the in-gate. "Let's go watch Kimberly's ride," said Bird. "Sox can come with us."

"I'm not leading him!" exclaimed Sally.

"No problem." Bird patted the gelding's face. *Come along, Sox.*

I'm scared! I want to go home.

You can't give up now. Sally needs to see how sensible you are. I'll be right here beside you.

Okay. But I don't like it.

Sally, Bird, and Sox got to the ring just as Moonie was walking in for her round. Kimberly saw them over her shoulder. "Wish us luck!" she yelled out.

"Good luck!" Sally called.

"You don't need it!" responded Bird. "Just feel the joy of riding!"

Kimberly grinned and gave them the thumbs up. She and Moonlight Sonata started a smooth, rocking canter and went through the starting timer.

They were off to a good start. Bird noted their pace and how well they were judging their distances to the jumps. It looked like it would be a very good round.

As Bird watched Kimberly and Moonie, she couldn't shake the uncomfortable feeling that someone was watching her. She glanced around, trying not to look obvious. Over by the stands stood handsome Dexter Pill, surrounded by his admiring students. He saw her looking at him and smirked. Then he mimicked Kimberly and gave Bird a thumbs-up.

Gee, thought Bird, recoiling. Could he look any more like an evil villain?

8 SURPRISE IN STORE

Show respect to all people and grovel to none.
— Chief Tecumseh, Shawnee

Tall Sox stood quietly beside Bird at ringside. He was getting more and more comfortable with the stimulation all around them. *This isn't so bad*, he messaged.

No, it isn't. Soon, when you're ready, you'll be out there jumping a course. And you'll be great.

Like Moonie? She's really good.

Like Moonie. And Sunny. And Sabrina. And Pastor. It's fun. You'll see.

Sox relaxed even more. His ears pricked forward and his eyes sparkled as he watched Moonie sail over the jumps and get her turns.

Kimberly rode with confidence and skill. Moonlight Sonata looked comfortable and keen. As a team, they appeared perfectly suited. They cut corners easily and kept a good pace without racing. Moonie's hooves skimmed over the rails without knocking any down. When they landed the final jump, Bird and Sally cheered.

"Great round, Kimberly!" yelled Bird.

"Hooray!" Sally applauded and stamped her feet.

Hannah was very pleased as she met them at the gate. "Very nice ride, Kimberly," she said proudly. "Take her back to the trailer and walk her out. Be ready for a jump-off."

Kimberly smiled broadly and nodded. "Okey-dokey!"

"Sally?" Hannah said. "Can you go help Kimberly? I've got to get Pastor and Liz over some jumps."

"Okay!" Sally patted Tall Sox, then turned to Bird. "Are you okay to stay with my horse?"

Bird nodded. She wanted to stay and watch anyway.

Sally ran after Kimberly, and Hannah returned to the warm-up ring.

Can we see some more jumping? Sox asked her.

Yes. Dexter and Glad are up next. They should have been in the ring already. Bird looked around for them.

Glad was balking at the gate. On his back, Dexter kicked and kicked, while Wanda and Ed Cage pushed and smacked his rump — to no avail. Glad had absolutely no intention of going into the ring. Dexter jumped up and down on the horse's back and flapped the reins on his neck. His face was dark with exertion and anger. Bird had seen that look before.

Beside Bird, Tall Sox began to shake. *That man makes me nervous.*

He can't hurt you anymore, Sox. She stroked his neck calmly. *You live at Saddle Creek now.*

Bird messaged over to Glad. *Relax, Glad. Just walk in. Don't worry.*

I can't do this! I'll knock down the jumps and it hurts!

At least try.

I used to be able to do this. I used to be good at it!

Then you can still do it!

Can you ride me instead of him?

Bird was surprised at the idea. Dexter would no doubt punish the horse if he allowed Bird to ride him. *I would love to, but not today. Can I see you trot?*

Trot?

Yes. Trot into the ring so I can watch how you go.

Glad trotted in. A half smile of satisfaction crept across Dexter's face as the elegant animal stepped out in a lively pace.

Bird continued coaching from the sidelines. *Now, move into an easy canter. Dexter will steer you toward the first jump.*

I'm afraid! If I do anything wrong, he gets so mad!

Don't worry, Glad. Nice and easy takes the day.

Nice and easy. The bay cantered through the starting posts and headed for the first jump. He sailed over it, but because he was trying so hard, he over-jumped and Dexter became unseated. He stayed on, but grabbed the mane and flopped forward. Bird could hear Dexter swearing at Glad, embarrassed in front of the crowd. When they landed, Glad was completely unhinged.

I'm sorry! I tried! I can't do this! Glad raced for the exit and could not be stopped. Dexter pulled on his face and tried to steer him, but Glad continued at a gallop. Dexter let the reins slacken as he decided to let the fence stop him, but the fence was not the problem. Glad leapt high.

The problem was that the bleachers were only one stride from the fence. The crowd shrieked with terror as the big horse came charging over the fence. Dexter screamed. People scrambled. Glad landed and veered away, mere inches from the bleachers. Dexter tumbled and landed hard on the grass beside the wooden benches.

Glad ran up to Bird and Tall Sox with his reins and stirrups flapping. He slid to a halt, out of breath and huffing. *Protect me, Bird!* he messaged. *He'll beat me for that!*

Sox sniffed at Gladiator's nostrils to comfort him. *Don't worry, Glad. Bird won't let him.*

Bird wondered what she'd gotten herself into. She did not have a plan, and Dexter was limping angrily toward her. Bird looked around for help. Hannah was far away, busy with Liz and Pastor, and there was no one else near. Sox and Glad stood huddled fearfully beside her.

Bird turned to face the seething trainer. "Hello, Dexter," she said with a fake smile. "Nice day."

"I don't like you one bit," Dexter muttered through clenched teeth. "You are nothing but trouble. Give … me … that … horse!" He stuck out his shaking arm.

"I don't have him to give," said Bird. "As you see, his reins are loose." She indicated the limp reins and the leather stirrup straps with steel footholds dangling at Glad's sides.

Dexter sneered at her, then reached down and snapped up the reins. Glad reared up in surprise, and the left stirrup swung wide, connecting with Dexter's head. Dexter yelped loudly and yanked hard on the reins, hurting the horse's teeth. Glad whinnied in pain and alarm.

Another voice entered the conversation. *Be calm, Glad. Be calm now.*

Bird knew who it was. The man. She didn't look around for him — she knew she wouldn't be able to see him unless he wanted to be seen.

Glad stopped moving. His ears pricked and his eyes were alert. Bird watched as his body began to relax.

From behind them, the man walked quietly up to Dexter. "Mr. Pill," he said humbly. "May I take your horse for you now?"

"Where've you been? Drinking?" yelled Dexter. "You're supposed to be working!"

Bird was stunned at the insult.

The man nodded meekly and took Glad's reins. Glad let out a huge breath and dropped his head. Together the man and the horse walked quietly toward Dexter's tent stabling.

"Lazy bum," muttered Dexter.

Bird watched them go. "How could you call him a lazy bum?"

"Because he is!" spat Dexter.

Bird stared at him. Dexter Pill had no right to demean the man, but she yearned to know more about him. "Does he work for you?" she asked.

"He started today. He'll be fired today, too!" Dexter stalked off, leaving Bird and Tall Sox standing by the fence.

The man is aboriginal, Bird thought, like me. And he has the same gift of speaking to animals. Are all aboriginal people able to do that?

Wanda stepped out from behind the stands, interrupting Bird's thoughts. "Bird, Dexter just fired me. Just now! I was looking for a different job anyway, but now I don't know what to do." The teenager with the red hair wiped a tear from her face with the back of her hand. She reminded Bird of a little child.

"What happened?" Bird asked.

"Dexter blames me for what Glad did and it's not fair! I tried to get him in the ring, but he wouldn't go. He's mad, too, because I told someone, well, maybe more than one person, that Glad hates water jumps, and it got back to him." Wanda looked at the ground.

"And that guy?" Bird pointed to the man walking away with Glad.

Wanda looked where Bird pointed. "Dunno. He just showed up. I guess I've seen him around. He got my job."

"My Aunt Hannah might know of a job somewhere," Bird said helpfully. She looked over to the practice ring. "Go ask her. It's time for me to get Sunny ready anyway."

The two girls and Sox walked away from the ring. Sally appeared, out of breath. "Thanks, Bird! Cliff is taking Sabrina home and he says Tall Sox should go, too."

"Why is the pony leaving now? Julia's class isn't finished and she'll miss the jump-offs."

Sally looked over her shoulder. "Your mother."

"My mother? What about her?"

"She called Hannah. She's very mad and wants Julia home *now*. Julia's upset."

Bird shook her head. How selfish of Eva to upset her daughter like this. "Typical," she said.

Are you ready to go home, Sox? she asked the horse.

Okay with me.

Bird gave Sally the lead shank and patted the gelding's neck. This had been a good day for him. He'd seen the show grounds. He'd had a scare but gotten over it. *You're a good horse. Next time we come, you'll be ready to compete.*

It looks like fun!

Bird grinned. She loved his positive energy, even after the bad start with Dexter. Dexter Pill. He was at the centre of a lot of horse problems. After all that Dexter had done, why on earth would the man go to work for him?

Bird stood beside Sunny in the trailer. She brushed him and got him saddled up, ready for their class. She watched Wanda and Hannah conversing by the mounting block. Saddle Creek didn't have an opening for a job, but Hannah knew most people in the show horse industry and would be an excellent resource for Wanda.

As Bird watched, Ed Cage walked by. Hannah's back was turned to him, so she didn't see the kiss he blew at Wanda. But Bird did. And Wanda blushed to the roots of her hair. What was that all about? Bird wondered. As far as she knew, Ed was married. She couldn't think about it now. She had a class to win.

Are you ready to go, Sunny? asked Bird.

I've been ready all day. Now I'm bored.

Do you want to jump or not?

Maybe. Maybe not. Sundancer yawned. *You've been spending a lot of time with Sox today.*

Bird considered this. *Yeah, but Sox needs help right now. Soon, Sally will be able to handle him.*

Sunny looked at her sideways. *And then?*

And then I can spend more time with you.

Okay. Then I want to jump.

Thanks, Sunny. Bird patted his nose gently. *You'll always be my favourite horse.*

Soon Bird was mounted, and she and Sundancer walked toward the warm-up ring. The air was clear, and the sky was blue. Bird breathed it all in. She was excited about her turn in the big grass ring.

Hannah showed up as they began to trot. "Get him warmed up, Bird," she shouted. "I'll wait for a jump and then I'll send you over a few. You're up in seven."

"Okay," called Bird. She kept Sunny in a nice trot for three minutes in each direction. She let him walk and stretch, then began a canter. By then, Hannah had secured one of the five jumps set up in the centre of the ring. Everyone took turns schooling over them, and Hannah had to wait until people finished before taking one over.

Sunny played a little with a happy buck, and Bird laughed out loud. She loved when he did that — it meant he was feeling good. They trotted toward the vertical. Sunny rocked back and used his haunches to lift them over the jump. He arched perfectly, then landed lightly and cantered away.

"Wonderful!" praised Hannah. "A couple more and you're good to go!

I'm feeling good, Bird! enthused Sunny. *Let's go win!*

All right, Sunny, but not too fast.

You're no fun at all. He did another little happy buck.

Bird smiled and patted her horse's shoulder. *You're feeling good!*

Bird felt ready and confident as they made their way to the enormous grass Grand Prix ring. As they walked, Bird took in all the sights of the show. There was a vast assortment of horses and ponies, all shined up and groomed to perfection. People of all ages rode them around rings, trotted them down the lanes, and lunged them in out-of-the-way corners. Scooters, golf carts, and bicycles moved people from stable to ring and carried saddles, cooler blankets, and accessories to where they were needed. Rows of tents that served as temporary stables were becoming adorned with brightly coloured rosettes, won in classes. Everywhere, people and horses were intent on going somewhere, doing something, working on skills, or merely resting before their next class. The entire showground was abuzz with energy. Bird felt alive just being there.

The classes and courses were posted on a big sign beside the Grand Prix ring. Bird found her course and studied it carefully. She looked at the jumps and went over the order in her head, pointing at them one at a time to entrench the course in her memory. There were some very tricky turns and some rather huge jumps. She breathed deeply and patted Sunny's neck.

Do you still want to do this? she asked.

Do barn cats kill mice?

Bird grinned. *We're up in five.*

Just beside them was a small dirt warm-up ring. They walked in and picked up a trot. It was busy, with close to a dozen horses jumping and cantering.

As they cantered around a corner, a big white cowboy hat caught Bird's eye. She took a second look. It was the man. He sat on the grass on the hill beside the ring, watching her. Why? she wondered. She cantered around again, and glanced to see if he was still there. He was.

It was worth a try. *Why are you watching me?*

To her amazement, she got a reply. *To warn you about something.*

Bird pulled Sunny to a halt. *Warn me of what?*

Keep working. Don't look at me.

Bird asked Sunny to trot on.

You have an enemy. Dexter Pill.

I know that.

Listen to me. He means you harm. You made him look bad just now with Glad. He will try to ruin your ride.

Should I scratch the class?

I leave it with you. Be very careful.

How can I be careful? I have to concentrate on what I'm doing. I can't be looking around for danger.

I'll help if I can.

Thank you. Who are you? What's your name? Bird looked up at the hillside, hoping for an answer, but the man in the white cowboy hat was gone.

As always happened, the crowd hushed when Sundancer trotted into the ring. His coppery coat glistened in the sun, and his muscled shoulders and rump moved with athletic rhythm and grace. His ears were pricked forward, and his energy was apparent with every springy stride.

He tossed his mane. *Let's do this, Bird.*

Are you worried about what the man said?

Why should I be? What could happen?

I'm with you every step of the way.

Bird pushed the man's warning from her thoughts. She asked Sunny for a canter.

They were through the starting gate. Sunny moved with energy and impulsion, using his entire body well.

The first fence was a solid flower box with three rails above. Sundancer and Bird came in to the centre and took off from the base, clearing it easily.

This is the life, Bird!

We're rocking this course!

Now, they turned slightly right and headed to a mess of coloured rails, called an optical illusion because it was difficult to find the right angle to approach it correctly. Sunny cantered to it and sprang. Up and over. A tight turn to the left and they sped to the in-and-out, constructed of two fences with red and white rails and bright blue wings.

They were over the first of the two fences, and had taken one stride. There was one more stride to go, and then they'd take off over the second.

They didn't make it. Between the two fences, Sunny let out a frantic whinny and reared. He twisted in the air, uncertain where to go or what to do.

I'm hurt!

Easy boy! You're okay.

I'm going home!

No, Sunny! Whoa!

But Sunny couldn't listen. He was terrified and unable to think. Bird held on for dear life as they raced to the in-gate. Several people stood there, hoping to stop him, but Sunny was panicked. He didn't slow his pace.

"Move!" screamed Bird. "Coming through!"

They galloped past staring people and spooked horses, sending carts and scooters flying as they sped through the gate, down the dirt lane, and up the grassy hill to the Saddle Creek trailer.

Once there, Sunny stopped. Bird slid down and patted his neck. *Are you okay?*

Something hurt me! Look at my rump. Am I bleeding? Am I going to die?

Bird stepped behind the worried animal and examined his rear end. *Which side?*

The bloody side!

There's no blood, Sunny.

There has to be blood. I'm a mammal!

Bird felt his coat carefully, but just like with Tall Sox, she found nothing at first.

I can't find anything.

It hurt! And it scared me! Something got me!

Bird continued to work her fingers through his silky coat. A small, hot bump was rising.

Here?

Ouch! That's it.

This was exactly what had happened to Tall Sox! Bird knew it wasn't a coincidence. Somebody was trying to do them harm. She considered what to do. Should she involve Hannah and report this to the Stewards?

The man, still wearing the white cowboy hat, came up silently and stood with them. He wore riding gloves, and held out a small black BB gun. "Look what was stashed beneath the bleachers."

Bird stared at it. "Wow."

"I couldn't get to him before he fired."

Bird's jaw dropped. "Get to who?"

"I'm not sure."

"But you're saying somebody actually shot Sunny with that?"

The man nodded. "I have no proof, but this gun tells a story."

She made a guess. "Dexter Pill?"

"Don't know for sure. I came around the stands to stay close to him, but I was too late. Sunny had already reared and run away. When I searched around, I found the gun." He looked at her earnestly. "I'm sorry I couldn't stop him."

"Someone shot Tall Sox, too, when Sally was grazing him. And now this."

The man frowned. "That's not all he's been up to. He needs to be stopped, and you can help."

"How?" asked Bird. "And exactly what are you talking about? What else has he been up to?"

"Let's take one step at a time."

Bird realized that the man was not going to elaborate. "Did anybody see him shoot at Sunny?"

"I don't know yet. His fingerprints might be on the gun, though."

Bird's eyes widened. "You mean we should call the police?"

The man smiled. "I am the police."

9 FRANK SKELTON

Out of the Indian approach to life there came a great freedom, an intense and absorbing respect for life, enriching faith in a supreme power, and principles of truth, honesty, generosity and brotherhood.

— Luther Standing Bear, Oglala Sioux, 1868–1937

Bird was still trying to comprehend what the man had told her when Hannah came running to the trailer. "Bird! What happened? Why did Sunny go wild?"

"Somebody shot him with a BB gun."

"No!" Hannah gasped. "How could that happen?" The man took off his white hat and slowly turned to face Hannah. "Hello."

Hannah stopped in her tracks. "Hello."

As they stood staring at each other, Bird looked back and forth between them, trying to figure out what was going on. "Do you two know each other?" she asked.

"No," answered the man, still looking at Hannah, "but I've heard of your aunt. She's well respected among horse trainers."

"And you look very familiar," Hannah said slowly. "Have we met?" The man paused, and spoke carefully. "It's not impossible."

Hannah's smile was just a little unnatural. "You certainly remind me of someone I used to know."

Something was wrong. Their conversation sounded like a play, with lines rehearsed. Bird couldn't remain quiet any longer. "Who are you?" she demanded of the man. "What's happening here?"

All at once it hit her. Hannah was acting more than a little strange. It was completely obvious! The man was from a First Nations community. He could speak non-verbally. He was brilliant with horses. He even looked a bit like her — his nose, his forehead, and the setting of his eyes. How could she have missed it? "You're my father," she blurted out.

The man stared blankly at Bird, clearly startled. "Pardon me?"

This wasn't the reaction she'd expected. Not at all. "Aren't you?" she asked, much less sure of herself now.

"Bird!" Hannah stepped quickly toward her. "Honey! Don't you remember? I told you, your father is … he died, Bird."

Bird shook her head. She knew what Hannah had told her, she just didn't want to accept it. "But he's just like me! Can't you see?"

Hannah gently placed her hand on Bird's shoulder. Bird shrugged it off and searched the man's face for confirmation. "Are you my father?"

He tilted his head. "Do you ask every man you meet that question?"

Bird's face reddened, but she felt a need to carry on, to explain herself. "But your belt! It has the initials F.S.! Those are my father's initials — Fred Sweetree!"

"They're my initials, too." His voice was cold. He turned away, and put on his hat. "We're not all the same."

Bird froze with confusion. She looked at Hannah's stricken face, then at the man. The truth sank in. She'd been wrong. This man wasn't her father. How could he be? Her father was dead. And now, this man, who she'd just met, thought she was totally crazy. And she'd insulted him.

Bird cringed, wishing that the earth would open up and swallow her. What had she done? Who goes around asking people if they're their father! Humiliated, she dropped Sunny's reins and ran. She didn't know what else to do.

What an idiot! She had to be more careful what she said aloud. When she was mute, she'd never had a problem like this. Speaking was too easy! Things crept out so fast and then you couldn't take them back. How many times would she have to learn that lesson? Maybe Eva was right. It *had* been better when she couldn't speak!

She ran across the field toward the tree line, passing horse trailers and trucks. There were fewer and fewer until she was running alone. Or so she thought until she heard hooves pounding.

You run fast for a girl.

Sunny!

What's your problem?

I just embarrassed myself completely. Bird slowed to a walk, but continued in the direction of the trees.

How?

I asked a complete stranger, a person who's actually been trying to avoid me, if he's my father!

That's more embarrassing than taking off like a rabbit?

Bird stopped walking. She felt even worse. *You're right.*

I'm always right.

Now what do I do, if you're so smart?

Depends.

On what?

If you want to go live in the woods. Like the wild man.

Bird flashed back to an image of Tanbark's tent down the escarpment in the woods, made from old horse blankets and strewn with garbage. *I don't.*

So hop on my back and we'll go for a ride. You'll look like all the other people here, not like some crazy rabbit.

Bird snorted with laughter in spite of herself. She adjusted the girth and found a tree stump to stand on. Sunny stood beside it as Bird put her foot in the left stirrup and threw her right leg over the saddle.

She had absolutely no desire to go back to the trailer. They headed down the hill in the direction of the Grand Prix ring. Her class was still going on, so they might as well see Dexter ride.

Her plan was to completely bypass the Saddle Creek rig. From the far side of the field she peeked over to see if the man was still there. Sure enough, he and her aunt were sitting on folding chairs in the shade of the trailer, deep in conversation.

What were they talking about? She rode Sunny a little closer, and stopped in the shadow of a spreading maple tree. Who was this man, anyway? He had said he was the police, and that she could help him with something. He spoke to animals, and he was from a First Nation. Plainly, he wasn't her father, but who was he? And what was he doing here? He was undercover, but what was he trying to uncover?

She needed to know what was going on. And besides, she couldn't avoid the man forever, especially if he was going to be hanging around the horse show world. Swallowing her pride, she rode Sunny over to the trailer and dismounted.

"Okay. I'm sorry. I'm sorry I said what I said." Bird ran up the stirrups, undid Sunny's girth, and removed his saddle. Better to face things head on, she thought. She slipped off the bridle and snapped on a halter so Sunny could graze. "What's happening?"

Hannah and the man stood up. They glanced at each other, then back to Bird. Hannah spoke. "I'd like to make an introduction, if I may. Bird, meet Sergeant Frank Skelton of the RCMP. Sergeant, this is Alberta Simms."

Bird felt her face redden again. Frank Skelton. Fred Sweetree. Same initials. Different people.

Frank and Bird shook hands. Bird said, "I'm pleased to meet you, Sergeant Skelton. I mean, officially."

Frank smiled. "I'm pleased to meet you, too. Officially."

Bird looked quizzically at Frank. "Why is the RCMP at a horse show? Are you doing the Musical Ride?"

"I'm here on assignment," said Frank. "We've been trying to get to the bottom of a string of, shall we say, 'incidents.' I'm here undercover."

"Incidents? What incidents?"

"I can't be more specific at the moment," he said. He and Hannah shared a look.

"And undercover?" Bird persisted. "Working as a groom?"

"Yes."

"And, by coincidence, you know all about horses?"

"That's no coincidence. My competence with horses is exactly why I was chosen for this duty."

Bird considered this information. "If you're undercover, why have you told us?"

Frank Skelton smiled again. "Because I need help, and you could be a great asset. I've been watching you carefully. If you agree to help, I'll fill you in."

Bird thought for a minute, then said, "I'd like to help."

"Thank you."

"But first, I need you to answer some questions for me."

"That's only fair. Please understand that I might not be able to answer fully."

Bird got another folding chair from the tack room of the trailer, opened it, and sat down. Hannah and Frank sat as well. When they were all settled, Bird asked, "Why exactly are you here?"

"I was chosen because I'm familiar with the area. I was here many years ago, when I was undercover on a different assignment." Frank cast his eyes over toward Dexter's stabling. "Look, I'm on a break, so I need to keep an eye over there. I don't want them to see me talking to you."

"Go on," prompted Bird. "There's more to your story."

"There's more to everybody's story. What do you need to know?"

"Maybe why you and Aunt Hannah were so uncomfortable when you met."

The sergeant sat back. "When I was here last, I met a lot of people. I wasn't sure if Hannah was one of them. If she was, I might have had a different identity, which might have been awkward."

It sounded somewhat plausible to Bird. "And Aunt Hannah? Why were you uncomfortable?"

"To be totally honest, at first glance Sergeant Skelton reminded me of your father. Until I remembered that it'd be impossible."

Bird took a quick breath. That made perfect sense, and she felt a whole lot better about her mistake. She turned back to Frank. "What were you doing here, back then?"

Frank shook his head. "Sorry, I can't say."

"Okay. I have one more question. For now, at least," said Bird. "You and I are both able to communicate … non-verbally … with people and animals. You are from a First Nation. So was my father. Is this a skill that all of us have?"

Frank smiled from ear to ear. He had a very handsome face for someone his age, thought Bird, especially when he smiled like that.

"No, Bird. Not all of us have that skill, no matter how romantic the idea. It's quite special."

Bird said, "Why can you and I do it, then?"

"I believe that all people have the ability, but few people allow it to blossom. Maybe the people who are the closest to nature are most likely to develop it. Plains Cree and Sioux in the West have nurtured their bonds with animals, horses in particular, but even among those people, this skill is quite rare. I consider myself extremely blessed."

"I do, too," said Bird quietly. "Although I've often wondered why I can do it. It makes me feel very different from everybody else. But in a good way."

"Me, too," Frank nodded. "And I don't know if you know this, but in much of ancient First Nations mythology, people and animals spoke easily to each other all the time."

"No, I didn't know that. I don't know much about First Nations, but I want to know more."

"If you want to learn, you will. Just like you learned to speak to animals."

"So did you. That's why I thought you were my father." She looked directly at him. "Do you understand?"

"I understand." Frank Skelton rose from his chair. When he looked down at Bird, his eyes twinkled. "Now, I must get back to work. I'll come to your farm tomorrow morning and explain what I need from you. I don't have to be at Moreland's until noon."

Hannah stood as well. "We'll see you tomorrow. If we're not at the house, we'll be at the barn."

Frank waved farewell. "I look forward to working with you both." He stopped, and turned to Bird. "Your special skills will come in very handy."

"I hope so," said Bird.

"Do you think you'll enjoy undercover work?" asked Frank with a friendly smile.

Bird smiled back. "Please understand that I might not be able to answer fully."

Hannah and Frank laughed. Bird laughed with them. If he wanted her to be a detective, a detective she would be.

The show was over, and it was time to pack up the Saddle Creek rig and go home. Cliff, Julia, and Sally had already gone with Sabrina and Tall Sox. That left three horses and their riders, plus Hannah.

"After you check the tack, fill the hay nets, Bird," called Hannah as she grabbed the pitchfork. "Liz, make sure all the brushes, boots, soap, and everything else is put away." She picked up manure from the trailer with the pitchfork and put it in the bin. "And Kimberly? Offer the horses a drink before you empty out the water buckets."

The girls continued with their chores, and were soon seated in the truck and set to go. The horses munched their hay, the trailer ramp was up, the drop windows were latched, and the air vents were wide open.

Kimberly and Moonie had gotten a first place ribbon, and Liz and Pastor had placed fourth. Bird and Sunny had been eliminated, but they were all in good spirits.

Hannah started up the engine. "It was a good day, kids. You all did us proud."

"Except for me," said Bird. "But I know it wasn't our fault."

"No kidding! I can't believe somebody shot Sunny with a BB gun! Why didn't you get another chance?" asked Kimberly.

"You sh-should've," agreed Liz.

"I guess I could've lodged a complaint," answered Bird, "but there were no marks and no way to prove anything. It looked like he just spooked and took off."

"He might have done that in the old days, but he hasn't misbehaved in quite a while," mused Hannah. "If it happens again, I'd guess that the judges would call an inquiry."

"I should hope so!" exclaimed Kimberly. "I'm so mad that somebody got away with doing that!"

Bird sat quietly. Dexter was *not* going to get away with this — not if she had anything to say about it. She thought about Frank Skelton, and wondered what she was going to be asked to do.

It was four o'clock when they drove up the lane to Saddle Creek Farm. Cliff came out of the barn to give them a hand unloading.

"Hi, Cliff!" called Bird. "Where's Julia?"

"Eva picked her up just a few minutes ago."

"And Sally?" asked Hannah.

"Gone, too," answered Cliff. "Her father picked her up an hour ago."

"Good." Hannah got down from the driver's seat. "Thanks for driving to the show today. Julia couldn't have come, otherwise."

Cliff dropped the ramp. "I was happy to see what you folks get up to. And you should've heard Eva swearing until I said I'd take the pony for Julia!"

Bird rolled her eyes. "Why do I feel like whatever Eva does is my fault?" She fetched three lead shanks, and each girl led her horse off the trailer.

"Because it usually is," grinned Cliff, punching her arm lightly. Bird pretended to fall over.

The horses were soon tucked into their freshly bedded stalls. They would eat their dinner of oats and sweet feed, rest for a few hours, and then be put out in their fields for the night.

Just as the saddles and bridles had been cleaned and put away, Liz's mother, Patty, pulled up in her car.

"Mom!" called Liz. "W-we got fourth!"

"Congratulations, sweetie!" she answered. "Kimberly? Can I give you a ride? Your mother asked me to get you. She's got a date tonight."

Kimberly winked at Bird. "So she's busy trying to work a miracle?"

Bird and Liz laughed. Hannah interrupted. "Careful, girls. You'll be our age some day, too!"

"I hope not," said Kimberly. She struck a pose with one hand on her chest, her head thrown back, and her other hand flung across her forehead. "I want to die young, very tragically. Men will come from miles away to cry over my beautiful body and wasted future."

"M-me, too!" cried Liz, slapping both hands to her throat.

"Get in, my tragic beauties." Hannah laughed as she opened the back door of Patty's car.

Liz and Kimberly jumped in and waved as they drove down the lane to the road. Bird and Hannah walked to the house.

"It's fun, isn't it?" said Bird. "To do what we do? Have a barn full of good horses, and go to shows with nice people."

Hannah nodded. "I wouldn't want any other job." She put her hand on Bird's shoulder as they walked.

"I've been thinking about Tanbark," said Bird. Tanbark Wedger was Hannah's half-brother. "When can we visit him again?"

"Funny you should mention him. Alison Wedger called just this morning."

Bird was all ears. "How's he doing?" Tan had been troubled and homeless for years, but since late June, he'd been getting treatment for bipolar disorder at the Centre for Addiction and Mental Health, or CAMH, in Toronto.

"Much, much better," smiled Hannah. "They've got his medication right. Alison said he's got his sense of humour back, and he's reading again."

"When'll he be able to get out of CAMH?" asked Bird.

"She doesn't know." Hannah smiled a little sadly. "I'm glad she called. She especially wanted to thank you, again, for all your help."

Two months ago, Tan had showed up in Caledon at the same time as a woman was brutally murdered. Because Tan was new, homeless, and considered strange, people in the community suspected that he had done it. Bird had helped prove his innocence.

"Can we go visit him tonight?" Bird wanted to know. It meant a lot to Tan to have visitors. Hannah looked at her watch. "It's already close to five. Visiting hours will be over soon."

"If we call now, can we see if they'll make an exception?"

"Aren't you tired? And hungry?"

"Yes, but every day gets so crowded up that we never get to see him. I know how much it means to him."

"I'll talk to Paul first, and see if he has plans, then I'll call. If we can't drive down tonight, we'll go tomorrow."

"Promise?"

"Promise."

When they got to the farmhouse, the message light was blinking. There were four messages. Hannah pressed PLAY and they listened.

The first one was from Laura Pierson. "Hello, Hannah dear. Pete is home now, and he's feeling much better. He had a piece of your delicious pie and told me to call. He said he wasn't sure, but he thinks he's gone to heaven!"

Hannah and Bird were warmed by Laura's cheerful voice. Bird said, "We should go visit them, too." Hannah nodded.

The second message began. Julia's voice spoke in a whisper. "Hey, Bird. Hi, Aunt Hannah. Mom doesn't know I'm calling. I'm sorry we had to go early. Mom's all upset. Can I come to Saddle Creek tomorrow? Please? Mom says I can't."

"Oh my goodness," said Hannah. Bird wondered if her little sister should come over that night — Julia sounded worried and lonely.

The third message was from Paul. "Hi, beautiful. I'm in surgery and can't get away. It's a tough one. Have dinner without me. Don't wait up. Love you."

Hannah's face registered disappointment.

"Look on the bright side," said Bird. "We can visit Tan."

The fourth message blared in their ears. "Pick up! If you're there, pick up! Julia's upstairs. She's crying and driving me nuts! She's so difficult! What have you been filling her head with? She refuses to talk! Call me!"

Bird and Hannah slumped into chairs at the same time. Eva had that effect.

"When Mom met Stuart, she seemed so … changed," said Bird. "Has something happened?"

Hannah shook her head. "I have no idea."

"Should you call her?" Bird asked. "Before she calls again? Maybe we should go get Julia. She'd be so much happier here."

"It's very tricky when Eva's in this mood," answered Hannah. "I'll suggest that Julia come for the night, to give your mom a break. She did say Julia was driving her nuts."

Bird nodded. "That might work."

"Go have a shower while I return these calls, and I'll scramble some eggs for us."

"And call about visiting Tan?"

"Let's see about Julia first."

"She can come with us."

Hannah smiled and rubbed Bird's cropped head. "You are persistent. I'll give you that."

"A good quality for an undercover agent, don't you think?"

By the time Bird had cleaned up and changed, Hannah had not only done the same but had also produced a large bag of packed dinner, and was writing a note. "Grab a jacket, Bird. It might be cool by the time we come home."

"Are we visiting Tanbark?"

"First, we're picking up Julia."

"Hooray!"

"And we'll eat as we drive to CAMH. Tomorrow, we'll go visit Pete and Laura."

"Wow! You're a great organizer."

"Thanks."

"Don't forget, Frank Skelton is coming over tomorrow morning, too.

"I know." Hannah nodded as she read over her note. "I don't want Paul to worry if he gets home before us." She glared at Bird, half seriously. "Something you should consider every once in a while!"

"Point taken," Bird said. "Do we have anything for Tan?"

"You bet. There's a separate bag inside filled with everything he loves to eat."

Can I come? Can I come?

Bird looked under the table. There lay Lucky, looking up at her with pleading brown eyes and thumping tail. She reached down and patted his silky brown fur. *We need you to guard the farm. We'll be gone a long time.*

Then you'd better let me out.

Good dog. Bird opened the screened door for Lucky, and watched as he trotted out and sniffed the air. "Oh, I have a letter to mail. Can we stop at a mailbox?"

"You wrote a letter? To Alec, by any chance?" Hannah teased.

Bird rolled her eyes and tried to look cool. "Maybe yes, maybe no.

"Okay, sweetie. Now, let's go. Julia's waiting and time's a-wasting!"

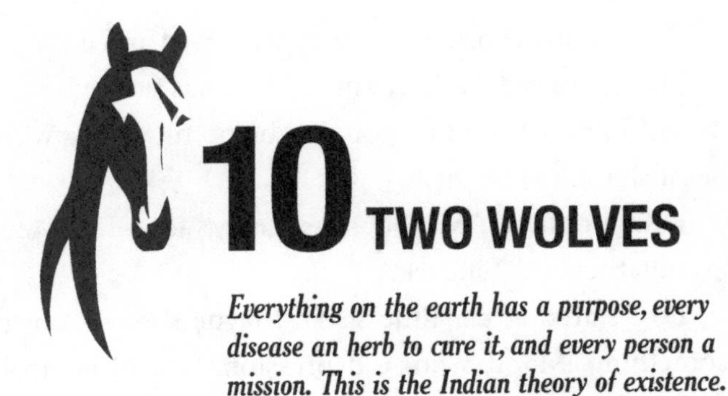

10 TWO WOLVES

Everything on the earth has a purpose, every disease an herb to cure it, and every person a mission. This is the Indian theory of existence.

— Mourning Dove, Salish, 1888–1936

The next morning, Bird and Julia were down in the kitchen early. They'd got home from CAMH around 9:30 the night before, and had both slept well. Now they cheerfully ate cereal and toast at the table. Hannah and Paul weren't up yet.

"What's up with Mom?" asked Bird. "Why's she being so weird again?

"Good question. I sure don't know." Julia chewed her toast thoughtfully. "She's worse when you're around. That's for sure."

"I know. I really get her mad. But she's so touchy! She explodes about nothing. Just like before she met Stuart." Bird spread more peanut butter on her toast. "Are they okay? You know, their marriage?"

"Stuart's crazy about her, but I think he's just as confused as we are. He used to be able to cheer her up with a hug and a joke. Not anymore. Even when he brings home presents."

"Does it make him sad? Or upset?" Bird asked.

Julia shrugged. "I don't know. He keeps trying."

"All I know is that it's going to be no fun living with her if she stays like this."

Julia nodded. "Maybe she's crazy, too. Like our grandfather and Tanbark."

Bird stared at her little sister. Maybe she was on to something. Mood swings, depression, lack of control. "Hannah says it's all on a spectrum."

"What's that?"

"Like a colour wheel. Shades of intensity. Some people are more affected, others are less."

"So if Tanbark is bright red, Mom might be pink?"

"Yeah," said Bird. "Like that. They *are* half-siblings."

"Both children of Grampa, and he's cuckoo." Julia made a twirling sign around her right ear.

"Totally," said Bird thoughtfully. "But I thought Tanbark seemed a whole lot better. Way less jumpy and weird. I'm glad we visited him."

"Me, too. He was glad to see us." Julia took another spoonful of cereal and spoke with her mouth full. "He loved the food we brought."

"He looked a bit sad when we left. That was the only bad part."

Julia nodded as she chewed.

"Do you think we'll be crazy, too?" asked Bird. "If everybody else is?"

Hannah opened the kitchen door. "I don't want you kids to worry about that," she said. "Every family has something to watch out for. Until Tanbark's diagnosis, we thought we were just eccentric." She smiled.

"But how will we know if we need help?" asked Julia.

"You will, now that you're aware of what mental illness looks like. You've seen how it works." Hannah put one hand on Julia's shoulder and one on Bird's. "You'll be fine. Don't worry."

"What if we're not?" Bird wanted a more solid assurance.

"Then we'll figure that out. Together."

Bird nodded. "Okay, I guess." She was a little uneasy with this new concern. "But do you really think I'll be fine? I can't talk sometimes."

Hannah put one hand on each girl's shoulder. "Yes. I really think you'll be fine. Both of you."

There was a light tap on the kitchen screen door. Lucky jumped up to bark.

Bird saw their visitor first. "Sergeant Frank," she said, and got up to open the door.

Julia stared at her sister, confused.

Hannah welcomed the man in. "Coffee? Tea? Have you had breakfast?"

"Hours ago, thanks, but I'll have a coffee with milk and honey." He smiled the smile that Bird had liked before. It warmed her somehow.

"What's your name?" he asked Julia in his soft voice.

"Julia Simms," she answered dutifully. "Why does everybody know you but me?"

Frank laughed kindly. "You'd already left the show grounds when I showed up, that's why."

Julia exhaled. "Oh, yeah. Mom had a meltdown."

"Did you misbehave?" he asked, his voice warm with mischief.

"No! I don't know why she left!" Julia was upset.

"I wasn't serious, Julia. You look like you never misbehave."

Julia studied him. "I do?"

"You do." Frank spoke simply and honestly.

"Who are you? And why are you here?" she asked.

"Julia!" Hannah sent a warning look in her niece's direction.

"No, no, Hannah. Those are good questions and I would like to answer them." Frank sat down at the table and accepted the mug of steaming coffee that Hannah brought over from the counter. "I'm here to look into some irregularities."

"What do you mean?"

"Some things are happening that shouldn't be."

"Here? At Saddle Creek Farm?" Julia exclaimed.

"Not at Saddle Creek Farm." Frank smiled again. "I'm here to ask for help."

Julia stared at him with widened eyes.

"I'm assuming that you will be discreet, and not mention my visit."

Everyone nodded, but Julia nodded most vigorously.

"Good."

Paul opened the kitchen door and stopped when he saw Frank. "Well! Good morning."

Frank stood, and offered his hand. "Good morning. I'm Frank Skelton, sergeant with the RCMP."

"And I'm Paul Daniels, doctor of veterinary medicine." They shook hands in greeting. "Hannah told me you'd be dropping in." Paul took a chair at the kitchen table.

Frank sat back down. "I'll get right to it. We're investigating events connected to show horses. Irregularities." He looked at each person directly and said, "Understand that this is strictly confidential." After everyone had muttered their assent, he continued, "To be exact, horses missing, injured, and killed for insurance purposes."

Bird covered her mouth. Insurance fraud. She'd become far too aware of that dirty business since her grandfather's misdeeds had come to light. This was worse than she'd imagined.

Frank continued. "I'm hoping that Bird can be helpful."

Paul raised his eyebrows and glanced at Bird. "Really?"

Frank nodded, but said nothing.

Hannah brought Paul a cup of coffee, and refilled Frank's mug.

"If anybody can help, you've got the right person in Bird." Paul sent a proud glance in Bird's direction.

The phone rang, and Hannah answered. "Hello? … Oh, Laura! … When is a good time? … We have company, but let me call you right back … Bye."

Hannah spoke to everyone. "Pete would like Bird to come over this morning to visit. I'm to call her back with a time."

Frank said, "Why not now? I need to talk to Bird privately. I can drive her over in my car."

Bird looked warily at Hannah, who nodded approval.

"Okay. I guess so," said Bird. She felt cautious. She was about to enter the sinister world of police work. She did not take it lightly.

"I'll pick you up in an hour," said Hannah as she pressed the Piersons' number.

Frank rose and shook hands with Paul and Hannah, and acknowledged Julia. "We'll see more of each other, I'm sure," he said. "Thanks for the coffee."

Once outside, Bird got in the passenger side of the old black Chevrolet sedan that Frank was driving. It was scratched and filthy, and needed a new muffler. It needed a new everything, Bird thought. "Nice wheels, Frank."

Frank laughed softly. "It's my cover, but I couldn't afford much better anyway."

"I wasn't insulting you."

"I know. You couldn't if you tried."

They drove out the lane and down the gravel road. The Piersons didn't live far away, and Bird waited for Frank to start explaining.

After a few seconds, he began to talk. "You have a gift with horses, Bird, and I'd like you to use it. I've taken a job with Dexter Pill to get inside his operation, and I'm learning what's going on."

That much she'd already guessed.

"His fingerprints don't match the ones on the BB gun."

Bird absorbed this new information. "Whose are they, then?"

"I'm working on it."

"I thought for sure they'd be his!"

"Me, too. But there's more. You know the horse Gladiator?"

Bird nodded.

"He's going to have an accident."

Bird jolted forward. "What?"

"He's fully insured at an inflated price. Dexter can't sell him. The horse is fried."

Bird knew what that meant. When a horse is so confused and insecure that he panics and fears everything, he's considered "fried." Only time and patience can help the horse regain his confidence and become able to work again. A fried horse is unsellable. Very few trainers were capable of reversing that mental condition.

Frank repeated, "He's going to have an accident."

"Holy. When?"

"Soon. We have to watch this situation carefully. My people have a saying: Never take your foot off the head of a snake."

Bird thought this was a good concept, and very descriptive. "I want to learn more about First Nations sayings," she said. "Can you teach me?"

Frank looked at the girl warmly. "Let me tell you about the two wolves."

"Two wolves?"

"Yes. It's a Cherokee legend. Two wolves live inside our heads. One is very bad — greedy, selfish, jealous, and evil. One is very good — loving, giving, kind, and generous. They always fight."

"They fight?"

"Yes, they fight."

"So, who wins?"

"The one we feed."

Bird sat and thought about Frank's story. It was a good one.

She'd try to remember it, and try to feed her Good Wolf as often as she possibly could. Even when her mother drove her crazy.

They pulled into the Merry Fields driveway and stopped at the kitchen door. Laura saw Bird through the window and threw open the door, smiling expectantly.

"I have to go, but how can I help with Glad?" Bird asked Frank, her hand on the door handle.

"I don't know yet, but I want you to be ready when I call."

She nodded. "I'll do whatever I can. Can we stop this from happening?"

Frank stared straight ahead. "Possibly, but we may need something to happen to Glad in order to put Dexter away. We need proof."

Bird's head was swimming. She waved at Laura, indicating that she would be there in a minute. "This is horrible. Glad's a good horse."

"So were the other horses, Bird, and so are the ones yet to be affected. We must stop him."

"Has Dexter done this before?"

Frank nodded. "Tall Sox? He was lucky that you and Sally stole him away."

Now Bird was even more confused. "Tell me what you mean!"

"Be careful what you believe and who you believe. Tall Sox was on the list."

"The list?"

Frank reached across Bird and opened her door. "Of vulnerable horses. Be ready when I call."

She nodded slowly and got out.

"Bird, dear!" called Laura as Frank turned the car around and drove off. "Come on in! Pete wants to see you!"

Bird shook her head. Astonishing. Tall Sox? Was he still in danger? She walked to the house in a daze.

"Bird, dear? Are you feeling well?" Laura's face was creased in concern.

"I'm fine. Really." She tried to smile.

Laura looked down the road in the direction of the disappearing sedan. "Who was that?"

"He works for Dexter Pill." Bird realized that she'd already fallen into her new job as undercover investigator. She hadn't lied — Frank Skelton did work for Dexter Pill — but she hadn't told the whole truth, either.

"You be careful who you take rides with, dear."

Bird smiled. Mrs. Pierson would feel better if she knew that he was a policeman, but Bird couldn't tell her. Horses' lives were at risk, and Bird had a job to do. She wanted to do it well.

11 PETE'S VERSION

In the beginning of all things, wisdom and knowledge were with the animals, for Tiraw, the One Above, did not speak directly to man.... he showed himself through the beast, and from them and from the stars and the sun and the moon, should man learn.

— Eagle Chief (Letakos-Lesa), Pawnee

Pete Pierson was sitting in his big armchair beside the kitchen fireplace when Bird entered the room. She smiled with pure delight at how well he looked.

"Bird, my girl. Come on over here." Pete reached out his arm and motioned for Bird to sit in the chair beside him. "How do I look?"

"A little better than you did in the hospital."

"Only a little?"

Bird laughed. "But *way* better than you did when I saw you on the hall floor."

Pete chuckled. "I should hope so." He patted her arm. "I feel better, too."

"That's good," said Bird. She squeezed his hand.

"So tell me what's been going on," Pete said. "I'm out of the loop."

Bird wondered how much to tell. "Well, Sundancer's in shape and ready to go. We had a little bad luck at the show on Friday, but there's another one next week. I'd love you to come if you can."

Pete grinned. "I'm on. Laura?"

Laura was at the counter. "I'm coming, too!"

"Where's the coffee and cookies? People are hungry!"

"I made banana bread last night with vanilla icing. Nothing better on earth with coffee. Or milk." She nodded to Bird as she carried a tray to the side table beside Pete, and began to serve.

"Pete first, of course," she smiled. "It's so good to have him home." Laura kissed him on the top of his bald head.

"And so good to have visitors," Pete added. "I was getting hard to please until you came over."

"Never!" said Laura. "You're always perfect!"

Pete turned to Bird. "You were asking me some questions at the hospital. About your father. I think I nodded off before I answered."

"You did. I'd love to know all about him." Bird took a big bite of the bread. "De-licious!" she mumbled through her mouthful.

"I don't know very much. He came to Caledon for a rodeo competition at the fairgrounds. It was a really big deal. Everybody knew about Indie."

"I remember!" exclaimed Laura. "There were posters and fliers and radio ads. He was unbeatable, and his advance publicity was huge. People lined up for autographs! He was very handsome." She studied Bird's face. "I always thought you took after him."

Bird tucked her feet under herself and settled in. She was ready to listen for hours.

"I met him, too," continued Pete. "I had an idea that he could give a seminar on horsemanship, but he was moving on and he had no interest. He was polite, but he declined."

"It would've been very helpful for a lot of folk around here," added Laura. "People need advice about horses, and who better to give it than the Indian Cowboy himself?"

"So, what happened then?" asked Bird.

"Well, the rodeo ended and the cowboys left town."

Bird waited for more, then asked, "That's all?"

"I told you I didn't know much."

Bird shook off her disappointment and probed Pete's memory. "Did Mom meet him then?"

"No, I don't think so. I think she met him later, in Calgary."

"What do you know about how he died?"

"Only what was in the papers. A small plane went down. There were no survivors."

Now Bird let the disappointment wash over her. It seemed that she'd never know more about her father than these few basic facts. Even when she'd Googled him, she only found a list of his rodeo championships. Nobody knew him except her mother, and Eva got upset with her for asking.

Laura tilted her head in sympathy. "Sorry, dear. That's all we knew about him until we heard the gossip about Eva being pregnant."

"Gossip from the gossipers," Pete said angrily. "You'd think nobody had anything else to talk about!"

"Eva's family took it hard, especially Kenneth. He was fit to be tied. Not Hannah, of course," Laura added quickly. "She didn't care if Eva's child was aboriginal."

Bird was taken aback. "What do you mean?"

"Laura!" chastised Pete.

"I want to know!" Bird sat up and stared at Pete and Laura. "Tell me!

Pete sighed. "The truth of the matter is this: People make generalizations. There's a stereotype out there. People make judgments."

"About what?" Bird asked.

Pete looked at Laura. "You tell her."

Laura folded her hands in her lap. "Back then, there weren't too many people in this community who weren't white," she said. "It's all changing, of course, as it should, and today it's a much different world than when you were born, but" — she inhaled and stared at the wall for a few seconds before continuing — "when Eva got pregnant, with an aboriginal man as the father, chins wagged."

It sure was different now, thought Bird as she pictured the variety of skin colours of the kids at her school. And the variety of religions, too. They were all just people to her. She couldn't imagine it being different than that.

"Chins would've wagged anyway, Bird. They always do when a young woman gets pregnant out of wedlock," said Pete.

"And Eva always caused a stir," added Laura. "One way or the other."

"True enough," agreed Pete. "Your mother got a lot of attention."

Bird brought the subject back to her father. "But you're telling me that people gossiped more because Indian Fred was aboriginal? Didn't you tell me everybody admired him? Asked him for autographs? Stood in line to see him?"

"Oh, yes," answered Pete. "Absolutely. It didn't make sense to me, but Eva was almost shunned over it."

Bird felt the unfairness of it. "Is that why she doesn't like to talk about my father?"

Laura nodded in thought. "It was a very difficult time for her."

"And is *that* why she didn't ever tell me that I'm First Nations? Is that why she wants me to be blond, like Julia?"

"I don't know about that, Bird," said Pete. "You'll have to have a real conversation with your mother about it."

"Right," snorted Bird. "Like that'll happen."

"More banana bread, dear?" offered Laura.

Bird shook her head. "So tell me, what are these stereotypes you talked about?"

"There's a problem with stereotypes, Bird," said Pete. "They don't usually fit."

"I want to know."

"They might fit one person but not the next, and we must always steer away from generalities, especially about groups of people, who are all separate individuals," Pete explained carefully, "with individual traits."

Bird knew he was trying to avoid her question. "I want adjectives."

"You're sure?"

"Yes. Just give me three."

Pete frowned as he spoke. "Lazy. Alcoholic. Unreliable."

"Wow," said Bird. Her stomach felt unsettled. She remembered Dexter calling Frank a lazy bum. And accusing him of drinking on the job. "But that has nothing to do with my father! He wasn't lazy *or* alcoholic *or* unreliable! Was he?"

"He sure wasn't lazy. I know that for a fact." Pete poured himself another cup of coffee.

"You mean he *was* an alcoholic and unreliable?"

"He wasn't an alcoholic, either," answered Laura. "But as for unreliable, I guess he didn't stay around to be a father to you." She murmured so quietly that Bird hardly heard her.

Bird inhaled deeply. She stood and picked up her plate and glass of milk. "Thank you both. I have a lot to think about."

"You're not leaving, are you?" asked Pete.

"Yes. I'm going to walk home."

"We've upset you, dear." Laura's eyes looked worried.

"You've told me the truth. I appreciate that." Bird put the plate and glass in the sink. "Nobody else has." She turned to go.

"But there are good stereotypes, too, Bird," Pete said firmly. "Preservers of nature. Wise. Spiritual. Brave. These are also stereotypes of aboriginal people, and also not always true."

"You're absolutely right," Laura said.

"Some of the best animal trainers I've known are Metis or First Nations."

"Is that supposed to make me feel better?" Bird asked. Her head was swimming. She needed fresh air. Then she remembered. Bird looked at Laura. "My father was killed in a crash. How could he be a father to me when he was dead?"

"He couldn't, of course, dear," said Laura hastily.

Pete tried to stand up, but he was too weak and sank back in his chair.

Bird couldn't stop. "If he was alive, he would've found me and been a real father to me. He and I would've ridden together, trained horses together. We would've understood each other! I wouldn't have felt like such an outcast my whole life!"

Bird felt the tears running down her face. She looked at the Piersons and realized that her outburst had upset them both.

"I'm sorry. It's not your fault. I'm sorry!" Bird ran for the door and darted out. She needed to be alone.

Once outside, she fled. Her heart pounded in her chest, and she had difficulty breathing. She stumbled along for a few minutes before she began to calm down. Finally, she stopped walking. She bent over, head down and hands on her knees.

There was rustling beside her in the bushes. She listened.

Bird girl. Fear not.

Cody! Where did you come from?

I sensed your unhappiness.

Thank you, Cody There's nothing you can do.

May I accompany you home?

Bird saw his head appear through the leaves, then his whole body. She felt a great weight lift from her shoulders. *Yes, Cody. I would like that very much.*

The small coyote and Bird walked together through the trails, taking a shortcut home. With each step, Bird felt better. Gossip never hurt you unless you let it, she reasoned. She should know that by now! She was proud of her father, and proud of herself. If Eva had a problem, it was *Eva's* problem, not hers. Unless Bird let it be.

She'd call the Piersons when she got home so they wouldn't worry. They hadn't meant to upset her. They had treated her like an adult, given her a history lesson, and told her things that were difficult to hear. She'd learned something about her father, and the conversation had also helped her understand her mother. Now she could begin to sort it out.

She'd been so deep in thought that she was surprised to see Saddle Creek Farm appear in front of her.

I go now.

Goodbye, my coyote friend.

Cody disappeared. Shoulders back and head held high, Bird marched into the farmhouse.

Nobody was there. Not even Lucky. She looked at the clock. Aunt Hannah had said she'd pick her up at the Piersons', so they must all have gone. The Piersons would tell them she'd walked home, but Bird wrote a note just in case, then ran upstairs to change into her riding clothes. Hannah would be pleased about the note, Bird thought with a smile.

The first thing she wanted to do was to check on Tall Sox. After what Frank had told her, she was worried about their newest boarder.

Bird pulled on her boots at the kitchen door and grabbed her hat from the peg. She headed outside.

Three horses grazed side by side in the front pasture. Charlie, Sunny, and Sox. Bird relaxed.

The handsome chestnut gelding lifted his head from the lush grass. *Hello, stranger.*

Hey, Sunny.

Are we riding today?

For sure.

Good. I'm a bit bored here.

Bird watched the other horses grazing together a short distance away. Things seemed calm and normal. *How are you getting along with Sox?*

He's okay.

Any problems?

None. Charlie and I like him.

Let me know if you see any strange people around.

Problems?

Maybe. I hope not.

Whatever.

I'll get your saddle and bridle and be back in a minute.

I'm not going anywhere.

Bird grinned as she ran up to the barn. She loved her horse and his dry sense of humour.

Cliff appeared at the barn door. "I thought everybody was gone. The car left a few minutes ago. In a hurry."

Bird opened her mouth to explain. Nothing came out. Not a sound.

Cliff took in what had happened. "Just relax. Take your time and try again."

She took a deep breath, tried to relax, and made an effort to speak again. Not a peep. This was terrible! Bird covered her face with her hands.

"Never mind, Bird," said Cliff kindly. "You know how it is. You can talk and then you can't. Don't sweat it." He patted her shoulder. "Your voice will come back again. It always does."

Bird appreciated his thoughtfulness, but really! Of course she'd sweat it! What was wrong with her? Why did this always happen to her? Was she crazy? Why did her vocal chords decide things without her?

She took her saddle off the rack, chose a saddle pad and girth, and pulled down Sunny's bridle from the hook where it hung. Trying to concentrate on anything but her speech, Bird raced down to the paddock where Sunny stood waiting.

I can't talk. Again! she messaged.

So what? You can still talk to me.

I can't believe it!

Sundancer bent his neck and nuzzled her. *Let's go for a ride down the escarpment. It always makes you happy. Me, too.*

Within minutes, Sunny and Bird were trotting past the barn and down the trails leading to the back of the farm. Sunny was right, Bird thought. She always felt happy riding back there.

Big solid rocks rose out of the ground randomly, and wildflowers sprang up in clumps of colour along the path. The air was filled with bird song, reminding Bird of the joyfulness of life. There was so much to be happy about.

Tell me I'm right.

You're right, Sunny. I feel much better.

They slowed when they approached the lip of the escarpment, where the path sharply descended. Small stones tumbled, rocketing to the bottom, as Sunny's hooves upended them. He became more careful of where he put each hoof, and kept them both safe as they made their way down into the cool, dark woods below.

Bird remembered meeting Tanbark for the first time last June. They'd been in this same spot. He'd come out of the bushes waving his arms, and Sunny had been so frightened that he'd spun and run right up the cliff again.

No Tanbark today, but Bird would never forget.

The wild man came out of the woods right here, Sunny messaged.

Bird patted his neck. *I was thinking the same thing.*

We think alike.

Bird smiled. They certainly did.

Cody appeared beside them.

Hey, Cody!

A man is at your den. I know not who.

Bird snapped out of her pleasant mood. *Where is he?*

In the field where Sunny lives.

Thanks. Sunny, we have to go back!

We just got here! We're having a nice ride!

Go now! Bird urged the horse to turn and run back up the escarpment. Sunny balked. *The man might try to harm Sox.*

Is this what you meant by problems?

Yes!

Sunny turned on his hocks and spun. He gathered speed and galloped up the steep incline. Once they were on firm land at the top, he retraced his steps to the barn in record time.

Bird could see a figure in the front field. A lone man. He was too far away to identify, but Bird suspected the worst. Charlie and Sox were running in anxious circles, heads and tails up.

Sunny ran past the barn, down the lane, and jumped the rail fence into the field. Charlie and Sox halted, tails high in the air, and snorted. The man stood still in shock.

Sunny skidded to a halt at the man's feet.

Bird stared right into the face of Dexter Pill.

"Be careful there!" he shouted angrily.

Bird tried to answer, but her voice refused to obey.

"Cat got your tongue?"

Bird ignored the comment. She didn't need her voice to deal with this. She urged Sunny on toward Sox and Charlie, who were calming down now that Bird was there.

How long has that man been here? Bird asked Sox.

Not long. We keep moving and he keeps coming. He's trying to catch me.

I move between him and Sox. Charlie added, *He makes us nervous.*

Bird stroked their necks. *Don't worry, boys. He'll go now.*

Charlie nickered. *Good. He left something at the fence.*

Where?

Sox looked over toward the barn. *There. On the ground.*

Bird couldn't see anything. She and Sunny trotted over to the spot that Sox indicated. Sure enough, there was a dark blue object in the weeds, barely visible. Bird slid down to the ground to take a look. It was a small, zippered cloth bag with a strap.

"Hey! That's mine!" Dexter ran toward them. "Get away from that!"

Bird had no idea what was in the bag, but judging from Dexter's urgency, she definitely needed to find out. She picked it up and crossed the strap over her shoulder, then used the fence to help her climb quickly up on Sunny. Together they galloped across the field, past the waving Dexter, and jumped out over the fence.

Bird glanced at the house. Nobody was home yet. Bag thumping on her back, she raced up to the barn, hoping Cliff was still there.

He was. "Bird! What the heck are you doing?" he called.

Bird pointed down the driveway to the front field, where Dexter was scaling the fence at the road.

"Who's that?" he asked, before he remembered that Bird couldn't speak. "I'd better go find out." Cliff jumped into the Rhino, a little four-wheel-drive farm vehicle. His Jack Russell terrier, Boss, leapt in beside him. Off they went, sending clouds of dust into the air.

Bird and Sunny ran along beside him, and got to the road just as Dexter sped away in his truck and trailer.

"What was that all about?" Cliff asked.

Bird shook her head.

"I'll tell Hannah when she gets home. Dexter has no reason to come over here like that."

Bird agreed by nodding her head vigorously.

"Crazy man!" Cliff exclaimed. "What the heck was he doing in that field without telling us? He has a lot of explaining to do." Cliff drove away with a brief wave to Bird as he sped past.

Normally, Bird would have examined the blue bag with Cliff, but now that she was a private detective, she wondered if she should give it to Frank. She was very curious, so maybe she would take a look herself, and then contact him. She walked Sunny over to the fence, removed his tack, and put him back out in his field.

Is this another mystery, Bird?

Might be.

Are you going to get all distracted and stressed like last time?

I hope not.

Will you be able to ride me in shows and concentrate?

I hope so.

You're distracted now, Bird!

Look, Sunny. This is important. Horses' lives are at risk.

In that case, go for it.

Bird patted Sunny's neck and thought again how lucky she was to have a friend like him.

Now, what was in the bag?

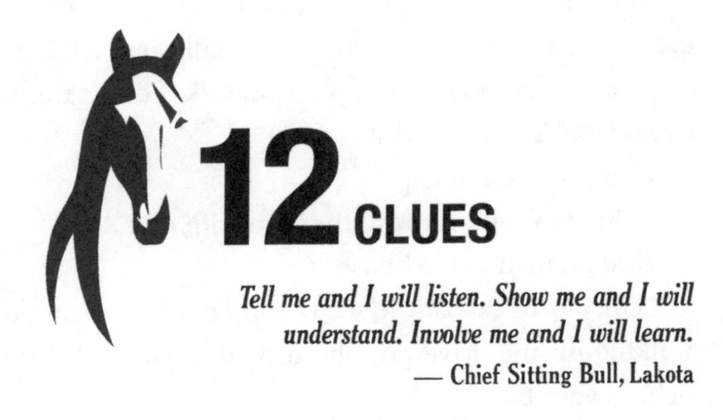

12 CLUES

Tell me and I will listen. Show me and I will understand. Involve me and I will learn.
— Chief Sitting Bull, Lakota

Just as Bird was opening Dexter's blue bag to take a peek inside, Sally and her father drove up the lane. She quickly hid it behind her back, and waved hello. The car slowed.

"Bird!" called Sally. "I came to ride Tall Sox. Can you help me?"

Bird nodded and smiled.

Sally opened the car door. "Thanks, Dad." She jumped out, smiling and eager.

Harold Johns turned his car around, and waved as he went past. "Hi, Bird! Bye, Sally! Call me when you're ready!"

Bird needed to see what was in the bag. She motioned for Sally to go to the barn, and mimed leading a horse so Sally would understand to get Sox's halter and lead shank.

Sally asked, "Why can't you talk?"

Bird knew it would have been useless to try to explain, even if she'd been able to try. Luckily, Sally kept talking.

"Wanda said sometimes you can't talk. I didn't think it was true. But it is, isn't it?"

Bird nodded unhappily.

"Why can't you come to the barn with me?"

Bird pointed to the house.

"Oh. Oh, okay." Sally looked at Bird oddly, but started walking up the driveway. She turned around. "What's behind your back?"

Bird brought the bag around to show her.

"Why were you hiding it?"

Bird shrugged, trying to appear like it was no big deal.

"So, why do you have to go to the house?"

Bird crossed her legs and hopped.

"Oh! Why didn't you say so!" Sally turned and ran up to the barn.

Bird sighed. She was new at this game. Obviously, she'd need to appear less secretive in the future, to avoid suspicion.

Bird unzipped the blue bag and looked inside. It was only a packed lunch! A bruised apple, a small carton of chocolate milk, a straw, some sugar cubes, and a squished chicken salad sandwich wrapped in plastic wrap. Dexter's lunch. Great private detective *she* was turning out to be!

Bird took the apple and sugar cubes out to give Sunny, and tossed the bag in the garbage. She started to leave, but had gone no more than a couple of steps when she stopped. Just a minute, she thought. *Real* detectives examine the evidence, no matter how trivial and commonplace it appears. She reached back into the garbage and plucked out the bag, replaced the cubes and apple, then searched around for someplace to store it. In the mudroom she found a white Styrofoam cooler. She got ice from the freezer and put the blue bag and the ice in the cooler. If Frank Skelton wanted to look at Dexter's lunch, at least she'd be able to show him.

Now she had to deal with Sally, who was happily striding down the lane with a halter and a lead shank.

Bird joined her at the gate.

"Tall Sox!" called Sally. "Tall Sox!"

The bay gelding with the four tall white socks lifted his head. He looked over at the girls, and resumed his grazing.

"Tall Sox!" Sally's voice hardened. "Come here right now!"

Bird motioned for Sally to walk out and get him.

"Dexter always told us not to. He said the horses would trample us.

Bird looked at her quizzically.

"I even saw it happen!"

Bird believed it. There were probably a lot of horses who wanted to trample Dexter Pill.

Bird opened the gate and walked into the field.

"Don't, Bird!"

Bird looked at Sally and shook her head. She continued out into the field. *Sox? Sally wants to ride you.*

I guessed as much.

Can you walk over to us? Slowly?

Can I finish this one little spot of grass?

Sure.

By the time the girls were halfway across the field, Tall Sox had stretched and was casually strolling over to them.

"You see? He's coming at us! He's going to trample us!"

Bird rolled her eyes at Sally and shook her head.

Sox? Can you stop walking?

Sox stopped. *Why?*

Sally's worried.

Tall Sox halted. Bird approached the puzzled horse and patted his neck. *Thanks, Sox. Sally needs to feel confident around you.*

Is it because I spooked at the show?

Maybe. But she doesn't know too much about horses yet. You'll have to help her. She'll learn.

Bird took Sally's hand and patted Sox's neck with it. Sally inhaled nervously. "Now what?"

Bird pointed to the halter.

"I can't do that, Bird. I don't know how."

Bird held the halter the right way and showed her where to put Sox's nose. Sally was tentative, but she managed to slip it on and do up the clip.

Bird grinned. She snapped on the lead shank, handed it to Sally, and gave her a thumbs-up.

"That wasn't so bad!" Sally beamed with pride.

Bird walked away.

"Where are you going?" Sally called. "What if he spooks and runs away?"

Bird shook her head and kept walking. *Walk slow, Sox, and stay close to her.*

"Look! He's coming with me! Bird! I can do this!"

Bird chuckled to herself. It always amazed her that kids like Sally, who'd been riding for years, had so few horsemanship skills. At the big show barns, the employees do all the work; the kids never learn to catch their horse, groom him, and tack him up, which is so important in establishing trust.

As they got to the gate, Paul's truck stopped beside them. Hannah and Julia were with him, and none of them were smiling. Bird could see right away that something was wrong.

Hannah opened the door, and Lucky jumped out wagging his tail. He licked Bird's hand, then caught a scent and was off.

"There you are, Bird!" said Hannah. "I'm afraid we have some bad news." She paused. "Pete's in the hospital again."

The hospital? Bird was stunned. She'd just seen the Piersons! She opened the palms of her hands in question.

"Mrs. Pierson called and told us you'd left, upset. We drove over, hoping to see you along the way. When we got to the Piersons', an ambulance was in the driveway. It looks like Pete had a minor heart attack."

Bird clutched her chest. A heart attack! She pictured Pete's face when she'd said she was leaving. White and stricken, with his eyes wide open. He was so upset that his heart couldn't take it! Bird felt terrible. She'd meant to call, too, when she got home, but hadn't.

Paul got out and came around the truck. "I can see you're blaming yourself, Bird. Please don't think it's your fault. Mr. Pierson has been having a real problem with his heart lately. And it wasn't a massive heart attack. It was more of a warning. They think he'll be just fine."

Hannah got out, too. "I shouldn't have dumped it all out like that, Bird."

Bird couldn't move. How could she make this all right?

Sally led Tall Sox out of the field. "Is Mr. Pierson the old man down the road? The one who comes to watch you ride?"

Bird nodded.

"He looks like a nice man."

Bird nodded again.

Hannah looked at Bird pointedly. "Bird?"

Bird looked at her.

"Aren't you going to say something?"

A tear rolled down Bird's face.

"Oh no, Bird. Not again."

Bird breathed raggedly as Hannah held her in her arms. "Don't worry about it, honey. It'll come back."

Exactly what Cliff had said, thought Bird. She lost her speech so often, nobody even worried about it anymore. Except her.

Julia jumped down from the back seat, and crept up beside Bird. She hugged her sister tightly. "It's going to be okay. You'll see."

Eva chose this moment to come driving up the lane. She stopped beside Paul's truck and rolled down her window. "I'm here to pick up Julia and I'm running late."

Everybody looked at her.

"Why the long faces?"

Hannah answered. "Pete Pierson is back in the hospital. Looks like he had a heart attack."

"That's too bad. Julia, we're late! Get in the car."

Nobody moved.

"What are you staring at?" Eva looked bewildered.

"Don't you think that's a little insensitive?" asked Hannah.

"Why is it always my fault? Look, I'm sorry. I'm sorry for Mr. Pierson, I'm sorry you think I'm insensitive. I can't seem to do anything right." Eva stayed in her car, her hands gripping the wheel so tightly that her knuckles were white. "Julia, for the last time, you have a dentist's appointment. Get in."

Julia did what she was told. Everybody watched as Eva drove her car right over the lawn and out to the road.

"Something's bothering your sister," said Paul.

"No kidding." Hannah stared after the car, concern drawing down the corners of her mouth.

Bird felt even more deflated than before. Her mother hadn't even looked at her. She tried not to care.

Sally broke the silence. "Can I ride now?" she asked, looking at Hannah for an answer.

"Sure, Sally. Sure. I'll give you a lesson. Tall Sox's sore is healing well. You go up and get him tacked, with an extra pad on his back. I'll be there by the time you're ready."

Sally grimaced. "I can't do it alone."

Bird sighed. She pointed to herself.

"Thanks, Bird. I'll be up in a few minutes." Hannah headed for the house while Paul parked his truck.

Bird and Sally walked up the lane with Sox.

"Wow," said Sally. "And I thought my mother was difficult. I know you can't say anything, but really, I don't know how you live with Eva!"

Bird didn't either.

Cliff met them at the barn door. "Bird, did you tell Hannah and Paul about Dexter dropping in?"

Bird shook her head. She'd totally forgotten — not like she could have "told" them anyway. She pointed to her throat.

"Oh, yeah, Sorry."

"What was Dexter doing here?" asked Sally.

"We don't know." Cliff began walking toward the house. "But I'll go tell Hannah now. She might just want to give him a call."

Bird helped Sally brush Tall Sox. She showed her how to pick his hooves, comb his mane and tail, and brush him. His bridle and saddle were in the tack room, and Bird taught Sally where they belonged so she could find them again. She showed her how to put the saddle pad on, how to place the saddle on it, and how tight the girth should fit. The bridle was a little trickier, but Bird thought Sally would catch on quickly.

Sally was thrilled. "I never knew how to do anything! Now I can come ride whenever I want!"

Bird smiled and nodded.

"Can you ride him first? In case he's too fresh for me?"

Bird shook her head.

"Please, Bird? Dexter always did that for me so I wouldn't get hurt." Sally appeared close to tears.

A transmission from Cody interrupted them. *Bird girl. The Listener wants to speak with you.*

Bird knew immediately that Cody meant Frank. He was a listener, both to animals and to people. *Where is he?*

At the end of the far field, waiting.

Thanks, Cody. I'll go now.

Bird looked at Tall Sox, all ready to go. She turned to Sally. She motioned that she would ride him after all.

"Oh, thank you so much! That would be so great! Dexter always rode him first, but Tall Sox never got calmed down so I never rode him!"

Bird put one finger in the air.

"Just this once? I get it! This is like charades!"

Bird snapped on the chin strap of her riding helmet and took Sox to the mounting block outside the door. She could see Hannah and Cliff leaving the kitchen. She'd have to hurry.

Sox, how are things?

Good. I like it here.

That makes me happy.

Where are we going?

Just to the edge of this field for a minute, then Sally will have a lesson on you.

Okay.

She's going to become a really good owner.

I think so, too.

Bird could see a man on horseback, just at the fence-line. It was Frank, on a horse she didn't recognize. She cantered up to him. *I can't speak out loud, so we'll have to talk like this.*

Fine by me. I have very little time. I'm exercising this jumper for Dexter, and have several more to ride. Cody told me that Dexter was here today.

Yes. He was in the field with Charlie and Sox. Sunny and I scared him away.

What was he doing?

The horses were running. It looked like he was trying to catch Sox. He left his lunch bag on the ground.

Do you have it?

Yes.

Can you give it to me?

It's in the house.

Good work. I'll take this horse back and get Glad. Can you meet me back here in one hour?

Bird nodded.

Frank and the horse turned and cantered away. As she and Sox trotted back to the barn, Bird thought how exciting it was to be a spy — exciting and productive. She was helping Frank put Dexter out of the horse business. This was good for any horse that might have the bad luck to fall into his hands.

Hannah stood waiting with Sally as Bird and Sox approached the barn. Bird slid down and patted the horse's neck. *Thanks, Sox. You're a good horse.*

My pleasure.

Hannah looked at Bird, confused. "Was there a problem?" she asked.

Bird shook her head.

"She just got him warmed up for me." Sally spoke up. "As a favour. Dexter always did that."

"We don't do that here, Sally. Everybody warms up his or her own horse."

"Well, Bird said she'd do it only this once."

"Bird said that?" Hannah's head swung around to look at her niece.

"No!" laughed Sally. "She didn't actually *say* it, but we do charades. I know everything she means!"

Bird handed Sally Sox's reins. She waved goodbye and headed down to the house.

"Oh, Bird? Can you ride Charlie next?" called Hannah. "He hasn't had a workout this week."

Bird nodded and ran. Perfect.

Once in the kitchen, she grabbed the blue bag out of the cooler and emptied the ice in the mudroom sink. She put Dexter's lunch bag in her folded jacket, then headed for the door. She had less than an hour to clean Charlie up, work him, and get over to the fence to meet Frank.

She was almost outside when the phone rang. Maybe it was news about Mr. Pierson. She ran back and picked up the receiver. She opened her mouth to say hello, but no sound emerged. Idiot! She'd forgotten she couldn't speak!

"Hello? Who's there? Hello?" A man's voice was on the other end of the line — a voice she didn't recognize.

"Hello? This is John Budd from Montreal. I represent Alain Morin. I'll call back." He spoke to someone who must have been next to him, "Somebody's playing games here. I hear breathing."

The line went dead.

Bird stood in the kitchen, receiver in hand. Who was John Budd? He'd said he was representing someone named Alain Morin? Was he an agent? A lawyer? Bird felt goosebumps on her arms. She wrote the two names down on a piece of paper to give to Hannah. The man had said he'd call back. At least she'd be able to tell Hannah that much.

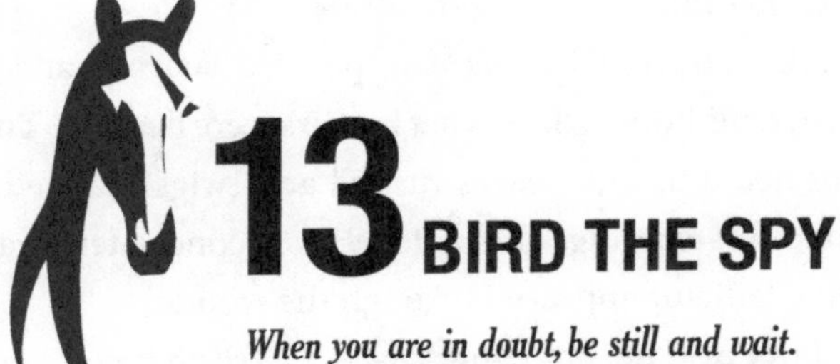

13 BIRD THE SPY

When you are in doubt, be still and wait.
When doubt no longer exists for you, then
go forward with courage.

— Chief White Eagle, Ponca, 1800s–1914

Exactly on time, Bird waited at the fence. She'd had a good workout on Charlie. They'd trotted one concession north then back again, and now the older black horse stood with his sides slightly heaving.

Keep me walking, Bird, or my ankles will swell up.

Bird chuckled to herself. Charlie was right. *Let's walk along the fenceline until Frank shows up.*

That's better.

Frank was late. Bird didn't have a watch, but it seemed like she and Charlie had been walking for hours. How much longer should she wait? She looked back at the barn. It was close to four, and Cliff was bringing in the horses. Bird's stomach growled. She'd forgotten all about lunch.

Bird? Can we go back? My dinner is waiting.

Can we stay just a few more minutes?

You're the rider.

Bird patted his neck. *Thanks, Charlie.* Sunny would've given her more of an argument.

All at once, Charlie's ears pointed sharply, and he twisted his body to face what his ears were hearing. Then Bird heard it, too. Leaves rustled and twigs snapped. A horse was coming, and quickly. A second later, Frank and Gladiator appeared through the woods.

I was held up, Frank messaged. *I have no time. Do you have the bag?*

Bird leaned over the fence and gave Dexter's lunch bag to Frank. *Someone named John Budd called Hannah today about someone named Morin.*

Alain Morin?

Yes.

What did he say?

Nothing. Just his name. Bird reddened at the memory of her muteness.

Morin's the man Dexter sold Tall Sox to, without Harold Johns knowing. Lots of things are happening. Today, Dexter bought Glad back from the Woodalls.

Bird's head was spinning. *Why?*

You can figure it out — but it's not your problem. Tall Sox is.

Insurance, of course, thought Bird. *What can I do?*

Keep him guarded. Here's a video camera. Frank reached into his saddlebag and handed Bird a small white sack. *Set it up in the barn, in case we need proof of anything.*

Sox has been staying out at night.

Alone?

No, with Sunny and Charlie.

Good. He has a better chance of getting away outside than in.

And what about Glad?

I'll guard him over at Dexter's. If he's in danger, he'll run over here.

Is that why you rode him over, so he knows the way?

Yes. Can you leave this fence open? Is there a gate?

Over there. Bird pointed to a rusted gate, hidden in overgrown weeds and brush. *I'll open it now.*

Frank rode Glad over to the gate to make sure he saw it. Bird dismounted and began to unwind the rusted wire. She noticed Glad's eyes; they were worried.

We'll look after you, Glad, she messaged.

I know you'll try.

Frank turned Glad back into the woods and was gone as quickly as he'd arrived. Bird heard them crash along the untrimmed paths and gallop away.

Bird's heart was pounding as she and Charlie made their way to the barn. She thought about how she could accomplish what Frank had asked. The field where Sox and the others stayed was right across the driveway from Bird's bedroom window. Maybe she could watch from there. But what if she fell asleep?

And poor, worried Glad. Dexter had bought him. He owned him now, and would get the insurance money if something "happened." The Woodalls would think that Dexter was doing the honourable thing, since he'd sold them the horse in the first place and it hadn't worked out. But now, Glad was much more valuable dead than alive.

Cliff waited at the barn door. "I thought you were gone for good! Where were you?"

Bird shrugged. One benefit of not speaking was that she didn't have to come up with lame excuses. But Cliff had to know that Tall Sox needed watching. She gave Cliff Charlie's reins and ran to the tack room to find a paper and pencil.

"What — are we a full-service barn now?" he joked.

Bird reappeared and began to write on the back of a shoeing bill. *Have 2 keep an I on Sox till we know Y Dexter showed up 2day.*

Cliff agreed. "I was thinking the very same thing."

Bird wrote, *Split night watch, like when mares foal?*

Cliff read the note and made a plan. "It's probably smart. Can you stay awake until three, then I'll take over?"

Bird nodded. She showed him the video camera, and wrote, *U know how 2 use this?*

Cliff examined it, and soon had it working. He showed Bird the on, off, record, and replay buttons. "We won't need to know more than that. Are you thinking of running it all night?"

Bird shook her head. *Only if there's something 2 film*, she wrote.

Cliff looked at Bird with admiration. "Good work."

Bird smiled at him, grateful for his unquestioning assistance. She untacked Charlie and put him in his stall to eat and rest. Later, he and most of the horses would go out for the night in the cool air.

"I'll stay up here for a while, Bird. I've got some things to do until night check. Then you're on your own until three in the morning. Okay?" Cliff's eyes twinkled. "Tap once for no, twice for yes."

Bird playfully held up a fist and shook it.

Sunny popped up his head from his grain bucket and stared at her gesture. *I don't want to know.*

Get some rest, Sunny. It's going to be a long night.

Sounds to me like you'll need rest more than I do.

Point taken.

Bird rubbed Sunny's nose and checked his water. Full to the brim. She checked all the horses before walking down to the house.

Hannah was stirring wild blueberries into muffin batter in the kitchen when Bird entered. Bird rubbed her tummy and licked her lips. She pointed to the bag of blueberries on the counter.

Hannah laughed. "I know, I know. More blueberries. You always say that." She dumped more of the tiny purple berries into the mix.

Bird nodded encouragement as she poured herself a large glass of milk. She chugged it down and immediately her stomach felt less empty. She reached into the cookie jar and pulled out a large oatmeal raisin cookie.

"A man called John Budd called just now."

Bird's eyes grew large. The cookie remained poised in the air.

Hannah continued speaking as she spooned the batter into the greased muffin tins. "He's a lawyer. He said he called before. Anyway, for some outrageous reason, he believes that we are harbouring a stolen horse." She licked some batter off her finger.

Bird stared at her, the cookie forgotten.

"This is ridiculous!" Hannah laughed. "Can you imagine?"

Bird reached for the pad of paper and the pencil beside the telephone. She wrote, *Tall Sox. Dex sold him 2 a man in Montreal before Sally moved him here. Alain Morin. Lawyer is John Budd.*

Hannahs smile disappeared as she read the note. She tilted her head. "How do you know that?"

Frank, Bird wrote.

"And nobody told *me*?' Hannah looked at Bird. "No, I don't expect an answer." She wiped her hands on a towel. She put the muffins in the oven and set the timer. Then she sat down. "So, this man, Alain Morin, thinks he owns Tall Sox? He bought him from Dexter?"

Bird nodded.

"Do Sally and her father know?"

Bird shook her head. At least she assumed they didn't.

"Then we'd better tell them." Hannah moved quickly. She picked up the phone and dialed.

Bird waited as the rings added up, and heard Hannah leave a message. "Hello, this is Hannah Bradley. Tall

Sox is fine, don't worry, but could you please call me as soon as possible?" She replaced the phone and sat down again.

"They might not be home yet. Harold picked up Sally about an hour ago, but they might have gone for groceries or something." Hannah sighed. Worry lines appeared across her brow. "I can't believe this, Bird."

Bird knew exactly how Hannah felt. She didn't know what to believe anymore, either. Things were getting more and more confusing.

"Cliff told me that Dexter was here this morning. What do you know about that?"

Bird shrugged and picked up the pencil again. *In the field & left. Nothing happened. Strange.*

'You're darned right it's strange." Hannah got up and began to pace. "Anytime Dexter Pill turns up, it's strange. He's not to be trusted."

The phone rang, and Hannah answered. "Hello? … Yes, Harold, I did call." She looked at Bird and pressed the speaker button so she could hear.

Bird crowded closer. She heard Harold say, "You said Tall Sox is fine? Was there an accident?"

"No accident, and Tall Sox is fine, but a lawyer named John Budd called. Do you know a man named Alain Morin, from Montreal?"

"No, I don't think so."

"Apparently, Mr. Morin believes he owns Tall Sox, and he's hired a lawyer to get him from us."

There was a silence from the other end.

"Harold?"

"Yes, yes. I'm thinking, Hannah. How could this possibly be?"

"I have no idea. I was hoping you'd be able to tell me."

"I knew that a man from Montreal wanted to buy him, but Tall Sox was never on the market. Do you have this lawyer's number?"

"No. I'm sorry. I thought it was so crazy that I didn't think to get it."

"Why did the lawyer call you and not me?"

"I don't know that, either. I didn't ask any questions. I just told him that we didn't have a stolen horse on our property." Hannah touched her forehead with her fingers and closed her eyes. "I thought it was all a mistake."

"I don't like the way this sounds."

"Harold, this lawyer will call back. When he does I'll give him your number, and I'll get his."

"That's all we can do for now." Harold's breath sounded like static on the phone line. "Maybe you're right and this is all a mistake. After today's ride, Sally's more in love with that horse. If there's a problem, she'll be terribly upset."

"I won't mention it just yet."

"And tell Bird not to talk to her, either."

Bird grinned at her aunt. As if.

Hannah said, "I'll call you as soon as I hear anything more."

Hannah and Bird sat in silence for a few seconds before Bird decided to show her the camera. *Cliff & I R watching Sox 2night 2 make sure Dex doesn't steal him,* she wrote.

Hannah's eyebrows shot up. "You think he'd do that?"

Bird raised her hands, palms up. Of course he would.

Bird wrote Hannah another note. *I'm going 2 nap so I don't fall asleep 2nite.*

"What about dinner?"

Bird stuffed the cookie in her mouth and grabbed another. *Wake me up at 8. Save me food!*

Hannah chuckled. "Yes, my sweet child. Things are so dull when you're not around!"

Bird didn't sleep a wink. She was too excited about the night watch ahead. She tried to rest, but every sound from outside her window caused her to jump up and look out. She fully expected to see Dexter sneaking around and trying to steal Sox right from under their noses.

Cooking smells from the kitchen finally ended her unsuccessful nap. Fried chicken, polenta, and fresh vegetables from Hannah's garden. Too much goodness to resist.

Bird hopped down the stairs and into the kitchen.

"That was a quick nap," said Hannah as she put a pot into the sink.

Bird grabbed a carrot stick from the table, noticing that the table was set for six. She pointed to it and looked at Hannah.

"Stuart called. Eva wants Julia to stay here tonight, so I invited them for dinner." Hannah scrubbed at the pot.

Bird sat down. She picked up a piece of paper and a pen. *What's going on?*

"Julia wants to stay here, and I said yes."

I mean Eva. What's up with her?

Hannah wiped her hands on her apron. "If I knew, I would tell you.

Bird sighed.

"Remember, Bird. Your mother was always very difficult, until she met Stuart. Then she changed and now we've gotten used to her like this. But that change was only last year. Why are we surprised that she couldn't stay like that forever?"

Bird could see Hannah's point. Changing was hard — she put her hand to her own throat. She ought to know.

Will Stuart B able 2 put up with her real self?

Hannah chuckled as she read Bird's note. "Time will tell, Bird. Time will tell."

Minutes later the screen door opened and Stuart, Julia, and Eva walked in. Stuart and Julia were dressed casually in shorts, and Eva wore a ruffly pink dress that was cut very low, and very short. Bird thought it made her look like she was trying to be sixteen. Bird cringed.

"Come in, come in!" Hannah rushed to the door. "You're just in time. Dinner will be on the table the minute Paul comes home." She indicated the chairs. "Keep me company in the kitchen while I finish up. Can I get anyone a drink?"

Bird thought she was being a little too cheerful. Eva obviously made her nervous.

"I'll have lemonade or orange juice, if you have it," answered Stuart.

"Me, too!" chirped Julia, trying to sound carefree. "Unless you'll pour me a scotch on the rocks?"

Eva frowned. "Not funny."

Julia's smile disappeared.

"Doesn't anybody offer alcohol around here?" asked Eva. She fluffed her blond hair and jutted out her chin. "To adults?" She sent an irritated glare in Julia's direction.

Hannah raised her eyebrows at the tone. "What can I get you, Eva? Wine? Beer? Gin?"

"A glass of white wine." She sniffed. "Chardonnay. Chilled."

"I'm on it."

Stuart had been looking out the window. "Are you getting some improvements done, Hannah?"

"No," Hannah answered. "Why?"

"There's a man taking pictures at the gate.'

Hannah and Bird exchanged a quick glance before Bird rushed out. A man was indeed standing at the road with a camera. He saw Bird and immediately ducked out of sight. Bird ran down the lane after him, but all that remained of his visit was a cloud of gravel dust.

Bird re-entered the kitchen and quickly wrote her aunt a note. *Man taking pics. Now gone.*

"What's going on?" asked Stuart.

Hannah showed him the note. "I don't know," she said slowly.

"Probably somebody out for a drive, and wanted a picture of an old Ontario century farm." Stuart smiled at Bird. "So, what are you up to, young lady? You look like you're up to something — more than usual."

"Bird can't answer," said Hannah. "Her speech is gone again."

"Oh, no," said Stuart with real empathy. "Not again."

Bird looked at her mother for her reaction, but Eva was busy studying her nails.

"I'll answer for her," Hannah said. "There's a lot of excitement going on around here —"

Bird knocked over her lemonade, spilling half of it on the floor. While everybody was gasping and running for towels, Bird grimaced at Hannah. Hannah nodded. She got the hint.

Once the lemonade was cleaned up, Stuart asked again, "So, what's so exciting around here?"

"Bird is all excited about the big show this weekend," Hannah said, with a reassuring smile to Bird.

"Wonderful!" enthused Stuart. "Do you feel ready?"

Bird smiled and nodded brightly.

"You'll win, don't worry. The only problem you have," said Stuart, "is that you're the best rider and Sundancer is the best horse around. People might get jealous."

Julia piped up, "They already are! Everybody convents him!"

Hannah stifled a laugh. "Do you mean 'covets'? As in wishes they had him?"

Julia sighed. "Yes, I do. I can't get it straight."

"It's a rarely used word, Julia," said Stuart kindly. "Good for you for trying." He looked at Bird. "If Sunny is so coveted, you'd better be sure he doesn't get stolen."

Bird took a short breath. Even joking about horse theft was too close to the truth.

"It does happen, sometimes," said Hannah lightly. She looked at the clock on the kitchen wall. "I wonder what's keeping Paul."

The phone rang on cue and Hannah picked up the receiver. "Hello? … Oh, hi! I was just wondering where you were! … Oh … No problem … Just take care of the mare and come home when you can … Yes! I'll save you some chicken." She hung up with a soft look on her face. "He works so hard."

"If you say so," Eva snipped.

Nobody spoke.

Stuart tried again to make normal conversation, and returned to the topic of stolen horses. "Hannah, do you really think that someone might actually come here in the night and take a horse like Sunny?"

Hannah spoke carefully. "It would be highly unlikely."

"And nobody could steal Sunny anyway!" exclaimed Julia. "He'd kill them first!"

Bird could picture someone trying, and laughed silently.

"Well, Bird," Stuart teased, "if you were ever worried about losing Sunny before the big show, you could always hide him in an 'undisclosed location.' Don't politicians do that when they want to avoid the press?"

As everyone but Eva chuckled, Bird's mind raced. An undisclosed location … Merry Fields! The Piersons' barn was empty. Dexter would never think of looking there. What a good idea!

Ur a genius! wrote Bird. *Now I know what 2 do in case of horse theft!*

"Glad to be of help," said Stuart. He made a play of blowing on his fingertips and patting himself on the back.

Bird and Julia laughed, but Eva stamped her foot. "It's elementary!" she said. "Even a fool would know that."

The kitchen went quiet again. Hannah stared at her sister in disbelief. Julia stood beside Bird with her head down, and Stuart exhaled slowly.

"And while I've got everyone's attention …" Eva spoke to Bird, a steely glint in her eyes. "If *anyone* has questions to ask me, I prefer to be asked directly." She turned to glare at Hannah. "And if anybody asks any questions that should be directed to *me*, don't answer on my behalf." She pointed her finger at Bird. "Tell *that person* to ask *me*."

Bird shrank back in her chair. Eva obviously knew she'd been asking about her father, and as Hannah had predicted, she wasn't happy about it. Still, Bird felt unfairly accused. She *had* asked Eva those same questions, and Eva had flatly refused to answer.

Eva picked up the glass of white wine that Hannah had poured for her and drank it down. She emphatically held out the emptied glass in Hannah's direction. "Another."

Stuart rose from his chair. "I'm sorry, folks. Eva, we should be going now."

"Don't you dare apologize for me!" she shouted. "If I have issues with my family, I'll discuss them! And I will go when I want to go and not before."

Stuart's face turned pink. He spoke so quietly that Bird could barely hear. "You're upsetting everyone. If you choose to stay here, you'll go home alone. And I will not be there." He walked to the door and took his car keys from his pocket.

Hannah said, "Oh, Stuart. I'm sorry!"

"No, I'm sorry. I was hoping that Eva could be reasonable tonight. I suppose that was wishful thinking."

"There you go, talking about me again!" Eva rushed to the door, as if she wanted to hurt him. "Get out of here!"

Stuart looked at her sadly. "Goodbye, Eva." He turned and walked out.

"Good riddance!" Eva called after him.

Stuart strode purposefully away. Hannah turned to Eva. "You really want to do this?"

"Do what?"

"Let him go?"

"He won't be gone for long. He'll come crawling back." Eva tossed her head. Bird knew Eva thought herself too beautiful for a man to resist, but right now, with her hard eyes and her down-turned mouth, she looked ugly to Bird.

"I guess we'll see," answered Hannah.

"And I meant what I said. I'm so mad that you told Bird about my affair with that no-good cowboy!"

Bird shook her head. She didn't want to hear anything more, and she certainly wasn't hungry. All the energy had left her body. She walked outside in time to see Stuart's car waiting at the end of the lane. He was giving Eva a chance to change her mind. If only she could speak, she would have yelled out to him that Eva wasn't worth it. Instead, she waved to Stuart and he slowly waved back. Then he drove away.

An urgent whisper came from somewhere behind her. "Bird!"

Bird turned around to see Julia waving at her from the upstairs window.

"Bird! Come here!" Julia waited until Bird got close enough to hear her whisper. "Mom wants me to come home with her, but I don't want to be anywhere near her. I want to stay here — that was the plan. Can you help me?"

Bird gave her a nod. Her younger sister wiped away a tear. She looked alone and scared. Bird understood how she felt.

But right now she had things to do. She held up her hands and formed a *T* for time out.

Julia whispered, "Thanks. Come back for me soon?"

Bird smiled and held up her thumb.

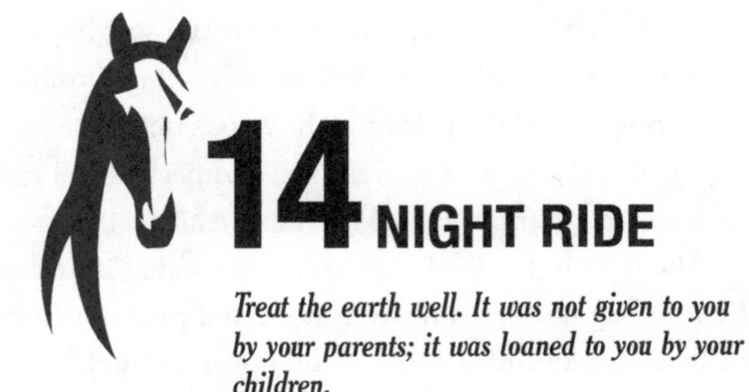

14 NIGHT RIDE

Treat the earth well. It was not given to you by your parents; it was loaned to you by your children.

— Chief Crazy Horse, Oglala Dakota Sioux

Now, Bird put her mind to her spy job. She'd have to let Cliff in on the new plan about moving Sox to Merry Fields — she didn't want him to wake up at three in the morning only to find the horse missing. And what about Frank? Would he be upset that she hadn't followed his orders?

But the more she thought about it, the more convinced she became that Dexter was going to make a move, and soon. By now, the lawyer in Montreal, as well as his client, would surely have called Dexter, wanting their horse. And what about the man taking pictures? It couldn't be a coincidence. She had to keep Sox safe, and Saddle Creek wasn't safe.

She hurried to the other side of the property, past the hedges, to Cliff's house. His truck was gone. She pulled out the pad of paper and pen that she kept in her pocket, wrote him a note, and left it on his door.

She walked back toward the farmhouse as the evening dusk was falling. In spite of all the pressure she felt and all the things she had to do, Bird took a moment to absorb her surroundings. She loved the musky scent of cooling air mixed with horse smells. The fields and the woods were alive with bugs and bats and birds, as well as all manner of small and large animals. Her spirits couldn't help but lift a little.

The light in the kitchen window reminded Bird that her mother and her aunt were alone and probably deep in conversation. Bird crept silently over to the kitchen window, which was open to let in the breeze. She got comfortable in the soft garden soil, trying not to crush any of her aunt's flowers. One thing Bird had learned over her years of being mute was that eavesdropping was an underrated skill. A person could learn a lot when people didn't know anybody was listening.

At first, there was no conversation at all, but soon, after a lot of cleaning up noises, Eva spoke.

"He doesn't really care about me. At all. Sometimes I wonder if he ever did."

So that's what's going on, Bird thought. Eva's marriage to Stuart is in trouble.

Silence from Hannah.

"He doesn't even try to be nice. I don't know why I should keep trying if he doesn't."

More silence.

"I went to see him today. He made me feel bad. He told me that if I couldn't find a way to get him out, I shouldn't bother coming again!

Went to see him? Get him out? Now Bird was confused.

Eva continued. "He even suggested that I seduce the jailer!" She began to sniffle.

It suddenly dawned on her. Eva was talking about her father. Bird should have known. Kenneth Bradley always had a big effect on both his daughters.

Now she could hear her aunt's voice. "Eva, listen to me. He's made his choices in life. They were bad, selfish choices. Don't wreck *your* life over him."

Bird thought about Frank's wolf story. She knew which one her grandfather kept feeding.

"If you're talking about my life with Stuart, I'm not! This has nothing to do with Stuart!"

"It doesn't? Don't you see how it works? Whenever you're upset about Dad, you're horrible to Stuart. Like tonight."

"No, I'm not! I'm just upset about the trial! You don't know anything."

"I don't? Why do you think I never had a real relationship until Paul came along?"

Eva sniffed. "That's your business. Blame Dad if you like." She sniffed again. Her voice became very quiet. "Maybe you're not totally wrong, Hannah. When I think about it. It does happen. I don't know why I get this way!"

"It's good you're starting to put it together, Eva. It's not easy." Bird heard Hannah push back her chair and walk to the window. When she next spoke, Bird was startled. Hannah's voice was right over her head. "The girls must be hungry. They didn't eat a thing."

"That's their problem."

Hannah paused before speaking again. "I haven't even gone to see him. I called once but he didn't want to see me."

"I'm not surprised. I always had a better relationship with him."

"You think so?"

"You're jealous, admit it. He wanted me around, not you. He always liked me better than you *and* Mom."

Hannah sighed deeply. "If that's how you see it, Eva."

"So how do *you* see it?"

Hannah paused, and said, "I don't think we have time tonight for that conversation."

Eva said, "Whatever. I know … and you know … that I'm his favourite."

"Totally true," sighed Hannah. "Uncontested. Now that we've figured out why you were so mean to Stuart, can we get to why you're so hard on Bird?"

Bird stiffened. This was what she'd been hoping for. She listened intently.

"Bird!" scoffed Eva. "How would you like those judgmental brown eyes staring at you? The girl hates me! I can't do anything right! I tell you, Hannah, she could be such a pretty girl if she'd do her hair and wear the clothes I buy for her. But no! Nothing I suggest is good enough for her!"

Bird had not expected such a tirade. And there was more.

"People can't believe I'm her mother — she's getting so tall! She's getting a figure, too. I'm too young to have a daughter with a shape. I'm still in my prime!"

Hannah spoke in a kind tone. "Eva, you have to listen to yourself. You almost sound jealous of your own daughter."

"How dare you!" Eva hissed. "That's a lie! You insult me! Jealous? What is there to be jealous about? Everybody says I'm a beauty. She doesn't look anything like me!"

Now we're getting close, thought Bird. Here it comes.

Eva's voice suddenly dropped to a whisper. "Every time I look at her I see Fred. Like she's there to remind me of my big mistake."

"You were young and in love, Eva." Hannah's voice took on a stronger tone. "Having Bird was one of the best things you've ever done. She's no mistake. Don't make her feel like one."

"I don't! I never tell her anything!"

"Maybe you should."

Bird waited, needing to hear more. She sat utterly still as several more seconds of silence passed. She even forgot to breathe.

Eva's next words were difficult to hear. She was crying now, hard.

"I'll never get over him, Hannah. He was my first, and maybe my only, true love. I never saw him again before he died!"

Hannah sounded comforting but firm. "Eva! You have a good husband who loves you. And two daughters who need you. Don't throw it all away."

Holy smoke.

Bird heard footsteps. Cliff. Bird guessed he'd returned and seen her note. She pulled herself together, and wiped her wet face. She needed time to process what her mother had told Hannah, but she'd have to do that later.

Quietly, Bird crept out of the garden and intercepted Cliff before he got to the walk. She motioned for him to stay silent, and led him away from the house.

Now she pulled out her pad and pen. *Why not take Sox 2 Piersons' 2nite?*

Cliff thought about it. "I thought we wanted to catch Dexter red-handed."

Film anyway? Set camera on the fence?

"How sure are we that Dexter is coming tonight?"

Not @ all.

"So we should leave Sox at Merry Fields? Or bring him here every day and back there at night?"

No plan after 2nite.

Cliff scratched his head. "I guess it wouldn't hurt for one night, if it would make you feel better. Will Sox be okay alone in the barn at Merry Fields?"

Bird nodded. He would if she explained it to him.

"Okay. You do that, and I'll try to work something out with the camera. I think I know how to do it." Cliff looked determined as he walked up to his workshop in the barn.

"Psst! Bird!"

Bird looked up at the second-storey window. Julia was trying to get her attention again. Bird put a finger to her lips and cupped her ears as she pointed to the house.

"That's what I've been doing all this time. Eavesdropping," Julia whispered. "All that's happening now is that Mom's bawling her eyes out."

Bird put out her hand in a stop position.

"You want me to stay here?"

Bird nodded.

"Are you going somewhere?"

Bird nodded again.

"I'm coming with you! I can't stay here!" Julia's head disappeared from the window.

It was getting dark now. Bird sighed. She had no choice — Julia would have to tag along.

Seconds later, the younger girl scooted out the front door. Bird motioned for her to follow.

Bird picked up Sox's halter and a lead shank, which was hanging on the fence at the gate, and walked out into the big field with Julia right behind her.

"What are we doing, Bird?"

Bird kept walking. She couldn't talk and she didn't feel like writing it all down. Julia would just have to figure it out as they went.

Sunny's head shot up from the grass as they approached. *What's up?*

Sox is in danger. He has to go to the Piersons' barn for the night.

Sunny nickered. Sox and Charlie looked up.

Sunny, watch out for any people in your field tonight. Give them a good scare.

My pleasure. Someone was here not long ago.

I saw him. Do you know him, Sunny?

No.

Thanks. Be safe.

Just let them try anything!

Bird rubbed her trusted horse on his forehead, and continued into the field. She calmly put the halter over Sox's head and patted his neck. *Dexter came looking for you today.*

Sox began to shake.

He might come again. Can you come with me? I'll take you to a safe place.

Sox rested his head on Bird's chest. *Yes.*

Bird thought the back trails would be fastest, and if Dexter was coming by the road with a horse trailer, she didn't want to run into him. Julia and Bird walked together to the far gate of the front field. Bird unlatched it, and closed it behind her after they were out.

Can you carry both Julia and me? Bird asked Sox.

I've never done that before. It might spook me.

Can you try? We can't walk as fast as you. If it's weird, we'll get off.

Okay.

Bird saw a log just off the path. She clipped the lead rope onto one side of Sox's halter, looped it over his neck, and tied the end to the other side, making reins. She pointed to his back and looked at Julia.

"You want me to ride him?"

Bird nodded as she led Sox to the log.

"And that's supposed to be the mounting block?" Julia stepped up, smiling. "This is fun."

Bird helped her up on the horse's back, then jumped on in front of Julia, who grabbed her waist. Bird held the rope and asked Sox to go forward.

How's this?

Not so bad.

They headed along the top of the ridge, overlooking Saddle Creek. The path would take them behind several farms, and up to the road that would lead them to the Merry Fields gate. The night was very dark, and Sox was careful about where he put his feet.

All at once, Sox jumped sideways. Julia shrieked and held Bird tighter. Bird patted the horses neck. *It's okay.*

It's not okay! It's a coyote!

Bird looked at the bushes, but saw nothing. *Is that you, Cody?*

Yes. I'm coming with you. Danger lurks.

Thanks, my friend.

It's my duty.

Bird tried to soothe the frightened horse. *Sox? It's a coyote, but a friendly one.*

If you say so.

They continued on along the trail. Minutes passed without incident, then Sox threw his head up in alarm. Julia shrieked again.

Easy, boy. What's wrong?

Something's coming fast.

This way?

Yes! Sox began to prance.

"Let me off!" squeaked Julia. "He's going to buck!"

Easy, Sox.

Now Bird could hear it. Hooves thundered closer and closer. Sox was close to panicked; there was no way he was going to listen.

"Please, Bird!"

Bird helped Julia down, and then slid off herself. Sox shook with fright. Bird led him off the path, and they stood in the bushes, waiting for the approaching animal.

Hello? messaged Bird. *Hello? It's Bird.*

The sound of hooves suddenly stopped.

Bird! It's Glad! I ran for my life!

Come slowly, Glad. I'm on the path ahead of you, with Sox and another human. A girl.

They stepped back onto the path and met Glad face to face. The two horses sniffed nostrils, recognizing each other from when they stabled together at Moreland Farm.

Bird patted Glad's neck. The animal was trembling and dripping with sweat. *Good boy! Come with us. We're going to a safe place.*

The Listener told me to go to Saddle Creek.

Frank had told Bird earlier that he would send Glad to her if he was in danger. Things had changed. Now, Saddle Creek might not be safe.

The Listener said not to stop.

It will be fine.

Okay.

Bird helped Julia back up onto Sox's back, and then hopped up on Glad.

"What happened, Bird?" Julia asked as they resumed their journey. "It was all so fast! We had one horse, now we have two. Good thing I came with you! But where are we going? What are we doing?"

In the dark, Bird couldn't even try to mime an answer.

"I hope you get your speech back fast. I hate talking to air!"

Bird hoped so, too.

Two girls, two horses, and a coyote arrived at Merry Fields a few minutes later. There were no lights on at the house or the barn. The entire farm appeared cloaked in black. It did not look hospitable.

"What are we doing here, Bird?" asked Julia in a tiny voice. "This place is giving me the creeps!"

Bird heard her sister's frightened tone. She patted her arm to reassure her.

"Something touched me!" Julia shrieked.

Bird sighed. It was impossible to communicate in the dark.

"Seriously, Bird! Something touched me! I want to go home!"

Sox messaged Bird. *I hope we're here. I don't want to carry this girl anymore. She's noisy.*

We're here. She'll get off in a minute.

Bird rode Glad toward the barn, and Sox followed along. As soon as they got there, the girls slid to the ground. Bird knew the layout of the barn from previous visits, and led the horses in.

"Can we turn on the lights?" asked Julia. "It's so creepy here!"

Bird shook her head.

"I don't know why we can't! It's not like anybody's here."

Bird shook her head again, harder this time. They must minimize any risk of detection. Someone driving by might see a light, and Bird didn't want to take a chance on it being the wrong person.

When Sox and Glad had settled into the stalls, Julia helped Bird get hay down from the loft and pump buckets of water from behind the barn.

Sox? Glad? We're going now. Do you need anything?

No.

No.

Okay. I'll be back first thing in the morning to feed you and give you water.

I'm happy I'm safe.

So am I.

Good. See you both tomorrow.

Bird and Julia left the barn and began to walk toward home down the lane.

Bird girl.

Yes, Cody?

I'll come back and check on them a few times tonight.

Thanks. That would be great.

My duty.

Bird took a deep breath of fresh night air and exhaled slowly. Mission accomplished. Was it possible that things were going to be okay, that Tall Sox and Glad were finally safe? For the first time all day, Bird started to relax — until a pair of headlights almost blinded her.

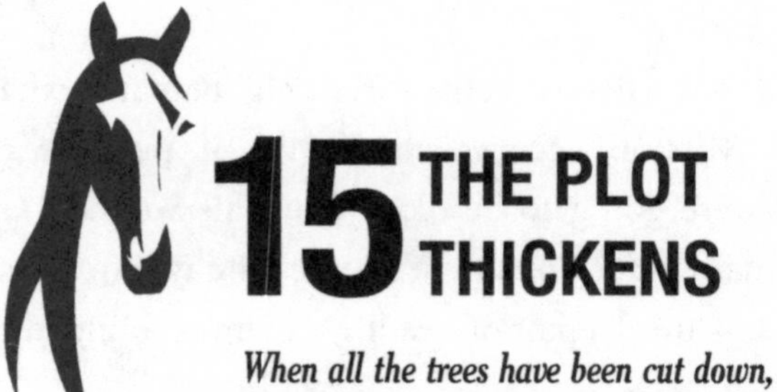

15 THE PLOT THICKENS

When all the trees have been cut down,
When all the animals have been hunted,
When all the waters are polluted,
When all the air is unsafe to breathe,
Only then will you discover you can't eat money.

— Cree prophecy

Bird and Julia jumped into a hedge and watched as an ambulance stopped at the farmhouse.

"Bird! What should we do! Are we in trouble?"

Bird put her finger to her lips.

The driver got out, walked around to the back of the vehicle, and opened the double doors. Another man got out of the passenger side and went around to help slide out a gurney with a person on it. Bird assumed it was Pete.

Laura Pierson stepped carefully out of the back. She picked her way up the walk to the kitchen door and unlocked it. Soon, lights came on, cheering up the whole place.

"That's way better!" sighed Julia.

The two men wheeled the gurney to the house and lifted it up the steps and into the kitchen. Minutes passed before they came outside, loaded the empty gurney in the back, got in the ambulance, and drove away.

"Now what?" whispered Julia.

Bird took her arm and together they walked up to the farmhouse door.

'You can't just walk up and knock, Bird! It's dark out. You'll scare them!" Julia dragged her heels.

Bird let go of her arm and strode ahead.

"You can't leave me alone!"

Bird turned and stared at her.

"Okay, I'm coming."

Bird climbed the stairs and looked into the window of the kitchen door. The kettle was on, and Laura was bustling around. Bird knocked.

At the sound of rapping, the older woman stopped and looked around. She hurried to the door and opened it.

"Bird, dear, it's you! I thought the men must have forgotten something. Come in!"

Bird stepped in, followed closely by Julia.

"And Julia, too! My, my! Come in, both of you."

"Thanks, Mrs. Pierson." Julia was suddenly very shy.

"Can I get you something?"

Bird could see that Mrs. Pierson was very tired. Her hair was all messy, and the lines on her face were deeper than normal. Bird shook her head no, then pulled out her paper and pen.

She wrote, *How is Mr. P?*

'The doctors think he'll be calmer at home. He's not a very good patient, I'm afraid." Mrs. Pierson's hand nervously touched her neck. "It was luckily quite a minor attack, and didn't damage his heart too much. He won't be bedridden, thank goodness, and should be able to move around the house as long as he doesn't overdo it." She giggled. "Which he probably will! Anyway, they've told me how I can look after him properly, and nurses will come three times a day to help."

Bird could see that she was unsure of how this would work out, and wrote, *Nobody can take care of him better than you.*

"I appreciate that, dear." She smiled briefly and sighed. "Now, why are you two here so late?"

There's a problem @ Saddle Creek Farm & we brought 2 horses. Okay if they stay here 2night? Bird scribbled.

Lauras eyes widened. "Is everything all right, dear?" She turned to Julia. "You can speak. Tell me what's going on."

Julia looked at Bird and wrinkled up her face. "I actually have no idea. I didn't want to stay with my mother tonight, so Bird took me with her. I really didn't know what we'd be doing."

Laura spoke to Bird. "Is everybody safe?"

Bird nodded, and quickly wrote, *People R safe. Worried about 2 horses.*

Laura put her hands on her hips. "I don't want to disturb Pete. He needs his rest. So I'll try to think what he'd do." Laura inhaled deeply as she thought this over.

"He'd tell you to leave the horses here. Then he'd solve the problem. But I can't do that because I'm not him and I don't know about horses."

Thank you! Bird wrote. *I'll B here in the morning.*

"Would you like a ride home?" Laura asked.

Julia's face brightened, but Laura was tired and Bird knew that it would be an imposition. She pinched her sister's arm. The younger girl quickly said, "No, but thanks. We're very happy to walk." She gave Bird a dirty look.

The phone rang. Laura was standing right beside it, and answered it at the first ring. "Hello? … Oh, yes, dear! Both of them are in my kitchen! … Come right over!"

Bird guessed that it was Hannah who'd called. She knew she was in a lot of trouble.

"Stuart will be here in no time to pick you up. That saves you the walk!"

Stuart? Bird had not expected this. The last time she'd seen him he was leaving Eva for good.

Thanks, Mrs. P. Bird wrote. *We'll wait outside & let U get back 2 Mr. P. Say hello 2 him 4 us. C U tomorrow.*

"I love deciphering your notes! What fun!" Laura said brightly. "Goodbye, girls. It was lovely seeing you. I'll tell Pete all about it. He'll have some good ideas."

Bird and Julia left the house and walked together to the road.

"What's going on, Bird?" said Julia.

Bird shrugged.

"Can you at least tell me later?"

Bird nodded. That would have to do for now, because Stuart's car was pulling into the lane.

Stuart called out the window. "Hello, girls! Jump in!" He sounded cheerful. That was strange, and Bird was also curious about why he was picking them up.

Julia got in the front and Bird in the back.

"How did you know we were here?" asked Julia.

"Process of elimination. Hannah called me, very upset, when she realized that you weren't upstairs where she thought you were, and Bird was nowhere to be found. I rushed right over. I was happy to have an excuse to go back, really. In spite of what I said back there, I love your mother very much and don't want to leave her." His voice sounded thick with emotion.

Julia reached back and squeezed Bird's arm. "I'm so glad. And Bird is, too."

"Thanks, Julia. And Bird. We'll work things out, whatever the problems."

Bird was surprised at how happy she was to hear that.

Stuart continued, "Anyway, Cliff came over and told Hannah you were coming here. We called here a few times, but Mrs. Pierson only answered now."

"They were at the hospital. They just got back."

"Oh." Stuart drove for a few minutes in silence.

"Are we in big trouble?" Julia asked.

"I don't think so. You'll see what's been happening while you were away."

Bird sat up straight. What was this? She tapped Stuart's shoulder.

"No, really, Bird. It's best you see for yourself."

The ride back to the farm was short, but every second seemed like an eternity to Bird. Finally, she saw the gates to Saddle Creek Farm.

A small, tagalong horse trailer and sports utility vehicle were parked off the road at the lane. Stuart turned his car and drove up to the house.

Two police cars were at the house, lights flashing. Uniformed officers stood by the cars.

"It looks like a TV show!" exclaimed Julia.

Bird's eyes scanned the field for the horses, but the lights were too bright at the house, and she could see nothing but blackness out there. She looked at all the people gathered at the house and picked out Hannah, Paul, Eva, and Cliff. Police Chief Mack Jones stood with the officers.

Bird searched the crowd for Frank, but she couldn't see him.

As soon as Stuart's car stopped, she jumped out of the back seat, hopped over the fence, and dashed into Sunny's field. Before anything else, she needed to be sure her horses were all right. She stumbled in the dark, and then stood still. She listened carefully.

A man moaned raspingly, "Help me! Help me!"

Sunny? Where are you?

Here.

Where?

Keep coming and you'll walk right into me.

And Charlie?

He's safe.

Bird walked slowly. As her eyes grew accustomed to the dark, she began to see forms and shapes in front of her. Nothing made any sense.

What's happening, Sunny? Who's there with you?

Frank messaged her. *I'm with him. Cody told me you brought Glad and Sox to Pete's.*

Now she could see what was directly in front of her. A man lay flat on the ground. Sunny held him down with his front foot. Frank stood beside them, and Charlie stood beside Frank. But what was on Charlie's head? He had on some kind of dark hood with straps hanging down.

What's up with Charlie? demanded Bird.

This man put on the hood to confuse him, so he'd get on his trailer.

Bird! messaged Charlie. *Get this off my head!*

Frank apologized. *Sorry, not yet. The police have to take pictures first. The hood will have evidence on it.*

Bird tried to decipher what she was witnessing. She looked more closely at the man on the ground. She had no idea who he was.

The man moaned again. He mumbled, "Get him off!"

Who is he? she asked Frank.

We'll soon know. He tried to kidnap Tall Sox, but captured Charlie by mistake.

Bird nodded. *Tall white stockings and blaze.*

Yes, messaged Frank. *They looked the same in the dark.*

Why can't he get up? wondered Bird.

Sunny won't let him.

Sunny whinnied loudly, and the man screamed.

Bird laughed silently. *You can let him go, Sunny.*

The big chestnut gelding lifted his foot off the man and reared up completely, standing on his hind legs triumphantly. *I waited for you to see what I did! Sox has been getting far too much time!*

You're a great horse! Bird patted his neck and rubbed his face. *Don't be jealous about Sox. He's in trouble, and I'm just trying to help.*

Sundancer pushed his head against her chest, then pulled her around to his side. Bird grabbed his mane and jumped lightly up onto his back. She leaned over and patted his neck firmly.

The man, newly released from the ground, stumbled to his feet. Frank cuffed his hands behind his back.

"I didn't do anything wrong!" the man wailed. "I told you! I was hired to pick up a horse!"

Frank spoke aloud. "Right. Tell your story to the police." To Bird, Frank said, "I didn't want to make a sound while Sunny had his foot on him. I couldn't risk him spooking and killing the guy." Frank chuckled. "Your horse was waiting for your command. He wouldn't listen to me."

Now that the man was standing, Bird realized who he was. *He's the same man who was here earlier,* she told Frank, *taking pictures of the horses.*

Thank you. Frank marched the prisoner toward the farmhouse while Charlie followed closely.

Bird asked Sunny to trot, and then they cantered joyfully around the field. It seemed that they went much faster in the dark, as the wind whistled in their ears. When they got to the gate, Bird slid down and hugged her horse again. *I love you so much, Sunny! You are a hero.*

She joined Frank and took Charlie's lead shank. She opened the gate, and closed it behind them.

Sunny whinnied proudly again.

One policeman took pictures of Charlie wearing his hood, and another donned latex gloves, removed it, and put it in an evidence bag. As soon as they were done, Bird led Charlie back into his field and let him go.

You're a good boy, Charlie. Thanks for your help.

I'm so glad it's over! I hated that thing!

How did that man catch you, anyway?

I'm ashamed. I fell for food.

Sweet feed?

Sugar cubes.

Bird rubbed his nose. *It's okay, Charlie.*

And apples.

Bird smiled. *Any horse would.* She patted his neck, and then watched him run to join Sunny.

She latched the gate and hurried over to the police cars. She didn't want to miss anything.

The cuffed man was still protesting, "But I swear! I was hired to pick up a horse! That's all!"

Mack Jones asked, "In the dark? In secret?"

The man nodded. "It happens. I was told the horse was stolen and my job was to get him back."

"Who hired you?"

"I don't know. My boss knows. I just did what I was told."

Mack pressed him. "Why were you here taking pictures earlier this evening?"

"My boss wanted to be sure the right horse was here."

"And he was?"

"Yes. A horse with tall white stockings on his legs and a white blaze on his face."

Frank stood beside Bird. *I believe him.*

Bird answered, *Me too. Where does this leave us?*

A little closer to the truth, but not as close as I'd hoped.

What happened with Glad? I met him along the trail above Saddle Creek, running scared.

Ed Cage was about to inject him with something. I pretended to stumble, knocked it out of his hands into the straw, and sent Glad running out the door. I told him to go to Saddle Creek.

Is Ed suspicious of you?

I don't think so. He always thought I was stupid, and now he thinks I'm clumsy, too. But I have the syringe. He's probably still looking for it! And we already know the fingerprints match the ones found on the BB gun.

Bird thought this over. *That means Ed shot the BBs. Will we be able to get Dexter? If he has other people do his work, and doesn't leave tracks?*

Frank put his hand on her shoulder. *We're getting there.*

They watched as two officers guided the cuffed man into the back seat of a cruiser and took off.

Mack turned to Cliff and shook his hand. "Good work, Cliff."

"Thank you, Chief," said Cliff. "I'm happy I could help."

Bird looked at Cliff with questioning eyes.

Cliff explained. "I rigged up the camera and recorded the whole thing. I guess it'll come in handy if anybody tries to deny it happened."

Bird grinned and gave him a high five. She was glad Cliff was helping the police. Last June, he'd been wrongfully accused in a murder investigation; now he was on the other side.

Paul came over to Bird. "It turns out that you were right to move him, Bird. Tall Sox was in actual danger tonight."

Bird smiled her thanks, but getting him away from Saddle Creek hadn't really made any difference. Sunny would have caught the kidnapper anyway, and Cliff would have had it recorded. Now that she thought about it, she'd accomplished nothing.

She saw Stuart standing with her mother in the garden near the house. They were holding hands and gazing into each other's eyes. Tears glistened on Eva's cheeks. Bird wondered if the chat she'd overheard between Eva and Hannah had made a difference — maybe Eva understood a little better why she was hard on Stuart, and maybe she'd even apologized. Well, Bird thought with a happy feeling, maybe something good had come out of the evening, after all.

She sent a message to Frank: *What should I do now?*

Go to bed. Feed Glad and Sox tomorrow. Keep them at Merry Fields for now.

What are you going to do?

I'm going to bed, too. I'll go to work in the morning at Moreland's and see what's up.

When will you know what was in the syringe?

Depending on how complex the solution, either tomorrow or in a few days.

Okay. Goodnight.

Frank looked at Bird with satisfaction. *You are a good partner.*

Thank you. Frank's praise meant a lot to her, more than she'd expected. *I hope we can solve this soon.*

The police cars were gone. The horses were settled. Eva and Stuart had left for the night. Hannah and Paul cleaned up while Julia and Bird hungrily ate chicken sandwiches in the kitchen.

"I almost starved to death!" exclaimed Julia with her mouth full.

"Heavens!" said Hannah. "Take it easy, girls!"

Paul laughed out loud.

Hannah gasped. "I haven't told Harold and Sally what's been going on!" she said. "I can't believe I forgot until now."

"A lot's been happening, Hannah," said Paul.

"No kidding." Hannah looked up the number and punched it in. "Hi, Harold, it's Hannah. Tall Sox is fine, but we had a little problem tonight."

Bird listened as Hannah told him about the botched kidnapping, and reassured him that his horse was safe at Merry Fields.

"Yes, of course, Harold. I'll tell you everything as soon as I hear." She hung up.

"Was he upset?" asked Paul.

"Not really. Just worried about what to do now."

"Anybody would be. His horse was the victim of an attempted theft."

The phone rang. Hannah answered it. "Hello?" Her left hand shot up to brush the hair from her forehead and her shoulders slumped.

Bird knew right away that it was her grandfather.

"Yes, Dad. The police have just left … Did she? … Yes, Eva's right, they're there … They'll be fine … Tomorrow? Of course I can visit … I'll see you then." Hannah sat down.

Bird jumped up and went to her. She put a reassuring hand on her aunt's shoulder.

Hannah looked drained. "Eva called Dad a little while ago, and she told him all about what happened, including where the horses are.

"Are you worried?" asked Paul.

"He makes me worry about nothing. It's stupid, really!"

"Stupid? Why? He causes trouble whenever he can, and you know it!"

"But he's locked up," Hannah smiled at Paul. "What can he do from jail?"

Bird didn't think Hannah's concerns were stupid at all. She wouldn't put anything past Kenneth Bradley, in jail or at large. Paul was right.

"Well," said Hannah, standing. "If you girls are finished, let's all get some sleep."

Julia yawned. "I'm stuffed and exhausted. I'm going to bed."

Bird felt the same. She yawned silently and trudged up the stairs, right behind Julia. She fell into a deep sleep as soon as her head hit her pillow.

Bird opened her eyes with a start. She looked at the ceiling. It was still dark.

Bird girl. Come now.

Bird sat up in bed. *Cody, what's wrong?*

Problems at the Good Old Man's barn.

Pete Pierson. Merry Fields. Bird pulled on a T-shirt over her pyjamas and stepped into her sneakers. She was downstairs in less than a minute.

Lucky jumped up from his bed in the corner of the kitchen. *Can I help? Can I help?*

Yes, Lucky. Listen carefully. Stay and guard the house. Do not leave the people alone. Okay?

Okay! Okay! The brown dog wagged his tail so wildly that he knocked over a chair.

Bird caught it just before it hit the floor. *Be calm, Lucky, and stay quiet now until I'm gone.*

Yes! Yes!

Bird patted his head and kissed his nose. *Good boy!*

She shot out the door to find Sundancer standing with Cody. *Sunny!*

At your service! I want to be part of the action! I've been feeling left out.

No time to lose. Cody began to run ahead.

Bird grabbed Sunny's mane, sprang with her legs, and leapt up onto his back.

The big gelding took off, following Cody down the grassy path to the trail above Saddle Creek. They wove through the tall grass, bushes, and apple and thorn trees. Avoiding rocks and holes and prickles, they galloped on. Bird held on to Sunny's mane with both hands and clung to his sides with her legs for dear life.

Within minutes they were charging up the driveway of Merry Fields. Spraying gravel, Sunny slid to a halt at the barn door. Bird dropped to the ground and ran in.

Too late. The stall doors were open and the horses were gone. Bird looked down to see tire tracks in a familiar pattern: a vehicle towing a horse trailer. It had been backed right up to the barn door.

Cody! What now?

Fear not. The tracks from the moving stalls have a fresh scent. Follow me. The small coyote ran off with his nose to the ground.

With trembling leg muscles, Bird used the mounting block and got back up on Sunny. As they trotted past the farmhouse, she saw with relief that all the lights were still out. The last thing she wanted was to wake the Piersons.

Cody turned left and ran up the middle of the road with Bird and Sunny right behind.

I hope they haven't gone far, transmitted Sunny.

Me too. I prefer a saddle for long gallops.

Trust me, so do I. You're flopping like a fish.

Sorry.

Nothing you can do. Well, maybe lean more on my neck.

Like this?

Yes. Try that for a while, then go back to the thumping.

The minutes seemed like hours, but very soon Bird saw a small black truck with the headlights off, pulling a dark trailer. She knew just where they were going. The truck pulled into the dirt lane beside Moreland Farm. It was headed to a shed. Bird guessed that this was where Sally had hidden Tall Sox when she was looking for attention.

Cody! transmitted Bird. *Slow down. Let's hide until they're gone.*

Good. The coyote vanished from sight.

Sunny, come this way. I know where we can wait.

As long as it's not in those cedars where the bugs will eat me alive.

We don't have a choice. Try to be brave.

Brave? You haven't seen brave until you've seen me!

Bird didn't respond. She was too busy watching what was happening from the little grove of cedar trees. She stared with shock at the scene that was unfolding. This was most definitely not what she'd expected.

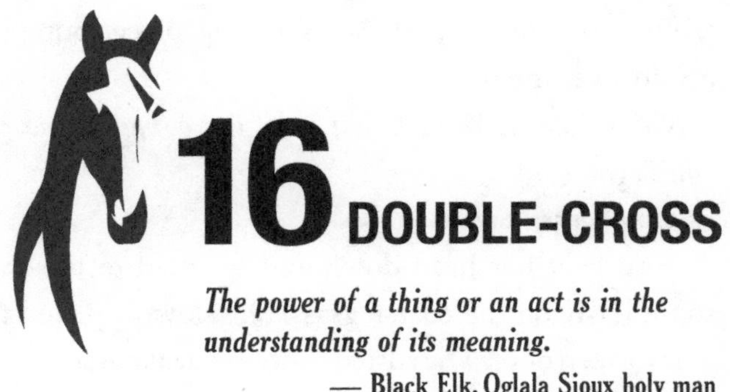

16 DOUBLE-CROSS

The power of a thing or an act is in the understanding of its meaning.

— Black Elk, Oglala Sioux holy man

Two girls stepped out of the truck — Wanda and Sally! What was going on? Bird's mind raced. Since when had they started hanging out together?

Am I dreaming, Sunny?

How am I supposed to know?

What I mean is, is this really happening?

Bird, I'm just a horse. I see some really delicious grass just over there …

No! Not yet! We can't be seen just now.

You and your mysteries! I'll just nibble on these nice cedars.

Bird ignored him. She stared, eyes wide, as Wanda and Sally dropped the ramp and unloaded Tall Sox and Glad. How did they know they were at Merry Fields? And why had they moved them?

The girls led the horses into the shed.

A few minutes later, they re-emerged and got back into the truck. Wanda expertly turned the small rig around and drove past Bird's hiding place, bumping noisily over the ruts.

Okay, Sunny. You can eat now. I'm going to find out what's going on.

Good grass. Sweet.

Bird kept her head down and sprinted to the shed soundlessly on the coarse grass. She slowly opened the old wooden door. The rusted hinges squeaked, sounding particularly loud in the quiet night. The smell of mildew and dampness assailed her nostrils. It was totally dark inside the shed, so she left the door open to let in a little moonlight. The dim light revealed four narrow stalls, each wide enough to hold a horse standing up. Two of them were occupied. Heavy chains hung at their rears, closing them in.

Sox? Glad?

Hello, Bird, messaged Sox.

Can you bring us some water? asked Glad.

The horses seemed relaxed and unharmed.

I`ll get some water soon, answered Bird. *I'm not sure where I'm going to find it, but I will. Are you okay for now?*

Yes.

Good. I need to think for a minute. Bird sat on an old bale of mouldy hay. A slow puff of fungus rose to her nose, and she sneezed. She moved to a bench.

Don't eat the hay, boys.

The horses nickered in agreement. Mould was bad.

Wanda and Sally together? wondered Bird. What were they doing? Bird was dumbfounded. She asked herself again — how did they know where the horses were? Hannah had told Sally's father that they were at the Piersons' barn. And Kenneth Bradley knew, too. Eva had told him.

But what should she do now? Should she leave the horses here until morning? Should she move them back to Merry Fields, or bring them home to Saddle Creek Farm? Or hide them somewhere else? Where was the safest place? She wished that Frank was there to give her orders.

Cody silently crept up beside her. *We have a visitor.*

Bird quickly stood up and headed for the door, but she was too late. Footsteps on the hard dirt lane were quickly approaching. The hinges creaked as the door was slowly pushed open. Bird ducked behind it, flattening herself against the wall. Something was digging into her back. Her right hand felt around behind her — it was a doorknob. She turned it and pushed a narrow door open, discovering a small room. It was likely a tack room or broom closet, but whatever it was, it had come in very handy. Bird stepped back into it just as the person stepped into the shed.

That was too close, she thought. She hoped she was the only person who could hear her thumping heart.

She listened intently. Quiet footfalls. Someone was sneaking around, Bird guessed, in an effort to avoid detection. She was pretty sure it was only one person. That was good, if it came to a physical fight.

"Bird, dear?"

Mrs. Pierson!

Bird peeked out of the tack room and saw a white vision floating at the other side of the shed.

"Bird?" Laura spoke rapidly and softly. "Are you here? I saw a trailer come to our barn and take the horses, and then I saw you riding and decided to follow. Are you in trouble? Can I help?"

Sweet Laura Pierson, in her cotton nightdress! Tears sprang to Bird's eyes. She walked into the hall of the shed, trying not to scare Laura. If only she could speak!

Bird rapped her knuckles lightly against the wall.

Laura gasped in fright and jumped.

Bird opened the door wide and stood in the dim light.

"Oh, my dear! You scared me!" Laura came up to Bird and hugged her. Bird had somehow expected a frail, bony frame, but Laura was sturdy.

"Are you all right?" she asked.

Bird nodded.

"Why are you out here in the dark, then, and not in bed where you belong?"

Bird wasn't sure how much to tell her, or how — no voice and no pen.

The elderly woman looked at Bird, her eyes narrowed in the dim light. In an instant, she guessed the problem. "Come to the truck, dear. I have something you can write on."

Bird followed the white nightdress to the truck, got in, and wrote: *The horses R here now. I don't know Y. R they safe here?*

Laura sat and thought. "It's a puzzle. You wouldn't have brought them to us in the first place if they were safe at Saddle Creek. And somebody didn't want them at Merry Fields, either. But that somebody obviously knows they're here, and you don't know if that person is to be trusted or not. Is that about right?"

Bird nodded energetically, waiting for Mrs. Pierson's advice.

Laura paused for a full minute before speaking. "I think you should take them home and put them in your back field. Is it fenced?"

Bird nodded.

"Good. That way, nobody will know where the horses are but you and me. And nobody would consider that you'd take them back to Saddle Creek, right? That might be the last place they'd look."

Bird smiled broadly. *Very sneaky*, she wrote, *& very smart!*

Laura hugged Bird. "It's called double-think. I use it only for double-crossers, and it sounds like that's what's going on here."

Bird was puzzled. *How do you mean?*

Laura answered, "I'm not sure, dear, but when things are this confusing, usually that's what's going on. Just an instinct."

She knew that Mrs. Pierson's instincts were pretty good.

"Can you get the horses to Saddle Creek alone?" Laura continued.

Bird nodded.

"Well, I'm off to bed, then." Laura started the engine. "I need my beauty sleep for Pete."

Bird quickly wrote, *How is he?*

Laura inhaled and said, "Still asleep. I have to get back."

Bird took her hand and squeezed it. She mouthed the words "thank you."

Laura smiled. "You're very welcome. Now get those horses home and keep us informed. Come over tomorrow and tell Pete and me what's going on."

Bird nodded. She stepped away from the truck and watched as Laura turned around and drove away. Now for the task at hand.

Sunny?

Here.

We're going home.

Give me a few more minutes. This is alfalfa and clover and something else we don't have at home. I quite enjoy it.

We have to go now, Sunny.

The chestnut superstar lifted his head and sighed.

Bird walked into the shed and released the chains across the standing stalls. *Sox? Glad? Follow Sunny and me back to Saddle Creek. It'll be safe. There's water and green grass.*

Okay, messaged Sox. Glad nodded his head and nickered.

As Bird turned to go, she received another silent voice. *Me, too?*

The transmission was faint and tentative. Bird looked around. She couldn't see a thing.

Where are you?

No answer. Bird peered into the shed's dark corners. There — in the very back of one of the standing stalls, she saw movement on the floor. She took a step closer and looked harder. An animal the size of a foal was huddled in the corner.

Are you all right? Bird asked gently.

I'm tired. The creature lifted its head. It was a very young horse.

Can you stand up?

The animal got his hind legs under him and used all his strength to hoist himself up. He was taller than Bird expected, but skin and bones. She guessed that he might be one or two years of age. Bird was shocked at the size of his bloated belly. He must be full of worms.

What's your name, boy?

I have no name. I have no friends.

How long have you been here?

I don't know. I sleep mostly. A man brought me here and forgot about me. I miss my mother and my friends.

Bird felt a pang of anger as she pictured what might have happened. The unwanted colt must have been dropped off by someone who'd decided to abandon him.

Bird reached out and the colt sniffed her hand.

Will you be my amigo? he asked.

Yes, I will, messaged Bird. *And will you be my friend?*

Yes, amigo.

Do you have the strength to come with us, Amigo?

I will try.

Bird dropped the chain and helped him out. Sox and Glad stood in the hall watching. Their eyes were soft and their nostrils flared. Both of their heads were low, and they stretched out their necks toward the young horse.

Bird led the way out of the shed. Sunny was waiting.

We have one more coming with us, Bird transmitted.

I heard. Sundancer sniffed Amigo and nickered. *Welcome! But I'm the boss.*

Bird climbed up on Sunny's back and started home. Sox and Glad stayed on either side of Amigo. Bird noticed that he was wobbly on his legs. He improved a little as they moved along, and as his legs got used to the exercise. Even though he was weak, he could keep up at a walk.

Bird wondered about the reaction she'd get when she brought yet another horse to Saddle Creek. Aunt Hannah would worry about Amigo bringing disease to the farm, and tell her that she couldn't save every horse on the planet. But what choice did she have? She couldn't have left him there to die. Hannah would've done the very same thing, Bird was sure. If Hannah wanted Amigo gone, she'd fix him up and get him healthy first, then find a good home for him. Amigo's life would be saved, in any event.

There was no noise except the plop and thud of horse's hooves along the gravel road, and an occasional owl or cricket, until they passed a swampy area. There, a million frogs came to life in a chorus of squeaks and chirps and croaks. All the horses startled.

Amigo leapt in fright. *What's that?*

Only peepers. They won't hurt you, answered Sox.

Amigo didn't know what peepers were, but he accepted Sox's answer and walked on.

Fifteen minutes later, the little posse rode up the lane at Saddle Creek Farm. Bird led them past the field where Charlie stood alone.

Hello! he called out in a whinny.

Quiet, Charlie. Don't wake anyone. We're going to the back field. Are you okay alone tonight?

I've been quite nervous. I'm nervous alone.

Okay, then Sunny will be there soon.

Thank you. Bird.

Bird organized her thoughts. Things would look more normal if Sunny was in the front field, and he would be a good lookout. Sox, Glad, and Amigo would keep each other company, out of sight at the back. *Sunny? I think you should stay with Charlie tonight.*

Okay with me, messaged Sunny.

She led the horses through the gate to the back field. The water trough was empty, so Bird hopped down from Sunny's back, closed the gate behind them, and went to get the hose. It was wound in a neat coil at the wall of the barn, attached to the pump. She lifted the lever, dragged the hose over, and twisted the nozzle to let the water flow. She first rinsed the dirt out of the trough, then let the water fill it up.

Amigo drank straight from the hose, with Bird stroking his neck until he got his fill. Already she'd grown attached to him. In the morning she'd take a good look. Paul could check him out for illnesses and give him his shots and worming medicine. In the dark, the colt's coat looked brownish, and he had two white hind socks and a narrow blaze down his face. Tomorrow, in the daylight, she'd find out what colour he really was.

As she waited for the trough to fill, Bird watched the dim shapes of Sox and Glad as they checked out their new area in the dark. They seemed content. When the trough was full to the brim, she turned off the water.

Okay, Sunny, come with me.

There was no answer.

Sunny? Time to go!

Another voice spoke up. It was Amigo. *The boss jumped out as soon as we got here.*

Bird shook her head. Of course he would. He knew where he was spending the night. *Thanks, Amigo. Have a good night, and I'll introduce you to Hannah tomorrow.*

Is she the human boss?

Yes. Bird smiled at Hannah's new title.

Okay.

Bird walked back to the farmhouse, suddenly exhausted. Her bed seemed like the most wonderful place in the world. She could hardly wait to drop her head onto her soft pillow and to cuddle up under her cozy covers.

As she passed the front field she glanced at the horses. Sunny and Charlie grazed side by side.

Good night, boys.

Good night, Bird.

Lucky ran up to her with his tail wagging. *All's well, Bird girl! All's well!*

Good dog, Lucky! Bird rubbed his ears and smiled sleepily. She hoped things would stay that way.

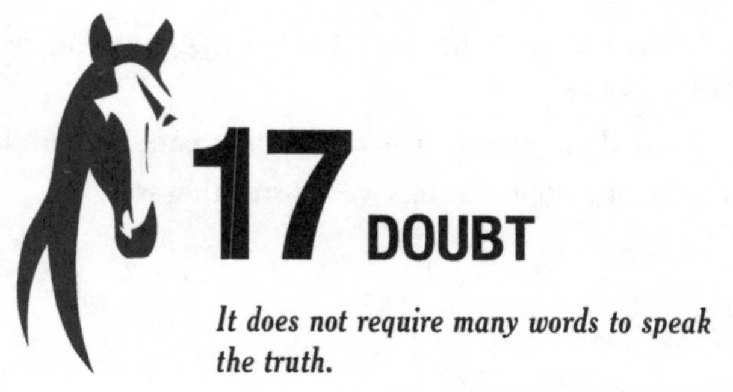

17 DOUBT

It does not require many words to speak the truth.

— Chief Sitting Bull, Lakota

The next morning Bird awoke from a deep sleep to the sound of the telephone ringing. Someone picked it up after a couple of rings, and Bird sleepily rolled over. But the smell of bacon cooking was too much for her. She opened her eyes. The clock read 9:00. She never slept this late! It was Sunday, and she had no chores, so Bird let herself enjoy the moment. She stretched from the top of her head to the tip of her toes, and yawned fully. She tested her voice and tried to hum. Nothing yet. Oh well. She'd have to be patient.

She thought about Alec, and pictured his handsome face with his engaging but lopsided smile. She pondered about what he was doing right now. Sunday was supposed to be a day off for the counsellors, so maybe he had a fishing trip planned with the guys. Or a canoe trip. She was really looking forward to his return. Only a few more weeks. Had he gotten her letter, she wondered? She hoped so, and really hoped he'd write back.

Amid the clatter of cutlery and plates in the kitchen, she heard low voices. She listened carefully. People were muttering, and nothing was clear, so eavesdropping was not an option. She climbed out of bed, got dressed, and went downstairs. Her mouth watered at the thought of a big breakfast of bacon and eggs.

Paul, Hannah, and Julia sat at the table. They turned to look when they realized Bird was there. She caught her breath. Something was wrong. Not one of them was smiling.

Bird glanced from one to the other. Julia kept her eyes down, but the two adults stared at her with questioning eyes. Bird's stomach twisted. Was Hannah mad about Amigo? She raised her palms as if to ask.

"Bird," said Aunt Hannah. Her face was strained. "We love you one hundred percent, and trust you. Completely. Please understand that. But we've just had a call."

Bird grabbed the pad and pen. *I can explain about the colt.*

"A colt?" Hannah said, distracted. She shook her head. "This is not about a colt."

Paul sighed unhappily. "We just got the call this minute, and know it can't be true." He looked at Hannah for support. "But help us with this, Bird. John Budd, the lawyer from Montreal, has been in touch with Harold Johns's lawyer about their lawsuit concerning Tall Sox."

He cleared his throat. "Apparently, it names you, Alberta Bradley Simms, as the seller. It also names you as the recipient of the money for the sale of the horse."

Bird shook her head to clear her ears. What was this?

"We know this is all crazy, and a misunderstanding," added Hannah. She reached out to pat Bird's arm, but she recoiled. She was stunned. Had she heard correctly? She plopped down in a chair.

Paul smiled supportively at her. "I don't believe it, Bird."

Hannah's voice cracked with emotion. "Nobody believes it, but you need to help us clear it up. And there's something else."

Julia exclaimed, "I know you'll be able to explain it!"

"Why didn't you bring Sox and the other horse back here last night," asked Hannah, "like you told Mrs. Pierson you would?"

Bird's eyes widened. *I did!* She scribbled.

"But they're not here, Bird." Paul breathed deeply. "Let's go back a bit. You and Julia brought Tall Sox and another horse to Merry Fields after dinner last night."

Bird glanced at Julia, who nodded wildly. "Yes we did. To save them from danger!"

Paul continued. "Then someone else came and moved them from there to the shed beside Moreland's around two in the morning. That's where Laura saw you. You told her that you were going to take them back to Saddle Creek."

Paul slowly and kindly made his point. "I know they're not at Merry Fields. You were sleeping late, so I drove over this morning to feed them. Mrs. Pierson told me what happened in the night. Then, I drove back here and looked in the field. They weren't here, so I drove to the shed, just in case you hadn't moved them after all. They weren't there, either."

Paul leaned over and looked right into Bird's eyes. "Tell us, Bird. We all know whatever happened you did for a good reason. We're just confused. Where did you take Tall Sox? And what about the other horse?"

I brought them here, I promise! Bird wrote. *With a starving colt that was in the shed. Amigo. I put them all in the back field!!!!*

Hannah sniffed back a tear. "Honey, we're not doubting you! In fact this whole thing is preposterous! But do you have any idea why they're not here now?"

Bird jumped up and ran out the kitchen door, not bothering to close the screen. She raced up to the barn and out to the back field, with Lucky close behind.

She couldn't see them.

She looked frantically in every corner. Hannah and Paul were right — the three horses were gone. There wasn't even any fresh horse manure to prove they'd been there.

Hannah, Paul, and Julia followed her up to the barn. They stood in a group, eyes searching the field.

Bird felt horrible. There was a hole in her gut the size of Canada. This looked bad. How could she make them understand that she was innocent? Even more importantly, how could they even imagine she was guilty?

Did they think she stole Glad and Sox to sell them? Her knees collapsed and she dropped to the ground, deep sobs shaking her body. It was hard to breathe.

Just then, Amigo came galloping into the field from the back. *Bird! I'm your Amigo! Don't be sad!*

Amigo! You're here!

'Look!" yelled Julia, pointing and jumping up and down. "A young horse! See? Just like Bird said!"

"Where did he come from?" asked Paul in amazement.

Tall Sox and Glad emerged next. The two big, handsome horses cantered across the field toward them.

"My heavens!" Hannah exclaimed. "Tall Sox and another horse! Bird, you told the truth!"

Bird's tears disappeared, instantly replaced by anger. Of course she'd told the truth.

Where were you? Bird asked the horses.

The apple trees are full of fruit, answered Sox.

Then Bird remembered. The gate. Frank had asked her to leave it open last night in case Glad needed to run to safety. She'd forgotten all about it. The horses must have wandered out when they'd smelled the apples from the trees behind the field.

Hannah turned to look at Bird. "I'm sorry, Bird. I'm sure everything else must have a logical explanation, too." She wiped tears from her eyes. "My darling girl, I love you so much." Hannah reached out to hug her. Bird felt resentful, but decided not to hold a grudge.

A vehicle drove up the lane and stopped behind them. Frank Skelton got out of his beat-up car. "I saw you and drove right up. I have news." Then he saw the horses. "Thanks again for saving Glad, Bird."

Hannah and Paul spoke together. "Who's Glad?"

Bird telegraphed quickly. *My name is on a document selling Sox and they think I got tons of money for him!*

Frank narrowed his eyes. *Interesting.*

But I didn't steal the horse or the money!

Of course not.

Frank answered Hannah and Paul's question. "That bay horse with no white markings is named Gladiator. I sent him running over here last evening when Ed Cage was about to inject him with a syringe."

"A syringe!" exclaimed Hannah.

"Yes. I was able to stop it just in time, send the horse off, and collect the syringe."

"What was in it?" asked Paul. His face had taken on its professional look.

"I just got the report right now. Air. And a little soft water."

It took a minute for anyone to understand. Paul got the significance first. "Air embolism."

Frank nodded.

Hannah looked from Paul to Frank and back again, waiting for an explanation.

"Air bubbles injected into a vein or artery create an air block, which stops the flow of blood," said Paul. "When the blood stops flowing, oxygenated blood can't get through the vessels into the organs of the body."

"It's a clever cause of death because it's impossible to detect, unless an X-ray is done before the autopsy, which is very rare," Frank added. "An X-ray would show the air block."

Hannah was astounded. "What are the symptoms?"

Paul answered. "Gasping for air, mainly. It appears very similar to a heart attack. The victim falls to the ground and dies a painful death from suffocation."

Hannah shivered. "Good thing you got there in time!"

Julia spoke up. "What's soft water?"

"Softened water means it came through a water heater. Hot water would expand the oxygen in the syringe to make it work more efficiently." Paul looked thoroughly disgusted.

"How horrible!" exclaimed Hannah. "You sent Gladiator over here? How did he know the way?"

Frank looked at Bird proudly, and put his hand on her shoulder. "Bird and I suspected that things were coming to a head. I brought him here earlier to show him the way. We left the back gate open."

Hannah and Paul gasped together. Hannah said, "Of course! That's how the horses got out!"

Frank continued. "It's good having Bird's help. She's proving to be a good partner."

Bird appreciated his praise, but there was no time to dwell on it. *There's more!* She needed Frank to know the whole story. *In the night, Cody told me there was trouble at the Piersons' and I rode Sunny over, but I got there too late and we followed a horse trailer to the shed beside*

Moreland's. It was Wanda and Sally, and they'd taken Glad and Sox there! Then I brought the horses back here.

Good information. Who's the little guy?

Amigo. He was in the shed and very weak so I brought him home. He would've died soon from thirst.

Frank's forehead creased. *He looks like one of the missing horses.*

What missing horses?

They're valuable racehorses, reported stolen, and the insurance company pays. We usually find the bones much later, and can't prove misdeed.

Bird shuddered. *Is Dexter involved?*

Dexter is most likely involved, but we need more proof. We know that at least nine horses have "gone missing." Amigo might be one. I'll look into it.

That's really disgusting, Bird messaged.

Paul inhaled and pursed his lips. "So, the gate was open. The horses were here all along." Paul looked at Bird. "I'm very sorry that you thought I doubted you. I never did, but it must've looked that way."

Bird smiled to let him know she was okay. She didn't care what people thought anymore. She was innocent, and she knew Frank believed her. That was enough. Right now, there were a lot of unanswered questions floating around in her head, and until those questions were answered, horses' lives were still in danger.

"So, what about this lawsuit, and Bird's name on the papers as Tall Sox's seller?" Hannah asked. Now that one problem was cleared up, she was ready to focus on another.

"Let's start at the beginning," said Frank. "Where did your information come from?"

Hannah's shoulders stiffened as she brushed the hair from her face.

Bird caught the familiar action. *Kenneth Bradley?*

"I was pledged to secrecy. I promised not to tell anyone, or he wouldn't tell me his news."

Frank nodded. "Understood. But let me guess. Your father, Kenneth Bradley?"

"Yes!" Hannah answered, taken aback but relieved that she could now tell Frank. "Harold Johns uses a lawyer at my father's firm," she answered. "My father called this morning from jail. He said his partner had received copies of the legal paperwork, and he wanted to give us a heads-up."

"And that Bird received money?" asked Frank.

"That information came from my father as well."

"How much money?"

"Thirty thousand."

Bird was amazed. Frank's eyes narrowed. "How did he get Bird's bank statements? They're confidential."

"I don't know," said Hannah, flustered.

"Harold Johns is the manager of the bank," said Paul, putting his arm around Hannah's shoulders. "We assumed that he'd taken a look at the statement himself."

Frank pursed his lips and considered this. "Assumed? Have you spoken to Harold?"

Paul shook his head. "We called and left a message. He hasn't returned it."

"How much did you tell him in the message?"

Hannah answered, "I just asked him to call us. I said it was important."

"It's Sunday," said Frank. "Hard to check with the bank or the law office until tomorrow."

Bird's head shot up. *Somebody's buying time.*

That's just what I was thinking, Frank replied.

Bird noticed a rustling in a nearby bush. *Cody?*

Bird girl. The man you call Dexter is at the place you were last night.

Frank heard what the coyote had said. He and Bird glanced at each other.

"I have to go to the shed beside Moreland's," said Frank out loud. "Paul, can you assist me? Bird, you come, too." Frank jumped in his car and started the engine. Bird got in the back. Paul looked at Hannah in surprise, but got in the front seat on the passenger side.

"What's going on?" asked Hannah.

"We'll let you know ASAP. Stay up here with the horses. And get Cliff over to help. I don't think anybody knows they're here, but you never know."

Cody? Will you stay to help?

It is my duty.

Thank you. Lucky? messaged Bird.

Yes, Bird girl? Yes, Bird girl?

This is very important. Help Cody guard Hannah and Julia. A bad man might be coming.

I will! I will! Lucky growled ferociously.

Good dog! praised Bird.

"Lucky!" scolded Hannah. "Don't growl!"

Cody telegraphed Lucky a response. *We will do more than growl if the bad man shows up.*

Yes, Cody! Lucky puffed out his chest with pride. The brown dog would take his assignment seriously, Bird was confident.

"Buckle up!" Frank drove quickly. In record time they arrived at the rutted lane to the shed. A small black truck and a navy blue trailer were there, in the process of turning around.

Frank parked his car at an angle that prevented the rig from leaving.

The driver slowed briefly, then decided to call Frank's bluff. He aimed his truck and sped down the lane, directly toward them.

"Jump!" screamed Paul. All three of them leapt out of the car, rolling into the tall grass. A split second later, the truck crashed into the side of Frank's car. Bird stared at the deep indentation for a moment before raising her eyes to the truck.

Dexter Pill's head rested on the steering wheel. He lifted it slowly, shook it, and blinked. He staggered down from the truck and made an effort to run away, but Frank and Paul grabbed him easily.

"Mr. Pill, do you wish to explain why you destroyed my car?" asked Frank.

Dexter smiled slowly. His words were filled with hostility. "About time someone smashed that piece of junk, you lazy Indian."

Bird was repulsed.

Don't react, Bird. Those words are pointed inward. They have nothing to do with you or me.

Bird understood, but Dexter's vileness felt like poison. She wanted more than anything to be miles away.

Paul took his cellphone from his pocket and held it up for Frank to see. "Shall I dial nine-one-one?" he asked.

Frank spoke firmly. "No. Bird, get the phone from the dashboard."

Bird quickly did as she'd been asked. The driver's side of the car was completely caved in, but the passenger door opened. She grabbed the cellphone and raced back to Frank.

Dexter lurched forward in a sudden effort to escape. Paul and Frank reacted by tightening their grips.

Press eight-one-one, Bird, and hold it to my ear.

Bird did just that.

Frank spoke into the cell. "Backup needed. Concession 10 and Second Line. Emergency #54378 Second Line."

"When did you get so smart?" sneered Dexter.

"You ain't seen nothing yet," responded Frank.

"Oh, yeah?" snorted Dexter. "We'll see who gets the last laugh."

Bird had a sinking feeling that they still didn't have the whole picture.

Within minutes, two police cars arrived at the scene. Paul and Frank handed over Dexter to the young officers in the first car. He was handcuffed and put in the back seat of the cruiser without ceremony.

Frank got in the second car and quickly rolled down his window. "Hannah is on her way to pick you two up. A tow truck is coming, too, but don't wait for them." He smiled. "I think it's time for me to get another car."

Paul laughed. "Might be!"

"I'll interview Dexter. If there's any news at all, I'll be in touch."

Bird nodded.

Frank began to roll up the window, but stopped halfway. "Bird? If we're going to get this solved once and for all, it's got to look like business as usual. Have you ever done a jumper derby?"

Bird shook her head.

"Well, you're doing one tomorrow. The Caledon Derby. You're already entered. Ask Hannah to help you prepare."

With that, he closed his window, and the cruiser sped away.

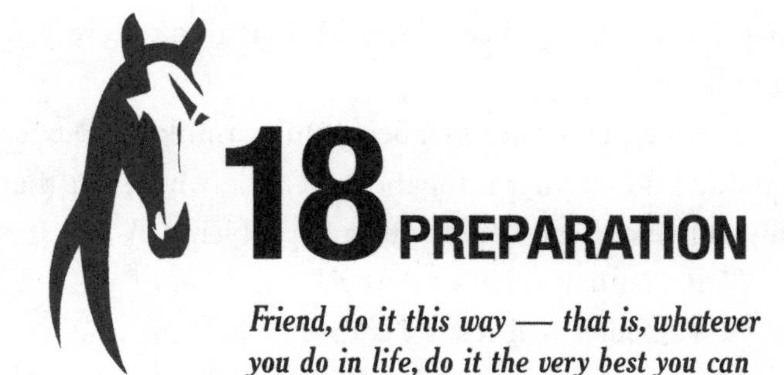

18 PREPARATION

Friend, do it this way — that is, whatever you do in life, do it the very best you can with both your heart and mind.

— White Buffalo Calf Woman, Lakota

"What's a jumper derby?" asked Paul, standing at the side of the road with Bird. "A hat? A race?"

Bird shrugged. She had a vague idea that it was a hybrid of show jumping and eventing, but she'd never seen one and wasn't entirely sure.

Paul looked down the road. "Here's the Saddle Creek Farm truck."

Hannah pulled in. Julia sat in the front seat, waving. "Hi, Paul! Hi, Bird!" she yelled out her window, but then stared in disbelief at the smashed vehicle.

"Holy smoke!" Hannah called. "What happened to Frank's car?"

"It's a wreck!" Julia exclaimed. The truck stopped, and she scrambled into the back seat.

"We'll tell you everything we know," answered Paul, getting into the front. "But first, is everything okay at the farm?"

"Yes. Cliff and Lucky and Boss are still up at the back field," Hannah said, turning the truck around. "But now that Dexter is in police custody, I don't think there'll be a problem."

Bird sat in the back seat beside Julia, thinking. Dexter couldn't do any harm for the next little while, but that didn't mean there wouldn't be any problems.

"Oh. Hannah, what's a derby?" asked Paul.

"It's an elite, skill-testing course. Why?"

"Because Frank wants Bird to compete in the Caledon Derby tomorrow."

"We don't have a derby horse!" said Hannah with surprise. "I wonder what he's thinking."

"Whatever he's thinking, it might be helpful to get Bird ready for it." Paul turned his head and grinned at Bird. "Frank already entered her."

"The nerve!" Hannah said with irritation. "There's no way to get Sunny ready for tomorrow! It's quite a specialty. It's really difficult and potentially dangerous. It's rarely held — the last one around here was years ago. There's a steep slope called the Bank that's really scary. It's about forty-five degrees, then once you're down there's a rail fence to jump. Very technical."

"I think I know! Does a derby have the Devil's Dike?" asked Paul. "If it does, I saw it on television from Spruce Meadows. And if it does, I agree: there's no time to get ready. And it's too dangerous."

Hannah was nodding. "Yes, of course you're right, it's too dangerous. The Devil's Dike is always part of the competition, and the Water Jump, too, with the fence on the inside and the water beyond. It's tough, for sure."

Bird leaned forward in her seat. This sounded fun! The more the adults thought she couldn't do it, the more excited she became. She tapped Paul on the shoulder and gave him two thumbs up.

"You want to do this?" asked Paul. He looked skeptical.

Bird nodded enthusiastically.

"No, Bird," stated Hannah. "No way. It's not safe. That's that." She set her jaw. "No more discussion."

An hour later, Hannah and Bird were putting together a course that was as close a replication as they could get to a jumper derby course.

"That Frank can talk a potato farmer into buying french fries," Hannah muttered as they built a jump at the top of a dip in the field. "I still think this is a bad idea."

Bird grinned as she helped. As soon as they'd gotten home, she'd gone right to the internet for course specifics. She'd printed out illustrations and measurements of past Derby challenges. Then they'd loaded the four-wheel-drive Rhino with tools, jump standards, and wood, and started looking for the right landscape for the various obstacles.

They found the perfect place for the Devil's Dike. Bird paced it out. Basically, it was three vertical jumps positioned over a hollow. One vertical at the top, two strides down a hill, a fragile vertical at the bottom with a ditch underneath, two strides up the hill, then another vertical at the top.

Bird stood with her hands on her hips. She could see the difficulties. Too fast, too slow, or not careful enough would lead to certain failure or a serious fall. Precision was needed.

Easy peasy.

Sunny! Bird hadn't seen him watching.

Easy peasy. Sundancer rocked back and leapt his fence. He trotted over to Bird to study the obstacle more closely. *What's the problem, Bird? You're not worried, are you?*

We'll have to go into this just right.

When it's ready, I'll give it a whirl. The big chestnut gelding put his nose into the grass and began to graze.

Bird patted his neck and chuckled. At least her horse was confident. That was half the battle.

It took about thirty minutes to complete the set-up. Hannah picked up the measuring tape, hammer, and nails, and began to pack up the Rhino. Bird figured out how to ride it in her head.

Sunny? Do you want to try this out?

Sunny lifted his head. *Sure.* He whinnied loudly, rearing up on his hind legs.

Hannah spun around. "What's *he* doing here?"

Sunny eyed the Devil's Dike and began a slow canter. He came at it squarely.

"He's not going to jump it, is he, Bird?" Hannah gasped.

Over the first hurdle, Sunny hopped. He took one stride down the hill and screeched to a halt at the ditch and rails.

Hannah shook her head. "What is that darn horse up to?"

Sunny backed up the hill and came again to the ditch. This time he cleared it. He took two strides up the hill, but ran out to the left of the top jump. He snorted, pawing the ground in frustration.

Easy peasy, big boy?

I'll get it. Just wait.

"Bird," called Hannah. "Stop him. He'll wreck the whole thing."

Bird pretended not to hear. It was far better for Sunny to figure this out himself than with her on his back — she'd make her own mistakes.

He came at the whole combination again, with quite a bit more speed and impulsion. Over the first jump, down the hill, over the ditch and rails, up the hill, and then crash! Sunny went right through the vertical at the top of the hill, sending the rails flying. The horse kicked out with both rear legs.

"Seriously, Bird! Stop your horse this minute! He'll hurt himself! See the skid marks and the cracked rail?"

Bird ignored her aunt and put the jump back together.

"You're not listening!" Hannah yelled.

Sunny picked up a canter and came around again. His speed was faster than it had been the first try, and slower than it had been the second. Bird could see how hard he was concentrating.

The big horse headed for the Dike. Over the first one he went, then down the hill and over the ditch and rails. He cleared it by a hair and powerfully cantered two strides up to the last vertical. Bird held her breath.

He cleared it!

Bravo, Sunny! Well done!

Easy peasy, Bird!

'Okay. You win. He did it." Hannah was exasperated, but she smiled at the gelding's skill. "Now, on to the forty-five degree Bank!"

What's that supposed to mean? Sunny transmitted.

Come with us and take a look.

Bird and Hannah climbed into the Rhino. Hannah drove past the barn and over to the edge of the far field. Sundancer trotted along with them. They stopped when the field ended abruptly.

There, right in front of them, was a steep drop. It was about twelve feet to the bottom, and looked almost straight down.

"This is as close to forty-five degrees as we have," said Hannah. "Unless you want to go down the entire cliff."

I can't do this, Bird. You know I'm afraid of heights.

Okay.

What? Okay? You think I can't do this?

Yup.

Watch me! Sundancer sat on his hocks and slid all the way down. *Got anything to say now?*

Good job, Sunny!

I guess so!

'That horse does nothing but amaze me, Bird!" praised Hannah. "You'd think he knew he was training for the derby!"

Bird stared at her aunt. Didn't she see? That's *exactly* what Sunny was doing — training for the derby. He wasn't sliding down hills and smashing through rails for nothing!

"Let's build a fence at the top and the bottom of this hill, like the picture." Hannah stared at the page. "One stride, only! My goodness."

Hannah and Bird erected the top fence with two standards and a rail. When it was built to their satisfaction, they slid down the hill with the materials from the farm vehicle and joined Sunny at the bottom. They paced out the distance, marked it, and constructed another set of standards with one rail sitting precariously on top.

"This is just like the picture," said Hannah dubiously. "But it looks so airy."

Airy and scary, thought Bird.

Not so scary, telegraphed Sunny. *Let me at it!*

Sunny scrambled up the rise and turned around. His eyes widened. His knees trembled.

What's wrong? asked Bird. *You slid down just a few minutes ago.*

It looks horrible with that jump at the top and one at the bottom. I'll break my leg!

Take it nice and slow and you'll be fine.

Easy for you to say! I'm way up here and you're way down there!

You have a point. We don't have to do this, you know.

Give me a minute. I'll trot away from the ledge and try again.

"I guess Sundancer's had enough." Hannah started to pack up.

Bird shook her head.

"Well, go up there and get him saddled up. You're going to have to try this sooner or later." Hannah began to climb up the hill to the Rhino.

Bird tried to stop her. She pointed to the top of the hill and made a galloping action.

"Sunny's not coming back, Bird. Horses won't do something like this on their own."

Hannah was interrupted by the sight of a determined-looking Sundancer, cresting the hill and coming down fast.

Bird grabbed her aunt and pulled her out of the way just as the big horse leaped over the top fence and slid past. Together they watched him gather his hind end under just in time to power himself up and over the bottom obstacle.

"Wow." Hannah was almost speechless. "Marvellous."

At dinner, Hannah explained to Paul what had happened. "We decided that Sundancer had done enough training himself. He was amazing! We didn't want to overdo things."

"So Bird didn't ride him at all?"

"No. No need, really. Bird knows he can do it. She'll just leave him alone tomorrow and trust him." Hannah tasted her chicken pasta. "Please pass the pepper."

Julia handed her the mill. "What time is the derby tomorrow?"

"It starts at ten. Bird and Sunny will ride over, it's so close. They should leave no later than eight-thirty, and we'll head over at nine. More salad?" Hannah lifted the wooden bowl and offered it around.

There was a knock on the screen door, followed by Sally's voice. "Hello? Sorry to come at dinner time!"

"Come on in, Sally," said Paul, rising from his chair.

"Are you hungry?" asked Hannah. "There's lots to spare."

Bird hadn't told them that it was Sally and Wanda who'd taken the horses to the shed. She tried not to bristle at the girl's presence in her aunt's kitchen. What on earth did she want?

"No, thanks," chirped Sally. "Mom just dropped me off to ride, but I can't find my horse."

"Join us, and I'll help as soon as we're finished." Hannah looked at Bird. "Or Bird could help you. It's either helping Sally or doing dishes. Your choice!" Hannah smiled at Bird, expecting her to jump at the chance to escape any form of housework.

Bird nodded. No problem. She took another forkful of the pasta as she watched Sally with interest.

Normally, Sally didn't drop over to ride like this. She still needed help saddling up, and she never rode except during lessons.

Lucky yawned and crawled out from under the table. He walked up to Sally, who was still standing at the kitchen door. She reached out to pat him, pleased to have something to do.

"What a nice dog!" she enthused. "His coat is so silky, and I love his white paws." She rubbed his head, which made Lucky very happy.

"We were just talking about the derby. Bird is taking Sunny tomorrow. You should come," said Hannah. "It should be quite something to see."

"Oh! Maybe I will!" enthused Sally, clapping her hands and jumping up and down with glee. Bird thought she was maybe a little overly enthusiastic. "It sounds like so much fun!"

"Are you going to sit down?" asked Paul. He'd been waiting for her to take a seat, and was too much of a gentleman to sit down until she did.

"Oh, no, thanks. I don't have long." She looked very awkward. Bird noticed that several times she'd glanced outside toward the road. "I don't want to bother you, really! Just tell me where he is and I'll get him."

Hannah sighed. Running a riding school and boarding establishment meant that she rarely had time to herself. Dinner was generally considered off-limits except by appointment. "Bird, why don't you run up with Sally now."

"No!" Sally yelped, immediately covering her mouth. "I mean, no, really, don't bother. You're eating. I'll get him ready myself, and ride him. Myself."

This was very interesting. Not at all typical. Bird leapt to her feet and pulled on her boots.

"Oh, you don't need to ride him, Bird," said Sally. "Just tell me where he is."

Bird looked at her, and Sally blushed beet red under her gaze.

Before another second passed, Bird dashed out the door and ran to the road. Just as she'd suspected — a truck and horse trailer were idling on the gravel shoulder.

And there was Wanda, sitting behind the wheel.

"Bird!" Sally came running up behind her. "I know what you're doing!"

Bird spun to stare at her. Did she?

"Tall Sox is my horse!" Sally stood with her feet planted and her arms braced on her thighs, trying to catch her breath.

Bird turned back to Wanda. The groom's face was expressionless. She was making a concerted effort to betray nothing.

"I want my horse!" demanded Sally. "You can't keep him against my orders!"

A deep voice spoke up. "Then you'd better call the police."

The three girls looked across the road. They'd been so involved in their argument that the quiet arrival of a sedan had gone unnoticed.

"Dad!" called Sally. "What are you doing here?"

Harold Johns got out of his car. "I'm going to ask you the same thing. Your mother has no idea where you are. She's been worried for over an hour."

Wanda suddenly reversed the rig, and then put it in drive. She tore off down the road in a big hurry, with the tires spraying out tiny stones of gravel.

Sally's face creased with worry and her mouth began to quiver. "I can explain everything, Daddy!"

"I hope so." Harold was clearly not pleased, but he was still calm. "Let's go talk to Hannah." He walked back across the road, got into his car, and drove up to the house, where Hannah and Paul stood outside watching. When Harold reached them, all three adults went inside.

Bird and Sally followed his car up the lane on foot. As they neared the house, a new black Ford Escape drove up behind them.

Bird.

Frank! Wanda took off, but they came to get Sox. Sally's father is here, and he wants answers.

Good information. Be nice. Play along with whatever Sally says. Tomorrow should be very interesting. Everything is set up. Are you and Sunny ready?

Yes. We'll be there early.

Good. See you tomorrow. Frank stopped his car, and backed it out the lane.

Wait! Are you going?

Yes. Sally should still think I'm a groom.

Okay. Is there anything I should know for tomorrow?

No. Just ride your best ride. Expect surprises, and adapt. Good luck!

"Who was that?" asked Sally. "Wrong farm?"

Bird shrugged.

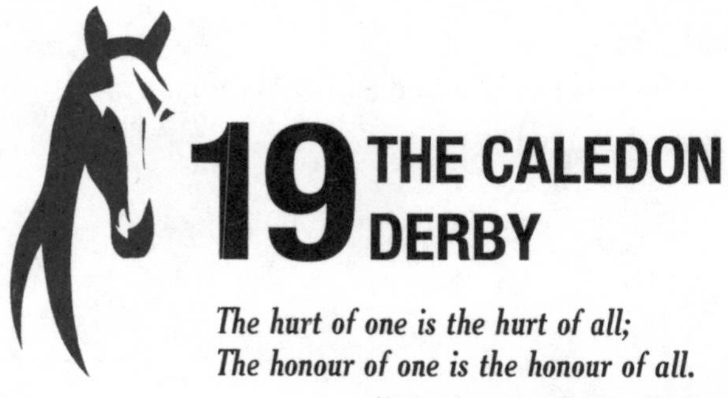

19 THE CALEDON DERBY

The hurt of one is the hurt of all;
The honour of one is the honour of all.

— **Native American Indian Traditional Code of Ethics, rule 6**

Bird sat on Sundancer, surveying the show grounds. They'd walked the few miles to the venue that morning, and had arrived in plenty of time. It was still early, but the cloudless day was already getting hot. Trucks pulling horse trailers continued to drive through the entrance, and the bleachers were filling with eager onlookers. Food stands were opening, and several tents were being erected to sell all manner of horsey items and souvenirs.

There was a buzz of excitement in the air. Bird could feel it. And smell it. The Caledon Derby was so rarely offered that it was a very popular event. Today, it would be closely contested. The calibre of horse and rider was high, and the prize money was huge. The Toronto-Dominion Bank was the sponsor. Fifty thousand dollars was to be divided three ways: thirty-five thousand to the winner, ten to the runner-up, and five to third place.

There had originally been a cut-off of twenty riders, but the organizers had accepted a few more at the last minute, including Bird. She was nervous about the derby, but extremely apprehensive about what Frank wanted her to do. She had no idea what was supposed to happen today. All she knew was that she trusted Frank completely.

Frank? Bird scanned the stands. It would be comforting to know he was somewhere close.

Bird did a double take. Pete and Laura Pierson were in the stands! Pete was in a wheelchair, and Laura, dressed completely in sky blue, was settling into her seat beside him. Bird felt a lump of gratitude in her throat. They'd always been there to support her, but now, with Pete in such poor health, it was more than she could've imagined! She was grateful that the heart attack had been so mild, and vowed to do her very best job for them.

All around, riders were getting mounted. Some were already working in the warm-up ring. Bird felt chilled with nerves, and her mouth was dry.

Hey, Bird! Don't worry!

How do you always know how I feel, Sunny?

That's easy. What's hard is knowing how you think.

Bird smiled in spite of her nervousness.

When do we get our chance?

We're last. It goes in the order of when people signed up.

Last? I'm ready now!

Relax. It's not starting for another ten minutes.

Then I can show them my stuff!

It's a tough course, Sunny! Don't be smug.

Easy peasy.

Bird hoped he wouldn't decide to take control and race too fast. It always ended in disaster.

Now Eva and Stuart were climbing into the stands with Paul and the girls from the barn. Julia peeked around and caught Bird looking at her. She grinned broadly and waved, then raised her hands together over her head like a champ.

Bird shook with silent laughter and waved back before returning her attention to the grounds.

She looked around for Dexter's rig. It was nowhere to be seen. And she still hadn't spotted Frank. *Frank?*

Nothing. Bird took a deep breath and squared her shoulders. Her job was to go into the ring and compete. She had to trust that Frank would do the rest, whatever that might be.

Hannah came up beside her with a rag. She briefly shined up Sundancer's coat and dusted off Bird's boots. "Are you feeling good?" she asked.

Bird managed a shaky smile.

"Do you know the course?"

Bird nodded firmly.

"Should we go over it again?"

Bird shook her head.

"Okay! Let's do a few practice jumps. Follow me." Hannah led the way to the warm-up ring, where a dozen riders were up and working their horses. Hannah kept an eye out for a vacant jump while Bird and Sunny warmed up trotting.

Bird tried not to worry as she began to recognize the competition. Some of Canada's top riders were trotting, cantering, and jumping right beside her. It was intensely humbling.

We can clean up, Bird. Totally!

Please don't get too cocky. Remember that time in June?

It happened. Get over it.

Will you listen to me today?

Will you brighten up and get a more positive attitude?

Bird chuckled to herself and patted his neck. *Deal.*

A few minutes later, the announcer called for the first horse. Bird was desperate to see how a fully trained horse and rider would manage the course, but she ignored the action in the big ring and dutifully jumped over the hurdles Hannah had set up.

Sundancer was in good form, and had just the right amount of energy and responsiveness.

"Good work!" called Hannah. "Walk around a bit and check back with me when the sixteenth rider goes in."

Bird nodded and faked a smile. She was more nervous than she could ever remember being.

"Oh, Bird! Pete asked me to tell you something. 'Damn the torpedoes, and seize the day!'" Hannah smiled broadly as she passed along Pete's words of encouragement.

Bird smiled back, somehow feeling a little better. She tried to breathe deeply as they walked over to watch the sixth horse go.

The course was huge. The Grand Prix grass ring had been expanded to include a steeplechase hedge, an enormous drop, and the Devil's Dike. Multicoloured jumps dazzled the eye in the bright sunshine. The lines to the jumps were anything but obvious, and the combinations were fearsome. Bird swallowed the bile that rose in her throat.

A big grey horse trotted in. His rider was a man in his late forties. Bird recognized him from *Horse Sport* magazine. She'd forgotten his name, but remembered that the horse was London Fog.

The man and his horse began their canter immediately, and went through the timer. The first jump was a red and white vertical made of wavy planks of wood, painted with a Canadian flag. They cleared it nicely and travelled toward an in-and-out with two strides in the middle.

He's going too slow, messaged Sunny.

He might pick up a little speed.

Bird and Sunny watched as London Fog cleared the first rail, but then lost momentum for the second and smashed through it.

He didn't. Sunny began to get excited. *I know how to do it!*

Stay calm. We need all your energy for out there.

The grey cantered on, jumping high over the water hazard. He gathered speed as he faced the purple oxer.

Horse and rider cleared it, then turned around the bend, jumped the solitary rail, and headed up the slope. London Fog got to the top and froze.

This was the dreaded Bank. The grey horse looked down, way down the forty-five-degree slope, the whites of his eyes showing. If he stepped back, even an inch, it would be marked as a refusal.

The rider urged him forward, but he wouldn't budge. The man smacked him with his crop, and still the horse stood firm. Suddenly, London Fog reared up and turned to go. The man stayed with him, but couldn't gather him before he had retraced his steps and jumped back over the rail. The horse and rider were off course and whistled out.

Bird began to shiver. How had the five who'd gone before done? Maybe it was better if she didn't watch at all.

She looked over into the stands. The bright blue of Laura's flowing sundress and floppy hat were immediately recognizable. Pete had a striped Hudson's Bay blanket draped over his legs. His face looked white, even from across the distance. He was always cold now, even in the August heat. Bird hoped that coming to this event wouldn't be too hard on him. Laura was right beside him, though, holding his hand. She'd take him home when he'd had enough.

Bird picked out Eva, too, who was in white pants and a hot pink blouse, with a lime green hat and bangles. At least she'd been smiling more often. She seemed nicer — at least for the time being. Her mother would always have her ups and downs. Bird didn't want to think about that now.

The next horse trotted in. It was a mare, Anastasia, ridden by Herb Vance. Bird had always liked this bay mare, and Herb had been ranked in the top ten Canadian riders every year for the past decade. Bird was eager to see them go, and curious about how they'd fare.

See it, Bird? Her back is sore.

I can't tell, but I guess she doesn't look too happy.

Anastasia cantered through the timer and on to the red and white flag jump. Her ears kept flicking back, and her tail swished.

She's going to refuse, Bird. Watch.

True to Sunny's prediction, the mare stopped. Her chest pushed the wavy planks to the ground as she skidded to a halt.

He should take her home. She won't jump today.

Good call, Sunny. But he probably doesn't know that her back is sore.

Herb backed Anastasia up as four men came running out to put up the planks. When they were finished, he brought her around again, smacked her rump with his crop, and aimed her for the flag. She stopped again. Herb doffed his cap and trotted her out. The mare's head was low. She looked embarrassed, but relieved.

Bird wondered again why Frank had entered them in the derby. Was something supposed to happen here? What was the plan? Bird looked around the grounds, checking for anything unusual.

The arrival of a large white car caught her eye. No cars were allowed past the parking lot, but this one drove straight across the grass and pulled up beside the warm-up ring. She examined it more closely. It looked expensive, like a Cadillac. Inside were two men. The licence plate was from Quebec.

Bird's heart began to pound. Montreal was in Quebec. Was it the lawyer, John Budd, and his client, Alain Morin? Could this be what Frank had been expecting?

Bird! Get a grip! Concentrate on the show! These guys are good. No trouble with the Bank at all.

That's nice, Sunny.

You've turned to stone. You're as stiff as a board.

I'll be fine.

You'd better be.

Bird watched as the men got out of the car. One wore a blue suit. He had a large belly and an imperious manner: he held his thick neck stiffly, and constantly jutted out his chin. He reminded Bird of a large rooster. The other, who was dressed more casually, was younger and slimmer.

In the big grass ring, another horse and rider had been eliminated. The announcer indicated that they'd had trouble with the Devil's Dike, but Bird hadn't noticed.

They made a mess of it, Bird. It was bad.

That's nice.

You're not listening!

What? The men were walking around, chatting with people. Someone pointed out Hannah. *Let's go, Sunny.*

Now? We're next?

No. Not into the ring. Over there. Hannah needs us.

I don't get this. Are we here for the derby or not?

Yes, Sunny. But first we have something to check out.

You and your mysteries, he grumbled.

They walked over to the edge of the warm-up ring, where Hannah was talking to the men. Bird positioned Sunny behind them, facing Hannah, to hear as much of the conversation as she could. Hannah glanced at Bird, but did not indicate that she'd seen her.

"So, where is the horse right now?" asked the large man.

"He's at my farm."

The younger man wanted clarification. "And why have you not allowed him to leave?" He spoke with a French accent.

"I'm sorry, Alain, but I don't have the authority." Bird thought Hannah looked very uncomfortable.

The large man clenched and unclenched his jaw. "We have had no response from Dexter Pill. He promised to send us the horse. I wired the money ahead of time in good faith because he's regarded as a good trainer, and was the agent in this deal. When the horse did not arrive and we heard nothing from Mr. Pill, we decided to wait no longer. We came to find out for ourselves."

"I bought the horse and now I want him," said the man Hannah had called Alain. "What is the problem?"

Hannah said nothing.

"We were told by Ed Cage that the problem lies with you and your farm, Miss Bradley." The large man puffed up his chest, looking more and more like a rooster. "We were told that you are hiding Tall Sox and will not allow him to be delivered to his rightful home."

Hannah paused before she spoke. "We need to find out who owns the horse, Mr. Budd, before we can determine who is authorized to sell him. The man who pays the board for Tall Sox at my stable believes he owns him, and has no knowledge of a sale. He's the one I must believe."

Mr. Budd considered this. "I see your dilemma.'

"Now what?" asked Alain Morin, who was becoming increasingly agitated. *"C'est un problem.* I paid for a horse and I get nothing?"

"We will figure this out," answered Hannah. "I promise."

Bird and Sunny stayed where they were as Hannah and the two men walked to the stands. Hannah seated them next to Pete and Laura Pierson, right in the front row.

Bird slid down from Sunny's back to give him a break. What was going on? Hannah had seemed nervous, but not surprised or upset. And how could there be two front seats left vacant in a packed house? Bird was beginning to feel like an actor in a play — but she didn't know her lines, and everybody else seemed to know theirs.

Ten more horses had taken their turns, and not one of them went clear. Bird was starting to understand why

Hannah thought they couldn't get ready in one day. This was beyond tough! It seemed that each horse had a problem with one or more of the obstacles. The fact that none of these amazing riders could get all of the elements right surprised her greatly. But nothing could have surprised her more than what happened next.

The announcer's voice rang out. "Our next contender is Frank Skelton, aboard Gladiator, owned by Dexter Pill."

Frank! Riding Gladiator?

Bird led Sunny over to the fence to get a good view. Yes, it was Gladiator himself cantering in, looking like a champion. The last time Bird had seen him, he was grazing quietly in the back field at Saddle Creek! Now, his ears were alert, his nostrils were flared, and his energy palpable.

And yes, Frank was riding him. Bird gasped. He wore beautiful old vintage clothes that looked as if they had been mended and cleaned countless times. His cap had turned brown with age, and his crop was topped with a highly polished silver knob.

Go, Glad! messaged Sunny.

Right on, returned Glad. He snorted loudly and reared. He looked confident and powerful. Bird had never seen him like this.

Frank rode beautifully. His hands never moved. He seemed like part of the horse, with his upper body flexible and his lower body strong. When they cantered through the timer and headed for the flag jump, they appeared to be one creature.

Bird watched in awe as they cleared the red-and-white and rolled on to the in-and-out. They had the correct impulsion, and sailed over with ease. The water hazard was no problem, and they seemed to be having fun as they soared over the purple oxer and galloped around the bend. They hopped the single rail and began the climb to the Bank. Glad paused only briefly at the top, then slid down and cleared the rail at the bottom. He appeared to be a little tired now, as they headed for the triple, but he gathered himself together and left all the rails up.

Glad's not in shape, Bird, messaged Sunny.

Can he finish the course?

I hope so. Well, I want to win, but, you know. I wish him well.

Together they watched as Glad and Frank started for the dreaded Devil's Dike.

This could be bad. I can't look, Bird.

I can't either.

But they did. And horse and rider got it right. They came in steadily, popped the first hurdle, cantered the strides down to the ditch and rail at the bottom, then came up two strides and cleared the jump at the top.

Glad's sides were heaving and his coat was covered in sweat. Frank slowed him to a trot. Bird knew he was thinking about retiring him from the derby.

But Glad wanted nothing to do with quitting. He neighed long and hard, and fought the bit. Frank laughed aloud. They continued on toward the huge steeplechase hedge. Over they went.

The terracotta sandcastle was next. Glad slowed and barely cleared it. The big horse was losing energy as he faced the green oxer. He couldn't push himself completely over, and the back rail of the oxer dropped to the ground. The entire crowd groaned together. Bird had barely noticed the audience until then, but she was pleased to realize how much the onlookers were supporting this team.

The last jump was a vertical, covered in vines, with flowery letters advertising an herbal shampoo. A huge plastic bottle replicating the product stood in the centre. Glad was flagging now. He tried valiantly, but couldn't quite get his hind end up and over, and the top of the shampoo bottle came down with a thud.

Eight time faults and four rail faults were the penalties, but this ride had been the crowd pleaser, and the best score of the morning. Nobody else had done as well on this difficult, skill-testing course.

Frank waved to the cheering crowd as he patted Glad's drenched neck. His beautiful smile and his athletic, agile bearing instantly endeared him to the crowd.

Then, above all the noise, Bird heard another sound — her mother's scream.

20 BIRD AND SUNNY RIDE

May your moccasins make happy tracks in the snow,
And may the rainbow always touch your shoulder.

— Cherokee blessing

Bird stared at the stands. Stuart stood in front of Eva, and Paul knelt beside her. Together, they helped her to a standing position and led her down the tiers to the ground.

A movement in the front row caught Bird's attention. It was Pete, flapping his hands to get Bird's attention. He pointed vigorously at the ring, and shooed her away with two hands, indicating that she go ride.

"Bird!" Hannah was shaking her shoulder. "Get up! They're calling for you!" Hannah helped her up onto Sunny's back. "Don't worry about Eva. She has lots of help. Now go! Have fun!"

"Last call! Alberta Simms and Sundancer!" the announcer called out. "Come into the Grand Prix ring! This is your last call."

Bird's stomach flipped. She was sure she was going to faint. Or vomit. Or both. And there was no time to see what was wrong with her mother. She was thoroughly scared as they trotted to the gate.

As Frank and Gladiator walked away from the ring, Bird saw a familiar-looking man approach them. It was Ed Cage, and he looked furious. Bird would have to check that out after her ride, too.

Bird! Concentrate! commanded Sunny.

She steeled herself. *I'm ready.*

I need help to get through this.

So do I. Why had her mother screamed like that? And what had Ed just said to Frank? Bird patted Sunny's silky neck, and put all of the questions out of her head. She tried to focus on the job ahead. *Here's to us.*

The bell rang. Bird and Sundancer both inhaled deeply before beginning their canter through the starting timer.

The Canadian flag jump came up fast. Sunny sprang high, and Bird was thrown a little off balance. She reached forward and grabbed Sunny's mane.

Thanks for letting me get my backside over.

No problem. If you pull back on a horse's mouth, Bird knew too well, their head jerks up and their hind end drops, knocking the rails down. A novice error.

Mere seconds later, they were facing the nasty looking in-and-out. All the rails were white, and blinding in the sunshine.

Steady, three, two, one, over, messaged Bird.

Land, one, two, OVER! Sunny replied, jumping over the second.

Suddenly, Bird felt at one with her horse. The tension left her body and calmness took over. She heard no noise except Sunny's steady breathing and his rhythmic hoof beats. Now, instead of jumbled panic, she looked forward to the challenges coming up.

The Water Jump had looked enormous from the outside of the ring, but with Sundancer's huge stride and confidence, it appeared now to be more like a blue puddle with a rail in front. They landed past the white line on the far side, and eyed up the purple oxer, deep in the shadows of a small grove of trees.

It was set a little off-centre, and Bird and Sunny adjusted their line to jump it squarely. All the rails stayed up.

Next was the Derby Bank. Bird focused on breathing as they travelled quickly along the grass track around the bend at the outside of the course. Sunny galloped.

There's a rail up ahead, then a sharp turn to the left, Bird warned.

I know. I've been watching this class for hours.

The chestnut gelding slowed two strides away from the single rail. He leapt it carefully, but with enough speed, and turned left in midair to save time. Up the hill they cantered, and slowed as they came to the crest of the Bank — the obstacle that had ended the hopes of many horses that day.

From Sunny's back, Bird thought the drop looked like an unforgiving precipice.

I won't look down.

Don't step back, Sunny. Keep moving forward!

There's nothing under my feet!

You've watched this for hours. You know what it is.

I watched it, but it looked easy!

Glad did it.

Sunny snorted uneasily, but continued forward. He plunged head first down the twelve-foot, forty-five degree angled hill, sliding his hind end under him. They got to the bottom, took one stride, and lifted off over the second single rail. He cleared it.

Bird's heart pounded in her ears. *Bravo, Sunny.*

Easy peasy. But he didn't fool Bird. Sunny's heart was pounding as hard as hers.

As the gigantic triple combination loomed, Bird felt Sunny's agitation. *We're okay. This pace is perfect, Sunny,* she reassured him.

As perfect as Glad?

Are you mad?

No! Jealous! Don't do that again.

It got you down the hill.

I'm better than Glad!

And you're proving it now.

Sundancer got to the first of the three jumps. He sprang over it with his knees at his nose, landed, and took a controlled stride. He jumped the next. He landed, took another stride, and easily cleared the last one.

Beautiful! praised Bird.

Better than Glad?

Way better!

Now they were heading for the dreaded Devil's Dike. Sunny and Bird both knew how essential it was to get the speed exactly right.

Not too fast and not too slow, Sunny.

You think I don't remember?

Aren't we going a little fast?

Probably.

Then slow down!

Sunny pulled against the reins a little to show Bird he had his own ideas, but he slowed in time to enter the Dike at the optimal speed. Over the first vertical he went, then down the hill to the ditch and rail at the bottom. Sunny got a little too close, so he popped it and landed clear. But because he'd landed so slowly, the stride to the top jump needed more impulsion.

Go, Sunny! encouraged Bird.

Fast now?

Fast now!

They flew over the fragile vertical at the top without rapping it, and were safely through the Devil's Dike.

Bird felt Sunny exhale. She did the same. But they remained vigilant as they faced the solid steeplechase hedge. Over they soared.

The terracotta sandcastle was right in front of them. From the back of a horse, it looked utterly strange — like something out of *Lawrence of Arabia.* Bird looked over it, not at it, and Sunny cantered on. He gathered his weight under his hocks, pushed off with power, brought up his knees, and jumped it clear. He cantered strongly to the second last obstacle, the green oxer.

No problem was posed by the distance or size, and they cleared it well. But they missed the sharp right turn to the herbal shampoo bottle and had to go around the Canadian flag in a large loop, which cost time.

I'll zoom! Sunny took hold of the bit and pulled.

No! Let's go clear! Bird held him back.

I can zoom and still clear it! He shook his head.

They had no time to argue. The shampoo vertical was only a few strides away. Bird let the reins go slack. *Glad knocked the cap off. I don't care if you do, too.*

Are you giving up? Sunny seemed to realize he was fighting only himself. Bird could feel him change his attitude, and start using his brain. He came in straight, lifted off nicely, and the rails didn't touch a hair on his ankles.

Nice, Sunny. Now zoom!

They galloped through the timer, and it felt so good, they galloped a little longer. Bird stood up in the stirrups to give Sunny's back a rest, and leaned on his neck. She revelled in the exhilaration of completing this extraordinary course, and smiled from ear to ear with the wind in her face. When they finally slowed to a walk, Bird was laughing out loud.

Bird?

Yes?

Try talking people talk.

Why?

You just made noise from your throat. I think you're back in business.

"Oh, Sunny! You're right!"

As soon as they were outside the big grass ring, Bird dismounted.

She was totally elated. Not only had they won the Caledon Derby, but she was able to speak again! She patted Sunny heartily and rubbed his face with the palm of her hand. *You're the best!*

Hannah tapped her on the shoulder. Bird turned, expecting praise. Her aunt's worried face brought her down to earth.

"What's wrong?" Bird asked.

"It's Pete. He's been taken by ambulance to critical care. The medics think it's another heart attack, and most likely worse this time." Hannah wiped away a tear. "He wouldn't let them take him until he'd seen you ride through the finish gate."

Bird felt her elation drain away. He should've stayed at home to recover, and he had only come to cheer her on. She felt a surge of guilt, and leaned against Sundancer for support. "Oh, no."

"Let's hope for the best. He's in good hands." Hannah gave her a hug and tried to cheer her up. "Congratulations on a brilliant ride out there! Nobody went clean but you and Sundancer."

"It was Sunny, all the way."

Hannah pulled away and stared at Bird, a hand on each of the girl's shoulders. "Are we having a conversation?"

Bird nodded. "Yes, we are!" They hugged again before Bird remembered Eva. "What's going on with Mom? Why did she shriek like that?"

Hannah shrugged her shoulders. "She's fine. I think she just overreacted to something."

"To what?" asked Bird. But before Hannah could respond, Bird's eye was caught by three police cars driving out of the grounds, roof lights flashing. She stared. "Why are they here? What's been happening?"

"While you and Sunny were winning the Derby, lots of things were happening — and exactly as Frank planned." Hannah's face lit up as she recounted all the excitement. "When Frank rode Glad out of the ring, Ed Cage started yelling. He's mad at Frank for taking Gladiator away from Dexter's barn, but Frank expected that, so he was ready, and taped the entire conversation. Including" — Hannah paused for effect — "admitting that he tried to give Glad an injection that night. And did you know Ed is the one who shot Sunny with a BB gun at the last show? Frank told me." Now her eyes squinted with anger.

"Yes, I know. Ed Cage," said Bird. "What a cad."

Hannah nodded.

"And so then Frank called the police?" Bird surmised.

Hannah looked up at the cruisers. They were pulling away from the show grounds. "Yes. Mack Jones is taking Ed in now."

"And Wanda?"

"What about her?"

Bird thought back. Did Hannah even know about Wanda's involvement? No. Now that she could speak she had to be more careful. Frank should be the one to divulge details as he saw fit. "I haven't seen her around, that's all."

"Neither have I, now that you mention it. Anyway, walk Sunny out a bit, and get ready to be given the grand prize. What will you do with all that money?" She grinned broadly. "They're going to bring out the podium and make a real fuss!" Hannah patted Sunny's neck and hugged Bird again. "I can't tell you how proud I am of both of you!"

Bird led Sunny around to the water trough, where the champion jumper wet his lips and drank.

Enough for now, Sunny. You don't want a tummy ache.

That's an old tale. I'm thirsty.

No, it's true.

Someone came up behind them. "Hi, Bird."

Bird turned to see Sally Johns standing there. Bird was surprised that she'd come.

"I know you can't talk, but congratulations." Sally appeared to have more on her mind than praise. She was looking everywhere but at Bird.

Bird decided to stay mute — this was not the time to say the wrong thing. She touched her cap in a response that she hoped looked humble, not comical.

"So," Sally spoke quickly, "I came to tell you, you rode great, but I know what's going on. Wanda told me. My father and Hannah — everybody thinks you can do no wrong, but Wanda figured it out." Sally pouted and tried unsuccessfully to stem the tears. "We came to make sure Tall Sox wasn't here, and now she knows where he is." Sally sniffed, and wiped her nose on her arm. She pushed out her chin and stalked off to the parking lot.

Bird thought fast. What did Sally mean? Wanda knew where he is? Tall Sox was innocently grazing in the back field with Amigo. Was she going to get him? He'd let Sally take him for sure — Bird had told him to be good to her! She had to move fast. She looked around for Hannah, but her aunt had completely disappeared. Where had she gone?

Frank? We have a problem.

No response.

Bird looked at her watch. Five minutes had already passed since she'd dismounted. Men were busily setting up the podium in the ring. The judges would be ready to present the prizes soon. Did she have time to dash home?

Bird looked at the line of trailers and cars leaving the lot. Wanda's car would be stuck in that jam for some time. Maybe the prize-giving would be over by the time they got to the farm.

Frank?

The heck with it. She couldn't take that risk, sitting around waiting to be given a prize while Tall Sox was taken off the Saddle Creek property! Once he'd gone, it would be extraordinarily difficult to track him down.

Bird cinched the girth and climbed up on Sunny's back. *Let's go home. We have a job to do.*

What about my victory lap?

Later!

Nobody noticed the girl and the chestnut horse vanish from the grounds. They trotted past the grass ring and broke into a gallop across the field to the road. They headed home directly through the fields, and jumped four fences along the way. They arrived at the back field three minutes later. Sunny hopped the split rail fence on the fly.

Sox! telegraphed Bird.

The sweet bay gelding with four white socks and a white blaze lifted his head from the grass. Amigo was right beside him.

Can you come with us?

Where?

She looked up to the barn. Cliff was on the tractor, taking the manure out to the pile at the back.

To the barn.

Can I come, too? asked Amigo.

Sure! Bird urged Sunny across the field, followed by the two horses. "Cliff!" He couldn't hear her. Sunny jumped the fence beside the barn, and they cantered up beside him.

"Cliff!"

He looked up, totally surprised. "Bird! Why aren't you at the show? And you just spoke!"

"Yes! We're about to be presented with top place, and yes, I can talk! Great and all that, but Wanda is coming to get Sox."

"Now?" Cliff digested this quickly. He shut off the motor and jumped off the tractor. "Frank warned me this might happen."

"Can you hide him?"

"I sure can!"

"And Amigo should stay with him or he'll be upset." Bird waited while Cliff clipped halters on the two horses and led them through the gate.

"Thanks, Cliff!" She asked Sunny to jump back into the field. "Watch him till I get back! Gotta go!" called Bird over her shoulder.

Cliff did a little jig holding a horse in each hand. "Top place, eh? You won the Caledon Derby! Wowee! Good on you!"

Bird's spirits rose with Cliff's jubilation. She whooped her thanks as she and Sunny galloped across the grass, hopped over the fence at the other side, and retraced their steps back to the show.

This is fun! Sunny whinnied. *I love to go fast.*

They crossed the road at the end of the show grounds, far from the crowd. Bird looked over to the lineup at the exit. It was still jammed. Wanda and Sally were probably stuck there.

The freshly painted white podium was now assembled in the centre of the grass ring, way across the field. Two horses with their riders were standing with wide ribbons draped across their chests, one blue and one white. People were craning their necks, looking for someone. Bird suspected that the someone was her.

She urged Sunny to run faster. He covered the ground in seconds and leapt the four-rail white fence that surrounded the ring. He landed softly, then began to slow. When they got to the middle of the ring, he came to a halt, right in front of the judge. He reared up, whinnied loud and long, then dropped his front feet back to the ground. He continued the downward movement into a graceful bow. Just like Dancer, his father before him. His knees bent deeply, and his nose touched the ground.

Silence. Then loud applause. People could not believe what they had witnessed.

Frank beamed his beautiful smile at her as he sat astride Glad. *Now, that was an entrance.*

Bird smiled back.

Where were you just now?

Wanda is on her way over to Saddle Creek to take Sox. Cliff hid him and is on guard.

Excellent job.

Tell me, Frank. Why did you want me to compete today?

To win. He smiled broadly. *But also to be on site to do whatever needed to be done. You've done that, and more. Thank you. We're almost done.*

Bird was warmed through and through by his praise. *I couldn't find you. Where were you?* she asked him.

Finishing what Pete started.

Bird was puzzled. *What did he start?*

You'll see.

The judge marched over and draped an elaborate red satin sash over Sunny's neck. He gravely handed Bird an envelope and a large silver cup on a wooden base. "Congratulations, child," the man said with an air of condescension. "You were almost too late."

Frank messaged, *You still would've won. Hannah was about to accept the trophy and award on your behalf.*

Sunny would never have forgiven me.

Sundancer reared up again and neighed. *This is the best part! I love a good victory lap!*

Bird tucked the cup under her arm and stuffed the envelope into the waistband of her breeches. Sunny led the way around the ring, with much fancy action and showing off. He high-stepped and strutted, and even threw in a few crowd-pleasing bucks.

Easy does it, big boy.

People love it!

Frank and Glad had come in second, and followed in Sunny's wake. Peter Roberts was third, aboard his smooth-gaited black mare, Malibu. The crowd cheered as the horses galloped and the riders waved and smiled. The male riders lifted their caps in a salute as they passed the judges, then all three trotted out of the big grass ring in single file.

For years to come, Sundancer's timely appearance and grand bow would be talked about. And for years, those who were stuck in the congestion leaving the grounds would say they'd seen a sudden bright flash across the field. The story was that they thought it was a comet, that he was going so fast that they didn't know it was a horse until he stopped to take a bow.

21 PUZZLE PIECES FIT TOGETHER

Walk in balance and beauty.
Love one another and help one another.

— Cree Elder

Bird wasn't at all prepared for the sight that greeted her outside the ring. Hannah, Julia, Eva, Stuart, Liz, and Paul stood together, waving an enormous, brightly coloured banner above their heads. A crowd of fans stood behind them, clapping their hands. Printed in huge green, blue, red, yellow, and white letters was, "Nobody Flies Like Bird!" Underneath it read, "Sundancer, Lord of the Ring!"

Bird was touched. She took her feet out of the stirrups and slid to the ground, still holding the silver cup. "Thank you, everyone!"

Julia ran to her. "Bird! You talked! But why are you crying?" She hugged her big sister around her waist. "You should be happy!"

"I am happy. Really, really happy. But Mr. Pierson is at the hospital, and I'm so worried."

Hannah stepped forward. She took the trophy out of Bird's hands. "We'll go see them right after you get Sunny home," she said quietly. "Pete told me to tell you not to worry about him. He said you should just savour the moment."

Tears fell from Bird's eyes. Of course Mr. Pierson would say that. For him, she would try. She waved at all the generous people who were cheering for her, and smiled with sincere gratitude.

Hannah hugged her. "Before he left, Pete said that you're the best rider he's ever seen. Even better than your father."

Bird was impressed. Better than Indian Fred, the Indian Cowboy? This was high praise indeed.

Can we go home now, Bird? This is getting old.

Be polite. These people are here to make us feel good.

I'm hungry.

Bird broke out laughing. She couldn't stop. For a moment she was afraid she'd start crying again.

From somewhere nearby, Frank messaged her. *Easy, girl. Keep it together. There's more to do today.*

Bird took a few deep breaths. *Thanks, Frank.*

I have to stay here and finish some business. I'll catch up with you later.

Okay.

With a great deal of difficulty, Hannah and the group turned the unwieldy banner around and led the way to the parking lot. Bird hopped up on Sunny and followed a few steps behind. When they got to their vehicles, people cheered again and waved goodbye.

"Walk him home, Bird. See you at the farm," called Hannah. "Take your time and cool that incredible horse out."

"Sure will!" answered Bird. "Then we'll go see Mr. Pierson?"

"Sure will!"

Bird and Sunny walked across the big field toward the road. They were halfway there when Sunny spooked sideways at a bush. Bird barely hung on.

Hey, Sunny!

Not my fault! Cody's hiding and I didn't know!

Cody? Are you there?

Bird girl! The coyote's head popped up between the leaves.

What is it?

Go home fast. Lucky and Boss and the Good Thin Man need help. Now.

Sundancer, still agitated from the scare, was only too happy to break into a canter. They followed the same path they'd taken earlier, and within minutes were again in the back field of Saddle Creek Farm.

Sunny soared over the fence with ease and galloped straight toward the barn. Bird strained her eyes and tried to figure out what was happening.

Boss was barking at one side of Wanda's truck, and Lucky was snarling at the other. Cliff was dragging split rails across the lane, hurriedly rigging up a barrier behind the horse trailer.

Panic grew in her chest.

Sox? Where are you? messaged Bird.

In the trailer. Can I come out?

Bird was relieved. Sox was still at Saddle Creek Farm. *Soon*, she reassured the horse. *Don't worry about a thing.*

Cliff lifted his head from his work as he saw them coming. "Bird!" he hollered. "I went to my house for a minute, and they loaded him! Where's Frank?"

"Still at the show!" Bird yelled back.

Sunny skidded to a halt at the fence. Bird quickly dismounted and removed his saddle and bridle. *Walk yourself out, Sunny. And don't gulp down too much water.*

And you're welcome. I won the trophy and brought you home faster than the speed of light and that's all I get?

No time for sensitivities. I'll rub you down later and feed you a big warm bran mash.

Okay, then. Sundancer sauntered off, pleased that he'd made his point.

Bird called as she ran toward the trailer. "Cliff! How can I help?"

"Call the police. Sally and Wanda are trying to steal Tall Sox."

Wanda stuck her head out of the truck window, smirking. "How is it stealing when it's Sally's horse?" She revved the engine and put it in reverse.

"Tall Sox is owned by Sally's father, and he wants him here!" Cliff continued to pile the rails on the driveway to prevent their exit.

Wanda spun her tires.

Cliff looked pointedly at Bird. "Run!"

Bird dashed into the barn. She opened the cupboard where the phone was kept, safely away from the barn cats. She couldn't remember Mack Jones's direct line and was about to punch in 911 when, through the tack room window, she saw a black car speeding up the driveway. Frank!

Bird ran outside in time to see Frank jump out of his car. He strode over to the trailer with his badge out and arrived at the same time as Bird.

Lucky? Boss? You can stop barking now.

Did we do a good job? Good job? asked Lucky. His tail wagged excitedly.

Yes! Good job, Lucky! Good job, Boss!

Lucky rolled onto his back. *I did a good job!*

Whatever, messaged Boss as he stalked away.

Frank ignored the dogs' chatter. He held up his police badge. "Wanda Jenkins and Sally Johns, please get out of the vehicle. Slowly." He sounded very official.

"You're the police?" asked Wanda. "You're a groom! You got my job!"

"We're not doing anything wrong!" sobbed Sally.

Frank looked at her sternly. "You may not think so, but you are involved with people who are. Please get out of the vehicle."

Sally and Wanda reluctantly opened the truck doors and emerged. They stood together like sullen schoolgirls.

"Dexter Pill and Edward Cage have been arrested and charged with multiple crimes, including insurance fraud, and cruelty to animals, going back several years." As he spoke, Frank became more and more angry. "Horses have had their legs broken, been given toxic weeds to induce deadly colic, been deprived of the necessities of life, and been subjected to cruel and unreasonable punishment. All of this to enrich the pockets of Dexter and Ed."

Wanda and Sally stood trembling. Gone was the sassy attitude. They looked scared, with their eyes wide and their mouths open.

"Wanda Preston," said Frank forcefully. "You are about to be charged as an accessory. Be very truthful with your answers. How would you define your relationship with Edward Cage?"

Her eyes darted as she spoke. "He works at Dexter's barn."

"I am aware of that. What is the nature of your personal relationship?"

"I just know him, that's all."

Frank paused, then looked at Sally as he continued. "Ed has informed us that he and Wanda have been seeing each other for months. Ed works closely with Dexter Pill in Pill's more secretive ventures. That includes, among other things, selling Tall Sox without your family's knowledge, and now needing to deliver him or get sued. You are abetting a crime."

Bird remembered the kiss Ed Cage had thrown to Wanda at the horse show, as Wanda sat talking to Hannah about a job. Very interesting.

Sally's face paled, but Wanda was furious. "You can't just say things that aren't true!" Her voice grew high-pitched and loud. "I'm helping Sally get her horse back! And Ed's getting a divorce! He and his wife hate each other!"

Sally took a step away from Wanda and stared. "It's true? You and Ed? You told me you weren't together!"

"So?" Wanda spat. "What does it matter? I'm helping you, aren't I?"

"It looks like you're helping Ed! That's why it matters! And Ed's helping Dexter!" Sally turned her head and looked hard at Bird. "Wanda told me that you sold Sox and got paid and kept the money. She said there was a contract and everything. Is that true?"

Bird shook her head. "No, Sally. That's a lie."

"Then why did you take him to the Piersons' that night, then steal him from the shed?"

"I was hiding him from Dexter and Ed. To keep him safe. Otherwise he'd be long gone by now."

Frank backed her up. "That's the truth, Sally. Bird has been looking out for your interests. Ed and Dexter got Wanda to help them by conning you."

Sally looked at the ground. "I'm so stupid! I should've trusted Bird."

"Bird's lying!" yelled Wanda. "I'm the one who's trying to keep Sox safe!"

Frank looked at Bird. *Is it possible that Wanda was duped by Ed? That she really thought you were the bad guy?* he messaged.

Possible, answered Bird. *How do we find out?*

"Okay, Wanda." Frank looked thoughtful. "Now we know that you're trying to help Sally keep Sox, and *you* know that Bird is doing the same thing. Right?"

Wanda looked uncertain. "But what about the contract?"

"Did you see it yourself?" Frank asked.

Wanda shook her head. "No, but Ed did."

Frank let a brief moment pass — just long enough for Wanda to realize that she couldn't trust what Ed said. She covered her face with both of her hands.

"So," said Frank briskly, "Sox is safe, and still belongs to Sally. Why don't we get him off the trailer and let him go back to his stall?"

Wanda dropped her hands and looked at Frank. Her bottom lip began to quiver. "I don't know. Ed told me to take him to that little lean-to barn beside the Stonewick Playhouse, you know? I promised." She looked at her watch. "I was supposed to meet the shipper there ten minutes ago."

I think she's just a pawn, messaged Bird.

Me, too.

Frank turned back to Sally and Wanda. "Things will go much better for you if you co-operate. Why not lead poor Sox off the trailer and back to the barn? He must be quite confused by now."

The girls dropped the ramp, untied Sox, and unloaded him. He was sweaty from tension, but otherwise fine.

"Girls," said Frank, "we'll need both of you, and your parents, to come to the police station for a statement. Can you come in before five?"

They nodded. Neither seemed surprised by the request.

As soon as they were out of earshot, Frank spoke quietly into his cell. "Wally? The lean-to beside the Stonewick Playhouse. Get someone there pronto.

Wanda Jenkins was to deliver the horse there. Detain the driver and confirm Wanda's story."

Cliff began to drag the split rails off the lane. "That was close," he muttered. "I was in my house for two minutes, and they showed up!"

"Thanks to your quick thinking, they didn't get away," said Frank.

"How did Wanda know where Sox was?" asked Bird. "Sally said someone told her."

"I told her when I saw her at the derby," Frank said. "It was a chance to catch her in the act. I knew Cliff would stop her." He tilted his head to his cell. "Excuse me. Wally just put Dexter on the phone from lock-up."

Lines appeared on Frank's brow. "Yes, Dexter. Thought you'd like to know, Tall Sox is not going to meet the shipper … Don't worry, your clients in Montreal have another horse … Yes, his name is Gladiator … Correct. The horse you sold then bought back from the Woodalls … So, they took him with them, and they're happy now … Oh, but you *have* been paid, Dexter … You have the money from the sale of Tall Sox. It's all even … No, the charges are another matter."

As Frank hung up, Bird asked, "Is that why you rode Glad in the derby today? So Alain Morin would see what a great horse he is, and take him instead of Sox?'

"Pretty clever, eh?" He smiled his beautiful smile. "It was Pete Pierson's idea."

"Clever for sure. Alain Morin already paid Dexter for Tall Sox. Dexter kept the money, but Sally still owns him. Dexter owned Gladiator. So giving Dexter's horse to Alain instead of Sally's horse makes perfect sense!"

"Pete came up with the solution. My job was to ride him and make Alain see he was getting the better part of the deal."

Bird smiled at him with admiration glowing in her eyes. "You sure rode him well. And he is a great deal. Sally and Sox are good for each other, and Glad really is more of a show horse."

"Which is what Alain wants." Frank looked happy. "He loves Glad." Frank, like Bird, cared a lot about matching horse to rider. "Nobody is disappointed."

But something was still bothering Bird. "How did Wanda and Sally know that Sox was at the Piersons' barn that night? Did Harold Johns tell them?"

"No. Your grandfather told Ed, and Ed sent Wanda to hide him."

"My *grandfather*? Does he know Ed?"

"Ed Cage used to work for him when he had horses. They keep in touch for when either of them needs a favour. Kenneth Bradley can't help himself. He saw a chance to make trouble, and he took it."

"And the documents and money supposedly in my bank account?"

"That, too. He made it up." Frank patted her shoulder. "I'm sorry, Bird. If I had a granddaughter like you, I'd be so proud I'd burst. But he had to make his point. He's mad that you helped get him arrested last June, and he's paying you back by making you look like a crook."

Bird believed it, and it made her sad. It wasn't fair. She held up her head and looked at Frank. "Thank you for being so honest. I'm glad they sent you here."

"Me, too. It was great working with you. And really good to get to know you." He looked at Bird fondly. "I'll have to be leaving soon."

"Are you staying around at all?" asked Bird hopefully. She suddenly realized how much she would miss him. "You could help me train Amigo."

"Sorry, Bird, but I'm off tomorrow. Another job. But I'll see you later at the hospital. I'm going to say my goodbyes to Pete Pierson."

Bird nodded and busied herself brushing off her breeches. Frank had become important to her. She didn't trust herself to speak.

Lucky and Boss began to bark as Hannah's truck turned in the driveway. Lucky ran as fast as he could to greet Hannah. Bird watched the brown dog's tail wag. He was so full of love that everything else seemed to matter less.

Hannah got out of the driver's side and met the exuberant dog with smiles and pats.

Eva stepped out of the passenger side. She stood to her full height as she glared up the lane toward Bird and Frank. Without a word, she stalked off into the house, with Hannah hurrying behind her.

"What's her problem now?" asked Bird. The last thing she needed today was more drama from Eva. She felt a wave of anxiety from Frank. She shot him a questioning look.

"I'll leave by the barn lane," muttered Frank. He didn't wait to explain. He hopped in his car, started the engine, and drove past the barn. Bird knew that he'd have to bump along the ill-tended tractor path to the road. Why would he choose to do that with a new car?

Wanda silently came up beside her. "Do you think Ed was using me?" Her eyelashes glistened with tears.

For once, Bird wished she were mute. "Yes. I think he was," she said simply. "But that doesn't mean you're stupid. It means he's a jerk."

Wanda took in a breath. "Yeah."

"You asked."

"I'm driving Sally to the police station."

"Good to get it over with."

"No, I really *want* to go. I'll tell them everything they want to know. I want Ed to get what he deserves!" Wanda stood tall and marched to her truck. "Sally!" she shouted. "Let's get moving!"

Sally came running from the barn and got in the truck. Wanda turned the rig around and then stopped. "Bird?" she called from the window. "Sorry for all the trouble I caused."

"Me, too," yelled Sally. "I'm sorry I didn't believe you."

Bird smiled. "It's all figured out now."

Bird waved to the girls as they drove down the lane. She thought back to all the grief Sally had caused since they'd met. No wonder Hannah hadn't wanted to get involved.

Bird stood alone at the top of the driveway, looking down the slope toward the farmhouse. It was quiet.

Never trust a married man who wants to date you, Bird thought. That was Lesson One. Lesson Two was always ask questions until things make sense. If Wanda had known Lesson One and Sally had known Lesson Two, none of this ever would have happened.

Bran mash?

Sunny! She'd forgotten all about him. *Right away!*

Bird mixed together a big scoop of bran with warm water, and added a few chopped carrots, apple slices, and sweet feed with extra molasses dolloped in. She brought out a towel and a brush and went to the fence.

Sunny! she called. *You'll like this.* The big chestnut strolled over to the fence.

This is more like how a champion gets treated.

While Sunny gobbled up the pail of goodies, Bird curried him from top to bottom with the brush. Then she took the towel and gave him a complete body rub, giving particular attention to the tendons on his legs.

You were unbelievably great today, Sunny.

Believe it! There's more where that came from.

Bird laughed out loud. She gathered the saddle and bridle from the fence where she'd left them earlier in her hurry. She hung the wet saddle pad on the top rail, and put the tack in the barn to clean later. Aunt Hannah had promised a hospital visit to see Pete.

22 THE HOSPITAL VISIT

When you were born, you cried and the world rejoiced. Live your life so that when you die the world cries and you rejoice.

— White Elk, Oto

The woman at the information booth gave them Pete's room number, and Bird ran up the stairs while the others pressed the button for the elevator. She couldn't wait.

She stopped running when she got to his door, and took a good look at him from the hall.

Pete Pierson lay quietly under a soft green blanket. Tubes ran from his nostrils and arms, and the life-saving machines hummed dully. His colour was grey. His skin looked like it would melt away. Oddly, Bird thought, he had no wrinkles. She thought of his laughing, smiling, lively face. Where had those wrinkles gone?

Laura sat in a chair by his side, holding his hand. She spotted Bird at the door and signalled for her to come in. "He's asleep now, but he wakes often," she said in a low whisper. "He's been asking about you. I'm glad you're here."

Bird crept to the bed and stared down at Pete. "Is he going to be all right?"

Laura smiled bravely. "I certainly hope so. He's my dear, sweet Pete, and I love him so much. I can't imagine life without him."

Bird couldn't either.

"Are the others coming?" Laura asked.

"As soon as the elevator gets here."

Pete opened an eye and saw her. "Hello, my girl."

"Hello." Bird felt a lurch of emotion. She had to fight to stem the tears.

"Don't cry. I have some … important things to tell you. Sit."

Bird did as he asked. She sat on the edge of his bed, careful not to disturb the tubes.

There was a rap at the door. Hannah, Eva, Julia, Paul, and Stuart stood in the hall.

"Laura, please … tell them to give us a … few minutes."

"I certainly will." Laura rose. As she passed Bird, she put a hand on her shoulder. "Come to the door when you're ready."

Bird nodded.

Pete licked his lips. Bird brought his water glass to him and helped him drink with a straw. When he'd had a few sips, he spoke haltingly. "You rode like your father … out there today. Very few … have your gift. Use it well … for the good … of horses."

"Thank you. I will."

"You and I … have always been honest … with each other."

"Yes."

"But you asked me … about your father. I was sworn to secrecy … for very good reasons … and I was … not truthful. I cannot die … with that … on my head."

"You're not going to die!"

"No time … I need to tell you this."

Bird wanted to explain that there were years and years to talk about this, whatever it was. Pete could not die!

"More … water. Please."

Bird held the straw to his lips until Pete had had enough. She could see the effort it took for him to speak.

"Your father, Fred Sweetree … was an undercover agent … for the RCMP … when I met him. He was posing as a rodeo star … which he truly was … but he was there to gather … information about the … mafia's drug and gun … racket."

Pete had her full attention. She listened carefully.

"His cover was blown … on the last day of the … Calgary Stampede. His life was … in serious … jeopardy."

A new picture was forming in Bird's head.

"All the work … he'd done … was compromised. His fellow officers … had to be protected." Pete's mouth was dry.

Bird held the cup for him as he sipped through the straw again.

"He was called … back. He had to … break all ties with his former … associates. That was the deal … going in. He had no … choice. He was … given a new identity."

"A new identity?"

"And his death was … faked."

"Faked? My father is alive?"

"Yes, Bird."

"There was no plane crash."

"There was a crash … and two deaths. But … Fred wasn't … on that plane."

Puzzle pieces were beginning to fit. Bird held her breath. She thought she knew what was coming next, but she needed to hear Pete confirm it. "Oh my god. Frank." She had shivers. "Fred Sweetree became Frank Skelton."

"Yes."

"Frank's my father."

"Yes."

Bird and Pete sat in silence.

Many things tumbled around in Bird's mind. She thought how much better her life would've been with him around. How many times she'd needed him and he wasn't there. Her stomach hurt. Her head swam. She couldn't think clearly.

"You might need … some fresh air," said Pete. "But please … come back. There's more."

Bird stood, nodding dumbly.

"One thing … to think about. Would you have … forgiven your father … for not being around … if you'd heard this … before you'd gotten to know him?"

It was too much. Bird ran out the door and down the hall, past her family with their surprised faces. She ran down the stairs two at a time and didn't stop until she was under the big tree beside the parking lot.

She flopped down on the grass and buried her face in her arms. Was this Lesson Three? Nobody is who you think they are?

How was this different than Ed using Wanda to steal Sox? Frank, or Fred, or whoever he was, had used Bird to help him uncover Dexter's racket. Would he have even wanted to know his daughter otherwise? And why had he never — not even once — made contact with her in all the years since she was born?

Eva's glare as she got out of the truck came into her mind. Now it made sense. She knew who Frank was. That's why she'd screamed at the derby. She'd recognized him when he'd ridden Glad out of the ring.

Bird's thoughts continued to race. The first day that Bird and Frank had spoken, she'd asked him if he was her father. He hadn't really answered. He'd asked her if she asked every man that question. He'd embarrassed her badly. She'd felt like such a fool that she'd run off. And what about Hannah? Did Hannah know who he was, too? Did Paul? Did everybody know except her?

Bird clenched her fists. She felt like a complete outsider. The joke was on her.

Tires rolled on the tarmac. A black Ford Escape stopped in the parking lot. Bird watched through the curtain of her dark hair as her father stepped out of the car and pressed the lock. She stiffened into a tight ball and made no noise.

Fred walked toward the hospital door, but suddenly stopped. He slowly turned around and stared in her direction.

I feel hatred coming from under the tree.

It's humiliation. Get your emotions straight.

Fred began to walk toward her.

Go away, Frank. Fred. Dad.

Fred stopped. *You know.*

Pete told me. Everybody knew ... but me.

I'm sorry.

Ha.

Can I explain?

Explain what? That you ignore me my whole life, then pop in so I can help solve a problem, then pop back out?

Is that what it looks like?

If it looks like a duck and quacks like a duck ...

I don't know what to say.

Then don't.

Fred turned again and headed toward the double doors. He had his hand on the bar when Bird messaged him again.

And what about Eva? Do you think you've been fair to her? You left her alone and pregnant and she thought you were dead! You left her to raise your child! You wrecked her life!

Fred stood still. A minute passed. *I'm sorry*. He quietly opened the door and entered the hospital.

Bird sobbed into her arms. There was so much pain in her heart that she thought she'd probably die. She cried for the father she never had, for the times she'd needed him, and for the father she'd found but couldn't have. She cried for her mother's loss, for her own loss, for her confusion, and for her despair at not knowing what to do.

In the end, she cried herself to sleep in the grass where she lay.

Bird girl. Time passes. A wet nose sniffed her face.

Bird lifted her head. *Cody. Why are you here?*

I felt your pain. I came.

Thank you.

What is my duty?

Oh, Cody, there's nothing you can do.

I'll stay until your pain passes.

Bird patted the soft fur around his ears. *It's about Frank. He's my father and I didn't know it.*

Is that a problem?

He didn't tell me!

You received your gift from him. Take the good and leave the rest alone.

Bird thought about what Cody said. Being able to speak to animals was indeed a great gift. But what about an entire childhood of not knowing her father? Shouldn't he have shown up before now?

But Cody, it's different for humans. We expect something from our fathers … a relationship.

But why?

It was too hard to explain. Bird sat up. *I need to talk to Pete. He's very ill.*

I know that. His spirit hovers.

Oh no.

It will be soon.

Bird inhaled a ragged breath.

His spirit is pure. Fear not for him.

Bird rose to go. She looked for Cody, but he was gone.

Her family was getting off the elevator when Bird walked back into the lobby.

"Bird!" said Hannah when she saw her. "Pete's very tired, so we left. But Laura said that you should go up. He has something to tell you."

"Where's Eva?"

"She's talking to Frank."

"Don't you mean Fred?" Bird snapped.

Hannah's eyes clouded with concern. "I didn't know either, Bird. Don't judge until we have a chance to talk."

Bird pursed her lips. She wanted to scream.

Stuart stopped her by saying, very quietly, "I understand how you feel, Bird."

Bird looked at his sad face. He'd been left out, too. How would all of this affect Stuart, she wondered? Eva had been madly in love with Fred, and now he was back. Did Stuart think she'd leave him for Fred? Bird's hostility vanished. She sniffed and rubbed her nose on her arm. "I think you do."

Without another word, she ran up the stairs and down the hall to Pete's room. She didn't want to be too late.

"Bird, dear," whispered Laura. "He's asleep again. Sit with me a few minutes."

Bird pulled up a chair. They sat in silence and listened to the steady rhythm of the machines.

"Pete was a very wise man," said Laura.

Bird shot her a quick look. "Was?"

Laura's chin trembled slightly. "I think so."

Bird stared at him. His breathing was very shallow. "But I need him. I need to talk to him. I have a big problem, and I need to know what to do."

"There will always be a problem, Bird, and Pete can't always be there to help." She smiled kindly. "Just ask yourself what Pete would do, and you'll have your answer."

"Hannah said he wanted to tell me something."

"We'll wait for a while and see."

"I've been wondering. How did Pete know about Fred being an undercover officer?"

Laura chuckled. "There's a lot about Pete that people don't know."

"I'm finding out there's a lot that I don't know, period."

"Not just you, Bird."

"But really, Mrs. Pierson. How did he know?"

"Pete was helpful to the government during the war. He was called on by the RCMP many times after that. He met Fred, your father, during one of those times."

That made sense. "And so he had to tell the same story? When I asked about my father, he told me what he was supposed to?"

Laura patted her arm. "Exactly. The world of intelligence and undercover police work is very complicated and dangerous. There are good reasons why secrets must be kept. But Pete felt terrible about it. I could see that."

"Did you know the truth about my father, Mrs. Pierson?"

"I only knew that Pete was troubled."

Bird took a deep breath. Maybe Cody had it right. Take the good and leave the rest alone.

Just then Pete opened his eyes. Bird and Laura sat forward.

"Bird, my girl … I need to tell you this.… All those years … your father kept in touch with me. He … wanted full … reports. He … loves you … more than you … can know. He's so proud … of you."

Laura let him sip some water from the straw. She rested her head on his shoulder as he drank.

"He came … to see you … ride … many times. It wasn't smart … because he was … undercover … but he came … anyway."

"Why did he talk to me this time?"

"He couldn't wait … any longer."

"What about Eva?"

"I don't … know. Not my … problem."

Laura put her hand on Bird's arm. "Pete is very tired, dear. I think it's best that you go now."

Bird thought fast. There was so much more that she wanted to know! "Mr. Pierson, why does he have to go again? Couldn't he stay here with me?"

Pete tried to smile. “It will be … what it is supposed to be…. Be strong…. You are strong.”

“Is that everything you wanted to tell me?”

“Did you like … how I got Glad sold … and out of harm’s way?”

Bird laughed. “It was genius. Alain will love him. And Dexter can’t complain about a thing!”

Pete smiled feebly. “Good on him.”

Laura stood up. “Bird, dear, thanks so much for coming. Now, Pete really needs his rest.”

Bird stood, too. “Thank *you* so much for letting me talk to him, Mrs. Pierson.” She looked at Pete. She knew in her heart that this would be the last time she’d ever see him. “You are the best person I’ve ever met. I’ll miss you.”

Pete said, “You’re … quite a girl. You … know that. Goodbye … I love you.”

“I love you.” Her throat was contricted, and her heart felt like it was full of lead. “Goodbye.”

“I love you, too.” Her throat was constricted, and her heart felt full of lead. “Goodbye.”

Bird left the room. She walked along the hall and down the stairs. She wandered through the lobby and out the front door. Somehow, she found Aunt Hannah’s truck. She got in beside Julia, who linked her arm with Bird’s. They drove home to Saddle Creek Farm. She didn’t remember how.

23 THE SILVER BUCKLE

Let me walk in beauty, and make my eyes ever behold the red and purple sunset.

— Chief Yellow Lark, Lakota Sioux, 1887

On the drive home Bird had been too preoccupied with thoughts of Pete to notice a thing, but as soon as they arrived back at Saddle Creek Farm, she felt an overwhelming need to see Sunny. She climbed the fence and walked through the field.

Sunny? Can we talk? I feel miserable.

What took you so long?

What do you mean?

Frank was here a while ago. He left you something.

Bird stopped walking, suddenly suspicious. *What?*

Don't be so grumpy. Do you want it or not?

I'll know when I see what it is.

Well, I can't use it. It might be nothing.

Where is it?

Sunny looked across the field to a birdhouse that was perched on a fence post. Purple martins had long deserted it, but nobody had bothered to take it down. *In there.*

Bird didn't move.

Don't be so stubborn! Go look!

Bird walked over to the birdhouse and peered in. At first she could see nothing but old straw and dried bird droppings. Then she saw a piece of white paper. A note.

She reached inside and pulled it out. It was wrapped around something heavy. She opened it up, and gasped.

It was a beautifully engraved silver bucking horse, the size of her hand. A belt buckle. She looked more closely. On the bottom, it read, "Champion of the Calgary Stampede."

Bird sank to her knees. She furiously wiped at her tears, wishing away all her complicated emotions. The paper floated to the ground.

She grabbed it and bunched it up. She wasn't ready to read her father's note.

Sundancer ambled up and stood over her.

Aren't you curious?

Bird reluctantly uncrumpled it. She read aloud, "To my only child, Alberta, with all the love that a single heart can hold."

Bird began to cry.

Why had she been so cruel to him when she found out he was her father? Why had she transmitted such harsh words in the parking lot of the hospital? He was her father. Her only father. She would probably never see him again, and her last words had been hurtful.

Then she heard his voice. It was far away, and totally unexpected.

Alberta. Bird.

Fred? I'm sorry for the things I said. I really didn't mean them!

I know. You were hurt. I hurt you. I'm sorry.

Will I see you again?

I'll come and go. I cannot promise more than that.

Do you understand why I asked if you were my father that day?

Do you understand why I didn't answer?

No, I don't.

Why does it matter what label I have, Alberta?

It does. I'm trying to understand things about myself and my family.

Some things must simply be accepted.

Can you stay, now that we know each other, and be my father?

I'm sorry, but I can't do that. My job takes me into dangerous places. When I'm called I must go. That's what I do and who I am.

Is it me? Am I not the daughter you wanted?

No! You're everything I could want and ten times more. It's me, Bird. My past would put you in harm's way. I cannot be what I am not.

I don't ask you to!

Please understand. I cannot be the father you want. I cannot become what a father means to you. I will not say that I will, to make you happy, then break your heart when I fail to live up to your expectations. But I can make two promises: I will always know if you are well and fine. And I will always love you more than I love myself.

But I don't ask any of that! I just need to know you. I need my father!

I'm sorry.

I've wondered about you my whole life.

Alberta, I admire and respect you. Never forget that. I look forward to watching how you live your life.

Will you come again?

I hope so.

Will I know when you're around?

Sometimes.

I guess that's it, then.

It's better this way. Please understand it is for your own good. I must wander in this world, not because I want to, but because I don't know any other way.

I do! I can help you!

No. You can't. I have to make my own journey. Like you must make yours.

But I have so much to learn from you! How can you go so easily?

My life has been anything but easy. There are reasons why I am what I am. I won't trouble you with them.

Then why did you come into my life?

Because it was time. I thought you were old enough to handle it.

I'll try. I'll try to handle it. I hope I'm strong enough.

I know you are. I'm very proud of you. I'll always be proud of you.

Your voice is fading. Fred? Dad? Are you still there?

I have to go. Remember to feed the Good Wolf.

I will, Dad! Goodbye!

He was gone. Bird felt completely empty. Hollowed out. Her throat ached and great sobs wracked her body. She felt more alone than she'd felt in her entire life.

A soft breath tickled the nape of her neck, and the familiar aroma of grassy breath reached her nostrils. Bird looked up. Sundancer stood over her protectively, his neck arched lovingly to her.

Then she felt coarse fur brush her arm. Cody stood on guard beside her, ready to attack any creature that might take advantage of her vulnerability.

My animals. My friends.

Bird girl. Despair not.

Oh, Cody. Fred is gone. I may never see him again.

At least you met him. That is good.

But it hurts! I didn't miss him before I met him!

Would you rather not have known this man who is your father?

Bird thought hard about Cody's question.

Sundancer nickered. *I met my father once. Dancer. A mighty horse. I'm glad I did. I'm proud to be his son.*

Cody touched Bird's nose with his own. *The Listener is good also, Bird, like Dancer. He knows the Language of the Animals. You got that gift from him. Ask no more. Take the good and leave the rest.*

Bird considered again her friends' wisdom. The more she thought about it, the more sense it made.

Her throat stopped aching so badly, and her breathing became more even. Would she rather not have met Fred? No. She was glad she had. She would have his beautiful smile and his gentle, wise ways entrenched in her memory. She had been enriched by knowing him, even for such a short time. As Fred had asked her, why did it matter what label he had? And he was right — her expectations for a father might be more than he could fulfill.

Bird sniffed loudly and wiped her nose on her arm. *Thank you, Cody. Thank you, Sunny. I'll try to take the good and leave the rest.*

That is good. Otherwise you get hurt by life, and become bitter.

Bird sat in the field surrounded by daisies, long grass, and clover. Cody settled in beside her, and Sunny grazed nearby. They enjoyed the quiet together.

A breeze rustled the leaves of the poplars along the fenceline.

A raven began to caw.

Another raven joined the first, and within a few seconds, there was an entire chorus.

Bird sensed that something had happened.

Cody lifted his head. He sat up. First he hummed quietly, and then he pointed his nose to the skies and began to howl. The howl was respectful and sincere.

Sundancer blew through his nostrils and drooped his ears. He lowered his head and closed his eyes.

Bird bowed her head. It was Pete. She knew from how her animals were behaving. A tear fell to her cheek. His spirit had passed out of this world and was going somewhere else.

He's gone, Alberta.

Fred?

At birth, we come from the east on the wings of the eagle. At death, we depart to the west on the back of the bison. Pete Pierson has gone to the west.

Is he okay?

His spirit is pure. He is at peace.

Thank you for telling me.

Be well.

Once more, the voice of the man she now knew as her father was silent. She trusted she'd hear it again. She just didn't know under what circumstances, or when.

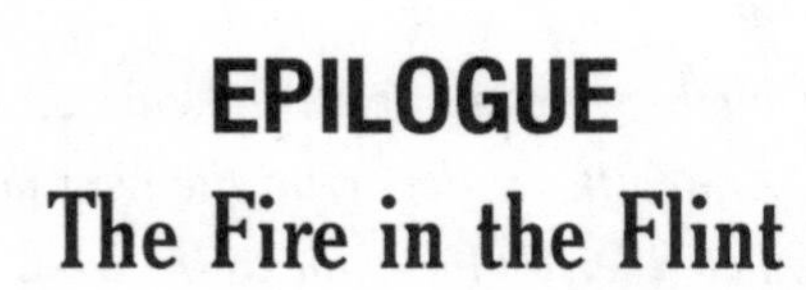

EPILOGUE
The Fire in the Flint

From nowhere we came; into nowhere we go. What is life? It is the flash of a firefly in the night. It is the breath of a buffalo in the wintertime. It is the little shadow that runs across the grass and loses itself in the sunset.

— Chief Crowfoot, Siksika Blackfoot, 1830–1890

At ten o'clock the following Tuesday morning, bells rang loudly from the little white church on Mississauga Road. It was a clear summer day, and rays of sunlight shone through the multicoloured stained glass windows of the Belfountain Church. The historic wooden building was filled to capacity. Chairs had been brought up from the basement and crammed into every nook and cranny.

In the front pew, Laura Pierson sat very still. Her face was serene. Instead of wearing the traditional black garb of a widow, she'd chosen to dress in white — her wedding dress — from head to toe. She'd worn it for Pete, she'd explained. Bird thought she looked like an angel.

Pete and Laura's three sons and their families had arrived at the hospital just in time to say their good-byes, and were now staying with their mother for a week. They'd gone together that morning to the crematorium. Bird imagined that their presence had been very comforting to Laura. Now they sat with her, all holding hands, as the minister intoned sympathetic and lengthy passages from the Bible.

Bird knew she should listen more carefully, but when Pete was alive he'd always avoided church. He said that his back grew sore sitting for so long on the wooden benches. Bird smiled a little at the memory. Somehow, sitting on wooden benches at horse shows, hockey games, horse races, and picnics was another matter.

For the obituary in the newspaper, Laura had chosen a passage from Shakespeare. Bird thought that it was totally fitting:

The fire in the flint
Shows not 'til it be struck,

It was from *Timon of Athens*, act 1, scene 1. Pete loved Shakespeare. He and Laura had enjoyed their yearly trips to Stratford to see the plays. Of all the countless lines in Shakespeare's sonnets and plays, Bird thought this one gave the greatest glimpse into Pete Pierson's soul. He had been such a measured and thoughtful man, but, like the matchbox in the quote, a person would've been warned to be careful if you struck his flint. Bird herself had witnessed Pete's fire on rare occasions, always when an injustice had been done.

Bird and her family had gotten to the church early enough to get the row behind the Pierson family. Hannah and Paul sat holding hands. Julia and Bird sat next to them, and Eva and Stuart tucked in to complete the row. On the other side of Hannah, Cliff wiped away a tear, his head bowed. Pete and Cliff had talked about horses and traded horse racing tips for years.

Three rows back on the other side, Abby Malone sat with her parents, Liam and Fiona. Abby had loved Pete, too. He had seen her through some very troubled times, and had helped her train Moonlight Sonata to win the Caledon Steeplechase the last year it was run. Her sad face mirrored Bird's own.

Hilary James — Mousie — and her husband, Sandy Casey, sat with their parents near the back. Mousie's grandmother, Joy Featherstone, and her husband, Robert Wick, were right beside them. Together they operated the Stonewick Playhouse. The James family had long been friends with the Piersons, and Pete had been a great supporter of Mousie's career. People in the area still asked for her autograph, years after she'd been the star of the show ring on her stallion, Dancer, Sunny's sire.

In the days since Pete's death, Bird had again asked Eva to tell her about Fred Sweetree. Finally, Eva had been honest about her feelings. She'd been dealing with her own pain of rejection, and believed she was protecting Bird. After she thought that Fred had died in the plane crash, she saw no point in discussing him. It had been her opinion that the less Bird knew about him, the less hurt she'd be. Bird wished they'd been able to discuss him years before. It would have been much easier to deal with then. But it was a start.

Eva had also opened up about Bird's grandfather, who was still in custody awaiting trial. Bird knew how Hannah felt about her father, but Eva had never spoken about him. Kenneth had been as destructive to his younger daughter as he was to his older one, doling out his affection in small amounts only when it suited him. He had treated both girls as objects, not people, and each still grappled with the impact he'd had on their lives.

What power parents have over their children's lives! Bird thought with vehemence. Why couldn't people just get past all the negativity and toss it out when they grew up? Bird would have to think about it. She didn't want to carry around any bad stuff from her mother or her father. She would try to take the good and leave the rest, as Cody had advised.

Maybe Fred was right to stay out of her life — at least if he didn't think he could be a good father. Maybe he would do less damage that way. Certainly a lot less damage than Kenneth Bradley.

Why did she expect more from Fred than he could give? She looked around the church, half expecting to see him, but he wasn't there.

Kimberly and her mother, Lavinia, rushed into the church late, but there were no more chairs. Lavinia was so strident that a man got up and gave her his. Kimberly was very embarrassed, but Bird winked at her. Bird chuckled quietly. Lavinia would never change.

As Bird scanned the crowd, Mack Jones and his wife smiled at her from the row just behind. Seeing Mack reminded Bird of all the intrigue that had happened in their little community in the last while. Pete Pierson had played a big part in righting all the wrongs.

How could Dexter, or anyone, have done those things to innocent animals, Bird wondered? Air embolisms, broken legs, induced colic, the unspecific accidents Fred had mentioned — all for money. She hoped that when Dexter got out of jail, he'd never again be allowed to have anything to do with horses. Ed Cage would get what he deserved as well. He'd said that he'd done what Dexter had asked because Dexter was his boss and he couldn't refuse, but Bird knew better. People *can* refuse to do things. Ed should have quit his job rather than injure animals. And the way he'd used Wanda was totally wrong. The whole thing made Bird feel queasy.

Tanbark and his mother, Alison Wedger, had driven up from Toronto for Pete's funeral. Pete had helped Tanbark when he was living wild in the woods below the escarpment. They sat halfway back, beside some neighbours. Tan and Alison were coming to Saddle Creek Farm for dinner later, with Laura and her family.

Sally Johns and her father, Harold, were at the funeral, too, sitting together quietly. Bird hoped that the whole incident with Tall Sox would soon be history, and that

Sally's problem with lying would cause no more trouble for Hannah.

Then she smiled softly. A letter from Alec had arrived that morning. She didn't need to look at it to remember each word, but particularly loved: *I think of you when I hear a bird sing. I think of you when the sun sets. I think of you when it rains. I can't get you out of my mind. All my love, Alec.*

Bird was startled out of her reverie by a great wail from outside the church. The minister stopped speaking. Everybody froze. The wail sounded again.

It was Cody. Bird was sure of it.

She got up as quietly as she could and crept quickly down the aisle along the wall. When she got near the door, she ran outside into the blinding sunshine.

Cody was sitting in full sight on the lush green lawn, bathed in light. His head was thrown back and his nose pointed straight to the heavens. He howled and wailed and howled again.

He was giving a proper send-off to the man he'd always called the Good Man.

Under the oak tree beside the road, a chestnut horse stood proudly at the fence. Bird gasped as she recognized Dancer, the majestic superstar. He was older now, and not as fit as in his prime, but there was no mistaking his elegance and his huge presence. Dancer pawed the ground. *We come to honour this man who understood the vast connections between humans, animals, and the earth.* The great old horse bowed deeply.

Moonlight Sonata — dark and silky, and beautifully proportioned — stood with Dancer, head down. She had borne two of Dancer's babies, both excellent horses in their own right.

Bird's gaze went to the tall gelding who cheekily stared back at her. Sundancer, the son of Dancer, and her best friend.

How did you get here? Bird asked Sunny.

Fences are meant to be jumped. You think we'd miss this funeral?

Then Sunny bowed, too, his nose touching the ground.

Cody humbly crept to his side and sat.

Bird, alongside the animals, dropped her head to her chin and grieved for Pete Pierson. Finally, out here in the open air, she could feel the sacredness of Pete's life and the solemnity of his death. He would not be coming back. Finally, with her animals, she felt the reality of it. In the church, surrounded by walls and people, she had not. Her tears began to flow.

She would miss him. A lot.

She remembered his words to her at the Caledon Derby just days before: "Damn the torpedoes, and seize the day." Then, when she and Sunny had won, "Savour the moment."

Bird vowed to try.

She thought about how much her father had admired Pete. He must be here, somewhere, on this day of Pete's funeral. Bird reached her hand deep into the pocket of her yellow cotton summer dress and pulled out the silver buckle he had given her. She held it up. She turned in a complete circle, to be sure that Fred could see it if he was close enough. *I'll keep this with me. Forever.*

Nothing.

Bird slowly dropped her hand, the silver buckle clutched so tightly that her entire arm began to shake. Pete was gone, and so was her father.

She wasn't alone, though. She had her animals and her family and friends. And she had been given tremendous gifts. The wisdom and confidence that both Pete and Fred had passed on to her were more valuable than she could fully understand.

She carefully put the silver buckle back into her pocket and wiped her nose on her arm.

Sunny pawed his right front hoof. *It's time to go.*

Bird took a deep, ragged breath. She walked up to the beautiful chestnut gelding and stroked his handsome face, enjoying how his satiny coat gleamed in the sunlight. She grabbed his mane with both hands, bent her knees, and jumped up on his back, her yellow dress draping his back and sides.

"Let's go."

The mighty Dancer led the way down the gravel road toward Saddle Creek Farm, followed by Moonlight Sonata. Cody was unseen but close by, and Bird and Sundancer completed the procession home from Pete Pierson's funeral.

Bird wondered if the pastor had even finished his sermon. She smiled. Pete would understand.

ACKNOWLEDGEMENTS

Many years ago, the germ of this story was planted by a conversation with a man who called himself Indian Fred. In the first book of this series I created Bird in his likeness to speak to Sundancer. Now, in *Dark Days at Saddle Creek*, the circle is completed when we meet the initial inspiration, Indian Fred himself. He's been dead for some years now, but I salute him with this book.

I sincerely thank Doug Gordon, who is Education Consultant for Native Studies and has been a friend for many years plus an exceptional educator all his life, for making the time to read this story and endow me with his quiet wisdom. James Bartleman, bestselling author, Canadian diplomat, policy advisor to the Prime Minister's Office, and 27th lieutenant governor of Ontario, was extremely helpful and generous. I thank him profusely for his thoughtful nuance and sensitivity.

My family, as always, with humour, patience and love, gave me the benefit of their encouragement and advice.

Thank you. I love you all.

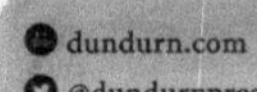